DOORWAY

A novel by Judith Hawkes

Also by Judith Hawkes

Julian's House
My Soul to Keep
The Heart of a Witch

Three unbreathing things paid for only with breathing things:
An apple tree, a hazel bush, a sacred grove.

                                    — The Triads of Ireland

⁜ 1 ⁜

Start with the end. With a human skull embedded in a charred tree, a silent riddle of wood and bone.

Start with the beginning. With a young man, white, listening to an old one, red. A spring evening in the year 1810, the two of them trading pulls at an earthenware jug outside the red man's shanty. The old Cherokee known as Jim Fox has heard the other whites in this rough Carolina settlement muttering against the young fellow, naming him trickster and rogue, but for a drink of whiskey Jim will tell his stories to anyone who wants to listen. He takes a swallow and starts to talk about a place he knew as a boy, a forest filled with *didanvdo.*

Spirits.

The old hunters tell the young ones to beware. They say the forest spirit has many faces – a deer, a tree, a stone, a beautiful maiden. If you meet one, it will tear out your heart and eat it. You may find your way home, but to the end of your days you will be hollow inside. Or you may never come back at all.

Either way, you are lost.

Start with the forest. The Noon Woods, the locals call it. Does the name suggest dappled shade, the drowsy twitter of birds? Imagine instead a brooding congress of furrowed trunks and low branches, roofed by a limitless fret of green where glints of light endlessly scurry and flee. The only sound is a pervasive rustle of leaves that reaches into the mind of the intruder, altering it little by little to an unknown frequency. The local people attribute the name Noon Woods o the notion that only at midday can the sun's rays penetrate the forest's dense canopy; but in truth it has nothing to do with the English word *noon*, or with matters of daylight at all.

Along with the old Cherokee legends come cautionary tales of the area's first white settlers – a hunter crushed by a falling tree, a pure white doe glimpsed at dusk, the bones of illicit lovers discovered deep in the forest, bound together by rioting vines. No one talks about the most recent tragedy, the one involving a group of rowdy boys on a Midsummer's Eve lark, but they all know there's only one good reason to brave the Noon Woods.

You've got to want something so bad that the wanting eclipses the fear.

Nearly three months have passed since Elizabeth Wyatt came home to Durwood to die. In her forty-odd years away, she hasn't forgotten the stories; nonetheless she's shaken by the obscure sense of presence abiding among the whispering leaves, the inescapable feeling of being watched by furtive shapes that dissolve into random configurations of branch and leaf. Forests alter a great deal in forty years and her memories are vague; it's taken at least dozen attempts, braving the observant green shadows and the secretive rustlings on every side, to find what she was looking for. Now, returning home, she heads straight to the kitchen, fills a jelly glass from the Mason jar of moonshine at the back of the cabinet, and drinks it down.

It's the only thing that can stop the shivering.

Or just start with Nick, freshly expelled from law school, using a staple gun to fasten a neon-green flyer to a tree.

•Revive a Durwood Tradition•
•Celebrate Midsummer the Ancient Celtic Way•
•Friends, Food, & Frolic•
•Join Us for the Festival of Oaks•

He steps back to admire the effect. The color's a real attention-grabber; he's glad he talked Morgan into it. And the image of the Green Man is pure inspiration – a little bit of nature magic disguised as trendy garden art. He's working his way down one side of Main Street and up the other, posting the flyers on the giant oaks that buckle the sidewalk with their roots. The trees are so imposing that at first they're all you see; only gradually do the weathered storefronts and houses huddled beneath them become visible in the shadow of the spreading branches.

Right now Nick's grateful for the shade. Today, like yesterday and no doubt tomorrow, is a scorcher, courtesy of the drought that's plagued this region for the past two years. Sweat trickles down his face as he makes his way down the street. In spite of the heat it's good to be out in the open air instead of unpacking boxes in the stuffy storeroom at Abundance – not that he won't be forever grateful to Morgan for rescuing him, offering him a place to live for the summer and a job at her store instead of having to slink home to Raleigh in disgrace. He's grateful as well for her take on his situation, one of her typical transmutations of negative into positive.

"Nothing happens by accident, Nicky. The Goddess brought you here, and I'm going to light a candle to Her as a special thank you!"

"How about a special thank you to Wake Forest Law? They're the ones who kicked me out."

"Law school – pfff! That was a mistake, a wrong path for you. I know you're destined for something more spiritual."

Spiritual isn't exactly how he'd define working as a cashier and stock boy at Morgan's health food store – but having made such a spectacular failure of his attempt at a law career, Nick's happy to trade a guilt-filled summer under the parental roof for one with his favorite aunt. He was twelve when Morgan discovered Wicca, old enough to dismiss his mother's snide comments about "Emily's identity crisis" and see that her younger sister, with her new confidence and new name, seemed happier than he'd ever known her. *It's a gift from the Goddess*, she says now whenever something good happens, and even his scandalized parents can't deny that the last few years have been good to Morgan indeed. After all, how likely is it that a store selling goddess candles and herbal teas, lime-cilantro marinade and goats' milk soap would become a booming success in a tiny place like Durwood, North Carolina?

Tucked away in the mountains amid forested ridges and tumbling creeks, Durwood is further isolated by rough roads, rickety bridges, frequent power outages, and clannish inhabitants; but stumbling upon it five years ago, Morgan had fallen instantly in love with the little town encircled by small farms and homesteads. The locals seemed wary of outsiders but not actively hostile. Left with a generous settlement from her recent divorce, she'd used the money to relocate and start her own business.

Nick's parents said she'd lost her mind. But over the next few years she'd talked up the place to her friends in the alternative community, and the news had gradually rippled outward. Acreage that had belonged to Durwood families for generations began to change hands: a decorative ironworker from Greensboro set up his forge in a two-hundred-year-old barn; a pair of schoolteachers from Hickory bought an abandoned farmhouse to restore during their summers; an Asheville artist and her wealthy lawyer husband built a lavish country home on thirty acres east of town. A craft store opened, a pottery shop, a vegan restaurant, and most recently a yoga studio. By now, to the mystification of all the locals and the distaste of a good percentage, the community includes a thriving element of crafters, pagans, and others for whom Durwood provides an antidote to the stresses of modern life.

For Morgan it means business is booming. A year ago she'd outgrown her narrow little shop on Main Street and bought land at the northern edge of town for a new building, and her decision to use local labor for its construction had significantly eased the tension between the natives and the more recent residents. Now she's cherishing high hopes for her latest brainstorm, a scheme to attract tourists to Durwood by a festival celebrating Midsummer.

"It's a huge project, Nicky. But with you here to help, I know it's going to be a success! And now that you've found the Goddess for yourself – "

Nick basks in the approval. He'd always thought Morgan's religion was cool – and last October, alienated and depressed by the law school grind, he'd impulsively attended a full moon circle sponsored by the small but lively neopagan group on campus. A crisp autumn night, a bonfire, and a welcoming kiss from a pretty girl with a pentacle necklace had felt like a welcome home. From then on, what intellectual energy he might have spent on his studies was diverted to total immersion in books on Wicca, Celtic customs, pagan practices old and new. By the end of first semester he was taking minor roles in the campus rituals but floundering in the classroom; by early February the dean had summoned him for a serious talk about grades; by April his law career was history.

Not that he's sorry. As Morgan says, it was the wrong path. He's not yet certain of the right one, but at least a summer in Durwood will give him some breathing space.

"What do the natives think about the festival?" he says.

"Hard to tell. Most of them don't have much to say to us outsiders, and that's anybody who wasn't born here. But the idea isn't new; we're actually reviving a local celebration that went belly up in the 1940s. You know CW Durwood, who runs the hardware store – well, he says when he was a boy, they celebrated Midsummer by choosing a King and Queen of the Greenwood to rule over a day of games and contests ending with a bonfire, food, music, dancing – "

"A traditional Celtic festival," Nick says.

"And that's not surprising, because practically everyone in these parts originally came from the British Isles. But even so, Nicky, Durwood's a little different. According to local legend, Roan Durwood, the founder, had some pretty unusual talents."

"Such as?"

"Such as shapeshifting and weather control, among other things."

Nick's eyebrows rise. "Wow. Lucky he didn't get himself strung up by the Christian establishment."

Morgan claps her hands. "Your mind works exactly the way mine does! Because don't you have to wonder – if maybe Roan and the others came to this remote spot precisely *because* they wanted to put some distance between themselves and the Christian establishment?"

"What are you saying?"

"Just that to me it strongly suggests they may have been pagans, maybe even Wiccans, looking for a place to practice their beliefs in peace. Of course it was two centuries ago, so there's no way to really *know*. But Midsummer is a pagan holiday – and there are those rumors of magical powers – and even after two hundred years, there's not a single Christian church in the whole of Durwood."

To Nick, that's proof enough; every Southern community, no matter how tiny or backward, has its church, sometimes half a dozen to accommodate doctrinal differences. He himself had begun boycotting services on his fifteenth birthday when, to his mother's horror and his father's disgust, he'd pronounced religion a giant bore.

"It's not that the local people are consciously, actively pagan," Morgan's saying. "They'd think that was sheer foolishness. But they've got this sort of

4

mystical relationship with the land, this legacy of respect for it as a living entity. They plant by the signs – the zodiac, the phases of the moon. They hunt only what they eat. The older folks even call the months by the names of trees – Oak Month, Ash Month, and so on.

"The tragedy is that it's fading with each new generation. Nowadays on Midsummer there are only a handful of people who put oak leaves on their hats or lapels; most of them don't acknowledge it at all. Imagine losing touch with such a deep part of your heritage, something that goes all the way back to pre-Christian times! But we're going to fix that. This year, Midsummer is making a comeback!"

Nick's got to admit it's a seductive notion: Durwood's founding fathers fleeing into the mountains to escape persecution for practicing the Old Ways. And why not? One of neopaganism's fondest tenets is that Goddess worship never really died out, that the old ways have been kept alive over the centuries by isolated pockets of believers who passed them down in secret. If Durwood was founded by such people, if a pagan tradition exists here, however fragmented by time – who better to revive it than the self-chosen inheritors of that tradition, people like Morgan who've found something special in this little community? Of course she'll say the Goddess led her here (her way of explaining a series of wrong turns on a drive from Raleigh to Johnson City), and who knows, maybe there's a case to be made for the Goddess having cynically exploited Morgan's total inability to read a road map.

If there's one thing Nick's learning as a fledgling pagan, it's that the Goddess works in mysterious ways.

The Hardware & General has always been the hub of Durwood, the place to go for news, and this morning is no exception. Avoiding the buzz at the cash register, Jared Gorton threads his way toward for the back of the store, down narrow aisles crammed with fishing tackle, shotgun shells, oil lamps, cookware, gaskets, switches, buckets, birdhouses, rubber boots, sacks of seeds and bulbs and fertilizer. Since he was old enough to walk, the Hardware & General's been his idea of paradise, the source of just about everything a body could possibly need to survive.

Which, for most people, happens to include gossip. But gossip happens to be one of the things Jared hates most about living in such a small community – everybody jawing and cawing like a bunch of crows in the treetops, making a lot of noise about nothing. Look at Pete and Ward and CW right now, huddled over a scatter of eye-popping green paper on the counter. Jared recognizes the color; the flyers are plastered all up and down Main Street, advertising some kind of shindig planned by Morgan Edwards and her crew of Bunny Dancers. It's got the old boys all in a twitch, and now Ward's twins have joined them. Jared busies himself among the plumbing supplies – his ma's showerhead is shot – ignoring the phrases that drift his way.

" – sorry piece of shit – "

" – ain't got the right to – "

"Jared!" CW's raised voice. "Where'd you get to? Somethin you need to hear."

Reluctantly Jared emerges from cover. He doesn't have time for a fussfest right now; he has to get to work and help Darrell with that timing belt job. But CW's jabbing a bony finger in the air, wire-rimmed spectacles riding the tip of his nose.

"I knew it! Soon's I woke up this morning, knot in my belly said trouble was on the way. Seventy-six years and that knot ain't never been wrong, not once."

Jared's known CW his whole life; the man's his father-in-law in everything but name, but he can't remember ever seeing him this worked up. He thinks of what Sally's been saying recently about her pa getting old, tending to fuss over trifles. He picks up one of the green sheets from the counter.

•Revive a Durwood Tradition•
•Celebrate Midsummer the Ancient Celtic Way•
•Friends, Food, & Frolic•
•Join Us for the Festival of Oaks·

The words give him a jolt. Those damn Bunny Dancers! Normally Jared is tolerant of the newcomers, even willing to admit they've done some decent things, like Morgan hiring local boys to build her new store. But it's typical of them to launch one of their cockeyed schemes without bothering to run it past anybody who knows anything – maybe think to ask why people in Durwood let Midsummer pass without fanfare these days.

He experiences a sudden savage wish that the whole blasted lot of them would get gone and leave Durwood in peace. Crumpling the paper into a ball, he looks up to find himself ringed by scowls. Even his childhood buddies Conley and Harley Cole look grim, and those two are notorious for fooling even at a burying.

"That ain't what we're talkin bout, here," Ward says. "Got us a way bigger problem here."

"What'd I say?" CW's fuming. "Trouble that happens during Oak Month is always extra bad. That's the old sayin: Oak courts the lightnin. Knot in my belly, I'm tellin you. Never wrong once."

⁙2⁙

"Last night," Star says, "I found *the perfect website*."

Morgan watches her wait for the side conversations to stop until she has the undivided attention of every woman in the circle. Even then Star doesn't speak; she lets the suspense build, the anticipation of what *the perfect website* might be. She has a flair for leadership, no question about that – a quality she's been putting to good use ever since she hijacked the planning of the Festival of Oaks.

Morgan asks herself if she's somehow created this situation by inviting her friends' input on the idea. But it had seemed like such a natural impulse, the organic growth of her connection with these five women. None of them are native to Durwood; they've gathered here as if by mystic confluence, drawn to a place where their common dream of an alternative lifestyle seems enticingly possible. About a year ago they'd formed a dream discussion group, a way of affirming one another and themselves. They share a vision of the earth as a wounded entity in need of healing, and their chosen pursuits reflect their commitment to the task: Tamara owns the Mother Earth pottery studio; Vivian supplies the breads for Morgan's health food store out of her home bakery and assists Chad, the yoga instructor at Durwood Body Arts; Molly and her husband Ben own the local craft store; Star and her husband Russ operate Durwood's only vegan restaurant, and Morgan runs Abundance.

They'd greeted her idea for the festival with enthusiasm, and at some point after that – she's not quite sure when – she'd realized it was Star running the discussions, Star the others were listening to, Star answering the questions and making the decisions. Morgan guesses she dropped the ball somehow, distracted by Nick's arrival and the need to get him settled. She really hopes Nick will stay in Durwood; he so obviously belongs here. She's never been able to fathom how her uptight sister Susan and that pompous ass Roland Rusk managed to produce such a rare and gentle spirit, and it's a continuing joy to her that Nick has found his way to Wicca, a choice that somehow it makes him more her child than her sister's, taking some of the sting out of her barren (in every sense) twenty years with Tim.

" – absolutely amazing," Star says, and Morgan realizes she's missed the latest great revelation. Glancing at the others' faces, hoping for a hint, she sees that Vivian and Tamara look thrilled, while Molly's mouth has the quirk that means she's withholding judgment.

"It doesn't sound like much work," Vivian says, and Tamara adds, "Not much at all."

Star rummages in her mammoth patchwork shoulder bag, pulls out her iPad and flips it to face the group. "Here's the image I downloaded last night."

Everyone leans in to see. Morgan wonders why Star has to hold the gadget herself – can't she just pass it around the circle? Craning over the clustered heads, she gets a glimpse of a raggedy green-clad crowd gathered around a flowery banner that reads *Jack-in-the-Green Celebration 2015*. They look happy, festive, and pleasingly pagan.

"You take an old bathrobe or sweatshirt," Star's explaining, "sew or pin a bunch of fabric scraps to it, any old rag as long as it's green, and poof! Instant festival finery! Stylish, reusable, looks like leaves without the mess – "

It's clever, creative, and ecofriendly, Morgan has to admit, and she knows she should be glad the group has embraced the idea of the festival with such enthusiasm. But it's her brainchild, a fact that seems to have been forgotten – and if she's honest, the worst thing is not Star's behavior but how it's eating at her. Morgan's accustomed to working with other women; four years in a women-only coven gave her plenty of exposure to high concentrations of estrogen. But the members of Womb&Folk were all about acknowledgement and support, not hijacking each other's projects.

Again laughter breaks in on her thoughts; again she reproaches herself for drifting. Vivian's said something funny and she's missed it. Searching the surrounding faces for clues, she sees Molly isn't listening either. One hand on her enormous belly, she's staring into space.

"Molly? You okay?"

Petite, dark-haired Molly emerges from her trance with a radiant smile. "The baby just kicked."

"Another couple weeks, huh?" Tamara squeezes her arm.

"That's what Sally says. But she also said since it's my first, it could come any time."

"How's it working out with Sally?"

"It's wonderful. I trust her completely. I was a little shy about asking her at first – you know how the locals can be – but I'm so glad I did. That peppermint tea she gave me got rid of the morning sickness in no time, and she's got me on red raspberry leaves to tone my uterus. She knows so much, and it's all natural medicine. I can't imagine having anyone else deliver my baby!"

Nods and smiles around the circle: CW's pretty redhaired daughter is Durwood's midwife and herbalist, and a general favorite. It's Sally to whom the children flock for a story or a song, who lends a sympathetic ear to the old folks' aches and pains and connects newcomers with a handyman or a load of firewood. Her office at the back of her father's hardware store, fragrant with hanging bunches of herbs, is the local treatment center not only for illness and injury, but for anyone in need of a cheering chat.

"Should we get Sally's input on the plans for the Festival?" Naturally Tamara's question is addressed to Star, and naturally Star gives a ruling.

"I kind of feel like this festival is our gift to the local community. They shouldn't have to do anything. And Sally's got to be pretty busy with her job, and Jared, and taking care of her family and all."

"Sally Durwood and Jared Gorton," Vivian says. "Now there's a cute couple. Why don't they just tie the knot?"

Molly shakes her head. "It's a pretty rocky relationship, from what Annie Sayles tells me – and just try shutting Annie up once she gets going! She says Sally's completely committed to the community and Jared just wants to get out and leave it behind. I think they genuinely love each other, but he's what my ex-boss back in Brooklyn would call a moody bastard."

Through the laughter Morgan says, "It might be partly to do with Tyner," and the others sober. None of them has ever met CW's son, who lives with his father and sister on the Durwood farm south of town, but they all know he's confined to a wheelchair. Morgan isn't sure if Tyner was born disabled or had some kind of accident; CW never talks about it and she wouldn't dream of prying.

"Okay," she hears Star say briskly. "Let's get back to business."

Seeing Sally's truck heading up Main Street as he's on his way to work, Jared wonders if the sight of his woman will ever fail to give him a buzz, even if they do spend half their time fighting about one thing and another. Taking advantage of the nonexistent traffic, they stop their vehicles in the middle of the street to chat.

"That ole baby get born all right?"

"Twenty-two hours and he was breech, but you got yourself a brand new nephew." Sally pushes a damp coppery curl off her forehead. "He's alive and whole, anyhow. I reckon that's all that matters."

The look they exchange recalls the hours they've spent hashing through her doubts and fears while she seesaws between loving her work and ruing the day she inherited her grandmother's midwife role. Two dead births out of seven in the past three years, limp little bodies sliding into her hands – and even worse are the deformities, like Jeff and Bonnie Durwood's baby girl born six weeks ago with no lower jaw, so pitiful it was a mercy when she died a day later.

Sally has two more impending births in her docket: Lissy Lewis and the Bunny Dancer called Molly. Jared knows she's not worried about Molly, who's young and healthy as a horse. But Lissy's forty, and this will be her first child. Sally's keeping close tabs on Lissy.

"Guess me and the boys'll have to get young Hubbard drunk tonight," he says. "Shelby doin okay?"

"She's fine. Hub don't look so good, though. I swear birthin's worse on the men than the women. Granny Dee always said they just ain't as tough."

"Tell me somethin I don't know." They laugh; Sally reaches across the space between them and Jared takes her hand. It's crazy how much he loves to see her smile. As it fades, he can see she's worn out.

"There's one thing, though." The words come slowly. "The baby's got a – a mark."

"A mark? What kinda mark?" He becomes aware that the fingers clasped in his are cold. She pulls them free.

"Little purple lines. All over his face."

"What the hell?"

"Just a birthmark is all. I told em it'll likely fade."

"Likely will," Jared says over the qualm in his gut. "Listen, you talk to your Pa this mornin?"

"He called over to Hub and Shelby's while I was washin up, all in a fret over some flyers Morgan's nephew dropped off at the store this morning. Some kinda summer festival?"

The smile is back and Jared lets her talk, knowing she needs to wind down from the birthing. "I told him, I said Pa, you gotta get aholt of that woman of yours, she's runnin wild. Well, he starts huffin and puffin, says there's no call for that kinda talk – but let's face it, he's liked the look of Morgan Edwards since she first got here. And I know she's a lot younger than him, but wouldn't it be kinda nice if . . . ? I mean, even if he always says Ma was the only one for him, they didn't have but eight years together, and he – "

She comes to a sudden stop. "What? How come you're lookin at me like that?"

Jared sighs. "I guess you talked to him before he got Ward's news."

For more than two hundred years, the members of this tiny mountain community have mingled and multiplied until they can't keep track of all the ways they're related. Back and forth among the households flows the news of marryings and buryings, housewarmings and harvests, accidents, illnesses, deaths and births. Childhood friends grow old to see their offspring fall in love and provide them with shared grandchildren, or a chance quarrel triggers a breach that lasts for generations. Cole, Lewis, Reese, Gorton, Vernon, Sayles, Wyatt, Tyner, Durwood: the names repeat and so do the faces, a certain sharp nose and determined chin, gray eyes and auburn hair shared along with stories of a legendary ancestor named Roan Durwood, said to have found here in the forest a door to a magical realm where none ever grew old, or felt the centuries pass away.

And now they share their new, unspoken fears. What's happening to Durwood's children? Even if nobody asks the question aloud, it's always there beneath the surface. What about Jeff and Bonnie's doomed baby, or little Hooper Tyner, born with a flipper in place of his right arm? What about the Preston twins? Whole and handsome and quick on their feet – but at six years old neither has ever uttered a human word, just sounds a pig might make. And then there's little Susanna Sayles, pretty as an angel, diagnosed with leukemia two years ago and now in precarious remission.

Is it any wonder pregnancies are becoming increasingly rare in Durwood? People wait in dread, not expectation, for their new arrivals. But nobody talks about it, and when Verna Lewis congratulates Tiny Reese on her new grandson, neither woman mentions how the pattern of purplish lines on his small face resembles the intricate forking of twigs and branches. Nonetheless, they're both thinking the same thing.

Only one tree could cast such a shadow.

Only one among nearly five thousand acres of root, bole, branch and leaf. Deep in the Noon Woods it stands alone in a clearing – a ruined oak with a scarred, twisted trunk. Hundreds of years have passed since the night a bolt of lightning struck it during a summer storm, splitting the young sapling nearly in two before sheets of rain doused the fire, leaving smoke wisping upward from the blackened wound. Over the years that followed, the two halves of the trunk rejoined, leaving an opening through which the wind sang songs as ephemeral as leaf shadows in moonlight. Cherokee hunters avoided the place, warning one another away with tales of hungry spirits, tales that lingered long after the whites had mercilessly driven their people from the land.

The second strike came only a few decades back, reducing the tree's luxuriant crown to a mass of splintered wood. Now it stands skeletal and bare of leaves, its lower branches festooned instead with an array of odd objects that stir in the fitful forest breeze. The cleft trunk itself is silent now. Where once the wind crooned its eerie refrain, a carefully shaped stone blocks the opening like a gag.

⁙3⁙

Slouched in the passenger seat of Tyler Vance's pickup truck, just yards from the looming edge of the Noon Woods, Gordie Durwood is talking to his dead momma.

"Lord, Momma, don't those slithery old roots look just like a mess of snakes? You told it true – this is an evil place."

Momma doesn't answer. He knows perfectly well she's dead; talking to her is just a habit that won't let loose. She's been gone less than a year, after all, and somebody like Momma doesn't fade out of your life. Not right away, maybe not ever. She'd be surprised to see him back in Durwood, but mighty pleased if she knew why he's here.

He fidgets on the lumpy seat. The Fawn Creek Logging rep is taking his sweet time in there – how long do you need to figure the value of a bunch of trees? Mister Tyler Vance had seemed surprised by Gordie's refusal to tag along – but however much Vance might know about trees, there's a lot he doesn't know about the Noon Woods. Gordie looks up the slope at the old cabin where he grew up, Momma insisting they live there because she didn't want to share the big family farmhouse with her in-laws.

"Looks like somebody's living in the old place, Momma. There's a beat up ole Jeep parked outside."

How many times did Momma warn him to keep out of the Noon Woods? Not that he'd ever really wanted to go in there. Yet some folks did; more than once he'd seen solitary figures skulking along the bottom of the field before vanishing into the dark mass of trees. What for? Finally he worked up the nerve to ask Momma.

"To worship the Devil, Gordie, that's what they go there for. They're Satan's children, and that vile forest is their temple of sin."

When Momma's mouth got tight like that and she started breathing hard through her nose, it was time to stop asking questions. Gordie'd already guessed the answer was connected with the witch balls, those globes of speckled green glass hanging along the edge of the porch roof, tinkling spookily when the wind blew. While he wasn't sure of their exact purpose, he knew they had something to do with the Noon Woods.

But what? The question gnawed at him. Early one morning, when he caught sight of Granny Dee and his redheaded cousin Sally at the bottom of the field, he ran down to watch where they went, but they'd already disappeared into the woods by the time he got there. He crept closer, holding his breath. Not a sound, not a sign – as if they'd been swallowed by the cryptic green stillness within.

Peering into the twilight of the trees, remembering Momma's tight lips and the whispering witch balls, all at once Gordie could see hundreds of hideous little faces peeping at him from the leaves. When a breeze like a small cold hand touched his cheek, he turned tail and ran.

It was the closest he'd ever come to the Noon Woods, and he'd never wanted to get that close again. Until today, when he's got a doggone good reason for being here. The best reason in the world.

Right, Momma?

Women cluster around the oak tree in front of Cole's Small Engine Repair, talking and laughing while they wrap its trunk with colored ribbons. Trying to imagine herself back in ancient Celtic times, Morgan is foiled by the litter of defunct mowers and chainsaws in the background. She'd argued for a tree in a prettier location – there's no shortage of oaks on Main Street, after all – to hold the winner's wreath for the Midsummer race, but Star had overruled her. *No, it's got to be that one. At that time of day, the sun lights it up like a pinball machine.*

Forlornly she notes that the decorating crew is made up entirely of Bunny Dancers, the locals' moniker for her and the other outsiders. She'd winced the first time she heard that devastatingly dismissive play on the name of her store; but really, isn't it natural for Durwood's natives to resent what seems like a takeover of their town, with half the local businesses now run by outsiders? Yet she's been clinging to the hope that some of the friendlier locals – Sally Durwood, Annie Sayles, May Vernon – would join in decorating the tree for the race, and by now that hope has vanished.

Watching Vivian prop a ladder against the trunk, she calls, "Viv! Not too high, okay?"

Vivian tosses her a mock salute and scampers up the ladder to hang the winner's wreath of oak leaves in the tree. They've woven red ribbon among the leaves to make it more visible – doubtless a departure from tradition, but this revival doesn't have to be an exact match of the original. The festival should reflect not just Durwood's past, but its present as well: a mix of tradition and innovation. Morgan wishes she'd thought to use that phrase on the flyer; it has a nice sound. Tradition and innovation.

So far, the Festival of Oaks hasn't exactly been a roaring success. By the official start time of 11:30, only two of the eight vendors who'd reserved space in Abundance's parking lot were in place to hear Ben Upshaw perform the event's musical kickoff.

She walked through the corn leading down to the river
Her hair shone like gold in the hot morning sun . . .

Privately Morgan found the performance disappointing, nowhere near as impressive in the open air as it had been in the Upshaws' living room when she'd impulsively asked Ben to officially open the festival with the bluegrass favorite *Fox on the Run*. But the words *hot morning sun* are certainly apt; like every other day since the middle of April, this one's a sizzler. Trying to stay positive, she tells herself the drought may have shriveled local creeks and withered kitchen gardens, but it's perfect weather for an outdoor event, a good omen for the Festival of Oaks.

She bites her lip. Although she woke up this morning convinced that the revival of the old tradition is just what's needed to unite Durwood's old and new populations, her certainty has been steadily dwindling ever since. The vendors' booths drowsing in the heat have drawn no more than a handful of sweating customers, and the petting zoo (a goat, two pigs, a goose and Tamara's ancient golden retriever) had to be shut down when the goose attacked the dog. The real disappointment isn't so much the locals' lack of participation as their utter indifference. They go about their business without so much as a curious glance at the events unfolding around them, as if their streets have been invaded by some cyclical pest that will move on once its ravages are done.

Morgan wonders if her idea is ahead of its time, or if it's just a bad idea. The event she envisioned as bonding the residents of Durwood is making her feel more like an outsider than she's felt since she first arrived. She consults her watch. Half past four. The race is set for six-thirty, with evening festivities to follow – a bonfire, food, music and dancing, along with face painting, fortune telling and free shiatsu massage. The thought of all the hours that lie ahead lends a mocking inflection to the phrase *longest day of the year*, and she can't help wishing the whole thing was already over. It seems like a lot of fuss for what's turning out to be a couple of dozen people.

There are only a few customers at May's Café this afternoon. May's nephew and his wife are at a corner table; Jared and Darrell are at the counter, grabbing a quick bite before they finish putting the new clutch in Burley Lewis's truck. Jared's got his nose in a book as usual, but Darrell keeps twisting on his stool to scowl at the people in shaggy green garments hurrying past the plate glass window.

"Oughta be ashamed," he says. "Somebody oughta stop this damn festival before it goes any farther."

Jared doesn't respond, but May stops wiping down the counter to put in her usual two cents. "Listen, Darrell, Morgan Edwards means well. I don't believe she's got the faintest notion bout what happened to Tyne."

Jared closes his book. "Hell, May, looks like she ain't got the faintest notion bout nothin round here, nor the sense to ask. Beats me what her and the rest of em are doin in this pisshole little town."

May pats a stray lock of hair, long faded from fiery red to soft apricot, back into her bun. "You maybe can't see it now, Jared. But someday you're gonna realize Durwood's a good place to live."

"Oh yeah, it's a regular paradise on earth." Jared leans across the counter and plants a smacking kiss on her cheek. "Long's you're here, anyhow."

May can feel herself blushing. Being kissed by a handsome black-bearded young man can still do that to her, never mind she's known Jared since he was in diapers. "You boys get on now," she says. "I got work to do."

◆◆◆

From the top step of the whitewashed wooden schoolhouse at the eastern end of Main Street, it's painfully obvious that the crowd is divided into two distinct groups. In the lively, voluble bunch clustered below Morgan, almost everyone is sporting a homemade Jack-in-the-Green costume of green scraps. Among them she sees her friends, their families, and other newbies like the Everdales and the Palmers, along with a few unknown faces – possibly tourists attracted by the flyers she asked friends to post in Raleigh, Hickory, and Asheville. Representing the native population are CW and Sally Durwood, Annie Sayles and her little girl, and May Vernon with her twin grandsons.

That's the first group. The second, stone-faced and drab in work clothes and plain dresses, consists of Durwood locals watching from the Shell station across the street.

The Midsummer race, centerpiece of the Festival of Oaks intended to unite Durwood, seems to have widened the gap instead. Star's two kids, teenage Rhiannon and ten-year-old Gwion, run valiantly back and forth, distributing sprays of oak leaves to everyone in sight. In the first group there are flashes of greenery as people wave them like flags; in the second, most of them lie discarded on the ground. Morgan winces at the recollection of the hours she's spent spinning fantasies in which the festival burgeons into a wildly popular annual event that brings prosperity to Durwood. A despicable prickling begins behind her eyes. In spite of the friction with Star during the planning process, there have been moments that recreated the warm camaraderie of her coven days, women working together to bring something wonderful into being.

Now it all seems like a pitiable charade. How can today be turning out so terribly wrong, when she was so certain they had the Goddess's blessing? She feels very much like a Bunny Dancer at this moment, frolicking hare-brained and all alone. Checking her watch, noting it's time for the race, she finds a ragged green figure at her shoulder – Nick decked out in his Midsummer finery.

"Who's that? She doesn't look like a local." He's pointing at Liz Wyatt, standing at the back of the friendly group, pale hair spilling down her back beneath a big hat with its sprig of oak tucked jauntily in the band.

"Oh, that's Liz."

"Liz?"

"Liz Wyatt. I forgot to tell you she lives here. Our token celebrity."

"Liz Wy – you mean Elizabeth Wyatt? *The* Elizabeth Wyatt?"

"The very one."

"Wow. I didn't know she was still alive."

"Nicky, this is a disaster. Is it too late to call it off?"

"What do you mean? It'll be fine."

In the wildly-popular-annual-event fantasy, Nick is her indispensable second in command. She sighs. "Okay, here goes nothing. Wish me luck."

Still gawking at Liz, he gives her cheek a distracted peck. "Yeah. Luck."

Morgan takes a deep breath and waves her arms at the crowd. "Welcome, everyone! Welcome to the Durwood Festival of Oaks!" To her, the words sound weak and despairing, but the friendly group erupts into cheers and applause. Among the upturned faces she sees Molly and Tamara beaming, CW with the sun glinting off his glasses.

"We're going to start the race in just a minute," she says as they quiet down, "but first I want to say a few words about this very special town." Scattered cheers from the friendlies, no response from the locals. Well, what does she expect? There's nothing to do but proceed.

"There aren't many places like Durwood left in the world today, places where people live gently on the earth, in harmony with the seasons, the way our species was meant to live. Now, I know some of you feel there aren't enough jobs to go around, and the roads are bad and the power's not dependable, and there's not much prospect of making a good living here. But those of us who weren't lucky enough to be born in Durwood feel blessed to have found it, and we want to do what we can to make this community flourish.

"Some of our older citizens can remember a wonderful tradition of marking the summer solstice, the longest day of the year. Back in ancient times, this was a day of tribute to the powers of light and growth and abundance, and today we're reviving Durwood's very own traditional Midsummer celebration.

"For those of you not familiar with it, the highlight is a footrace. The runners will race down Main Street to the oak tree in front of Cole's Engine Repair, where we've hung a crown of leaves. The first one to reach the tree, climb it. and claim the crown will be our King of the Greenwood. He'll choose a Queen, and together they'll preside over some festivities we've got planned for this evening outside Abundance.

"Let's hope that today's Festival of Oaks will represent not just the revival of a time-honored tradition, but the dawning of a new era of prosperity for Durwood!"

Out of breath, Morgan stops. There's a spatter of applause, bolstered by a lusty cheer from her friends. It's time to stop talking and get things moving.

"Runners, line up!"

Nick and Rhiannon unroll a green streamer across Main Street and the contestants line up behind it – all the newcomers like Ben, Russ, Chad, Mark, and Jason, along with couple of the putative tourists. Mariela Everdale is whispering vehemently to her husband, the prominent Asheville attorney, but he's not budging from the sidelines. Nor do the locals show any sign of joining.

Lounging on the benches outside the Shell station service bay are the young men of Durwood, bearded Jared Gorton and ponytailed Darrell Reese in their coveralls, Darrell's shy younger brother Hub, the Cole twins and Spencer Sayles and young Skip Vernon, all of them ideal contenders for the role of King of the Greenwood – their expressionless faces concealing, Morgan's willing to bet, pure contempt. She winces inwardly. The Festival of Oaks is turning out to be no more than a performance by and for the Bunny Dancers, and she's helpless to salvage it.

"Step up, folks," she calls. "Everybody's welcome!" She sees Nick, Goddess bless him, take his place among the runners. But it's a sorry showing compared to CW's description of the days when every male thirteen and older had eagerly vied for the King's crown.

She can't wait for this to be over.

"On your mark!" she cries. "Get set!"

The crowd quiets as the runners crouch forward. In the sudden silence the twittering of birds in the branches overhead is clearly audible, and then an angry bellow breaks the stillness.

"You got one hell of a nerve showin up here today, boy!"

Everyone turns to look. From her vantage point on the steps, Morgan can see two men in confrontation behind the runners. One of them is CW Durwood, whose shout stills hang in the air. She doesn't recognize the other; he's young and neatly dressed in chinos and a button-down shirt, his thinning strawberry blond hair combed in an aggressive side part that she instinctively associates with the Christian Right.

He rocks back on his heels. "Well, hey to you too, CW."

"You think we ain't heard what you're up to? Loggers in the Noon Woods! You crazy, Gordie?"

"Golly, CW, why get so riled up over a bunch of trees? It's not like you don't have plenty more woods around here."

"You got no right to log in there! Them woods don't belong to you, nor nobody else neither!"

"Well, now . . . " Gordie smoothes his hair. "I gotta tell you, CW, my lawyer over in Asheville says different. He says now Pa's gone, those woods are my legal property."

Without warning CW backhands the smirking face, knocking Gordie to his knees. It happens so fast that before the spectators have a chance to react, he's already moving in for another shot. Sally Durwood jumps between them.

"Get up, Gordie, and get gone. Pa, you made your point. Don't spoil the festival."

There's a tense pause. Then, with a crisp nod to the openmouthed contestants, CW marches over to take a spot on the starting line. A cheer breaks from someone in the crowd, swelling to a chorus of shouts and applause as, one after another, the young men of Durwood follow him to join the race.

◆◆◆

Them woods don't belong to you, nor nobody else neither. To Nick the emotion in the crowd is all but palpable, natives and outsiders miraculously united by CW's words. When the local men step up to the starting line, he cheers himself hoarse. Whoever this Gordie is, whatever his reason for showing up today, for this brief interval he's managed to fuse the two mismatched communities into one.

"Get set!"

Nick's ready. How can he resist the chance to take part in an event that still carries the flavor of an ancient Celtic tradition, however diluted by time? A celebration of youth and strength and fertility, of human life intertwined with the cycles of nature . . . Sadly those days are long gone, wiped out by the repressive era of patriarchy, but just knowing they once existed is enough to –

"Go!"

The crowd shrieks as the runners charge forward, hats flying off to be trampled underfoot. Jostled from his reverie, Nick discovers himself alone on the starting line and sets off in belated pursuit. Not the most auspicious of beginnings – but it doesn't take him long to find his stride, and after a few moments he'd settled into a smooth rhythm. As the cacophony of cheering fades behind him, he tries to dismiss everything from his mind but the thump of his feet hitting the pavement and the staccato wink of sunlight through the green branches overhead.

The pace is faster than he would have expected; nonetheless, before long he starts to gain on the pack, and by the time they reach the four-way stop sign at the center of town, he's at their heels. People are beginning to drop out – CW Durwood heading for the sidelines, Russ Barrett limping along in his sandals, offering a good luck wave as Nick blows past; and most of the local boys who joined the race at the last minute are now straggling along at a halfhearted jog. Nick threads his way through them, setting his sights on the leaders – a hybrid clump of hats and bare heads, Midsummer costumes and overalls. No one's exactly dressed for running; his own improvised robe is an old bedspread dyed green and torn into a ragged fringe along the edges, fluttering and billowing with every step he takes. But it's all part of the charm, the magic of the day, and he advances steadily until he's just behind the leader, a local man clad in work boots and grease-stained coveralls.

Lengthening stride, Nick pushes forward. Now the two of them are running side by side, legs pumping in unison. A sideways glance shows him an unfamiliar bearded profile and an awesome tatt of leaves covering the guy's forearm from wrist to elbow. He's panting as he runs, striving to win this contest he seemed ready to scorn a short time ago. And he's not the only one feeling the pace; by now Nick's lungs are burning, the pavement sucking like mud at his feet. He grits his teeth and forces his legs to keep moving.

There's about a block and a half still to go when it occurs to him that the winner of the race should be a local guy, that it's only right for a Durwood native to wear the King's crown. He's letting his pace slacken, allowing the other guy to pull ahead, when the noise of the following crowd hits him like a seismic wave – a ragged roar of pure bloodlust that bypasses reason and triggers the instinct to flee. He can't help himself. As they head down the final stretch, he pounds into the lead.

Ahead of him the tree stands resplendent, aglow in the light of the sinking sun, its chambered crown pierced by blinding rays that shine straight into his eyes. All at once he can see nothing – but lost in the dazzle he seems to perceive everything with stunning clarity, to understand that he's running not down a street in a little mountain town but along the inner curve of a living sphere ribbed with trees, a woven vessel of green branches and invisible roots enclosing Durwood, sealing it off from the rest of the world. He's filled with the sudden certainty that in this infinite, luminous web, he forms a crucial strand

and then his legs are snatched from under him and he's flung violently forward, arms windmilling as the street rushes up and slams into him.

He blinks. All he can see are green spots that slowly resolve into pitted blacktop a scant inch from his nose. He rolls over and sits up, still dazed. What happened? He tripped, fell – and now he sees the culprit, a long strip of fabric from his costume that's managed to wrap itself around his ankles. Tearing it loose, he can feel his scraped palms and bloody knees beginning to burn.

A dozen yards away the local man's already halfway up the tree. Nick picks himself up and limps the final distance. Just as well he wiped out; hadn't he decided to let local guy win? Above his head, the wink and gleam of afternoon sunlight through green branches is somehow conspiratorial, hinting at some fleeting revelation that's already slipped away; and watching his rival snatch the wreath from its branch and start his descent, he finds himself grinning like an idiot. What an awesome way to salute the summer solstice! Scraped knees notwithstanding, he wouldn't trade places with anyone in the world right now. But for the hand of the Goddess, he'd be clerking in some stuffy law office, counting the minutes until another dull summer afternoon dragged to its end.

He's looking back down the street, watching the remaining runners approach at a perfunctory jog, when the new King of the Greenwood drops from the tree to land beside him.

Nick offers his hand. "Hey, man. Great race."

The local guy grunts. "Do me a favor, huh? Take this damn thing." Thrusting his prize into Nick's outstretched hand, he strides away.

"Wha – hey, come back here! Hey!"

But by this time the other runners have reached the tree, and the cheering crowd follows close on their heels. Clutching the victor's wreath, Nick's mobbed by men pounding him on the back, women pushing forward to embrace him. His efforts to explain are lost in the hullabaloo; at last he gives up and accepts their accolades, picturing the real winner's obvious annoyance at having let himself get carried him away. That's just wrong; the King of the Greenwood shouldn't resent his role.

Take this damn thing.

All at once the crowd recedes and he stands alone, surrounded by a hush. An old woman and a little girl approach hand in hand. He recognizes them as locals; Morgan must have managed, riding the wave of unity, to recruit them for the roles she and Rhiannon were slated to perform. The old woman – Mrs Reese, isn't it, who runs the grocery store? – takes the crown from him and gives it to the frail blond child. For an instant he sees himself reflected in those round blue eyes: the winner of the race, tall and strong.

King of the Greenwood.

Maybe it was meant to be.

The old woman's hand is on his shoulder, a feathery pressure, and he kneels, not feeling his scrapes. As the little girl sets the crown on his head, the tickle of leaves sends a shiver through him. A voice speaks, startlingly near.

"King of the Greenwood, choose your Queen."

He blinks. The faces encircling him now are all women's. Old and young, known and unknown, smiling or grave, their eyes upon him. In this moment, strangers all. He rises to his feet, robed and crowned in green, dazed by the sense of another identity overlaid upon his own.

King of the Greenwood, choose your Queen.

His questing gaze catches on one face and holds.

Hal Everdale heads for his car with a sense of relief. So much for the Durwood Festival of Oaks. Very quaint, very picturesque.

Having put in an appearance at this hillbilly hoe-down to humor his wife, he can now go home and have a drink in peace on the porch overlooking his pond. He and Mariela came in separate cars; she's planning to attend the evening leg of the festival as well, besotted as she is with the bizarre blend of yokels and New Age types who make up the Durwood scene.

And besotted with Chad, the yoga guru: softspoken prettyboys are Mariela's favorite dalliance. Not that Hal minds, or has for the last decade, but in addition to being softspoken and pretty, Chad is black – as if Mariela needs to keep upping the ante to see just how much Hal will take. It irritates him that Chad's skin color seems a matter of indifference not just to the hippies in Durwood but to the locals as well; he'd enjoy seeing Yoga Boy reminded of how things used to be in this part of the country.

Of course, Hal can't afford to express such feelings in today's social climate. Instead he's paying the rent on Chad's studio, the pretentiously named Durwood Body Arts, so Mariela can have her daily yoga fix along with the other New Age fruitcakes who live here. But credit where credit is due: it was Chad who'd introduced Mariela to the alternative community in Asheville, which eventually led to Durwood and Hal's introduction to the most beautiful and unspoiled country he's ever seen. He'd lost no time buying thirty acres on a ridge east of the town and hiring a dependable Asheville contractor to execute the plans for his dream house.

Completed just over a year ago, it's perfect in every detail, paid for by years of hard work for his corporate clients. The crowning touch is Mariela's studio, located on the far side of the pond and modeled on a Japanese teahouse. Along with the studio and the gallery in Asheville, this new sculpture kick of hers has set him back a small fortune, all so she can concoct a bunch of plaster and wire objects that look vaguely gynecological to Hal. But as long as it keeps her occupied . . .

He brushes a drift of dead leaves from the hood of his Lexus. What with the drought, it's more like fall than summer around here. A gob of something sticky beneath the leaves resists his cursory effort to rub it off; he gives up, climbs in, and slams the door. Pulling out, he notes pandemonium at the far end in of the street; some oaf has won the race and the crowd's going wild.

The Durwood Festival of Oaks. What a farce. And as if the event isn't tedious enough in its own right, who should come blundering into the middle of it but his newest client, the obnoxious Gordon Durwood.

When the young man had showed up in his office last week, dropping Buck Pawling's name and saying he needed to confirm his legal title to a piece of land, Hal had immediately detested him – one of those fervent, sweaty-palmed Christians convinced that Jesus Christ is micromanaging the universe on their behalf. Nonetheless, Gordon Durwood stands to make a hefty profit from timbering the old growth tract known as the Noon Woods, and Hal never lets his personal tastes interfere with potential income.

From today's confrontation it's clear there's a lot of local resistance to the destruction of the trees, but that's immaterial to Hal; he's been careful to purchase enough surrounding land to insulate himself no matter who does what around here. And he has to admit it gave him a certain pleasure to see young Durwood flattened in the street by an old man.

❉ 4 ❉

Lit by the sinking sun, the witch balls glint along the edge of the porch roof. Liz Wyatt passes beneath them and lets the screen door bang behind her, stowing her walking stick in its customary corner without breaking stride, heading straight for the kitchen cabinet where she keeps Ward Cole's moonshine.

It's a new jar, nearly full. She unscrews the lid and tips a generous measure into a jelly glass. Normally she limits her trips to Durwood to once a week for groceries – the less time she spends driving, the better; she hasn't had a blackout in a while, but she knows they can happen any time. Today's visit to the Festival of Oaks was a whim, an impulse to support Morgan Edwards, whom she's grown to like in the few months she's known her. But the news of the proposed logging has spoiled the day, and instead of staying to watch the race Liz has come home to fret.

Glass in hand, she makes her way to the sagging sofa in front of the fireplace. Minnie jumps onto her lap and begins to purr; Liz strokes her, sipping the moonshine. She'll have a fire later, in the evening chill that falls over the mountains like a blessing on even the hottest days.

When she'd come back to Durwood three months ago, looking for a place to stay, CW had offered her his old family cabin and she'd accepted his generosity without bothering to confide that it would likely be her last home on earth. Not that it would have been likely to make a difference; Durwood people, like country folk everywhere, take death in their stride.

But not every death. Not the death of the Noon Woods.

Unconsciously her fingers dig into Minnie's fur and the cat shoots off her lap, landing with a thump on the hearthstone. Settling back on the sofa, Liz feels something in the pocket of her skirt and extracts a crumpled ball of paper – one of the flyers advertising today's event. She flattens it over her knee.

The Durwood Festival of Oaks. Below the fanciful font is the image of the Green Man, the nature spirit whose leaf-wreathed visage was spread across Europe by medieval craftsmen, a pagan interloper carved into the wood and stone of Christian churches, no two quite alike, their expressions ranging from merry to menacing.

This one sits somewhere at the middle of the spectrum. While she sits staring down at it, the sun's rays lengthen outside, gilding the hayfield, deepening the bordering shadows. A mourning dove calls and subsides and the first crickets begin to sing.

At last Liz bends down and picks up a chunk of charcoal from the hearth. Turning the paper over, she begins to sketch on the back. The first few lines are hesitant, fragile as root tendrils, tentatively breaching the blankness of the page. Slowly they gain force, each stroke more robust than the last until they're spreading with lightning speed, smears and smudges adding weight and depth to the lines. Liz bends closer in concentration, oblivious of the cat slinking away, ears flattened and tail tucked. The only sound in the house is the scratch of charcoal on paper.

When it's done, she sits back to survey the first real drawing she's made in sixteen years. She's oddly out of breath. *Green Man.* Not a carved motif. Not a garden ornament or an image on a flyer. This is the guardian spirit of the Nood Woods, present in every root and bole and branch and leaf.

Outside the cabin, the witch balls are singing in the wind.

On the drive back to Lenoir in Vance's truck, Gordie's tongue keeps probing the raw place on the inside his cheek where CW's fist ground it into his teeth. He can see Vance sneaking looks at him, no doubt thinking he's a sissy for letting an old man slap him around, wondering what all the fuss is about. But this logging is something he's got to do. The idea may have come from Buck Pawling, but Gordie knows Buck was just the instrument. It's all part of the Savior's plan.

Buck's an acquaintance of Gordie's from church, a slick real estate guy who's always smiling and winking and talking fast around his chewing gum. He's a regular customer at Arlen's Fashion Footwear in the Biltmore Square Mall, where Gordie works as a salesman. He's also a big fan of Sealed in the Spirit, the gospel group that's going to make Gordie a star.

Sealed in the Spirit has come a long way in the eight years since Gordie and the Cochran brothers and Willy Howell were all pimply Youth Fellowship members at the Blood Bought Baptist Church in Asheville. Momma let them practice in her garage, and they performed at church picnics and summer tent revivals. Even though Gordie can't play an instrument, he has another skill: he can stand up in front of a crowd and witness to the glory of the Lord, a talent developed during those miserable childhood Sundays when Momma made him preach scripture outside the Durwood Hardware & General.

Unlike the folks in Durwood, the gospel crowds love him. He brings the mike in close and lets his voice go husky as he talks about growing up in a lonely place back in the mountains where him and his momma were set apart by their love of the Lord. There were times, he'll say, times when he downright hated Jesus (gasps from the crowd), yes folks, hated Our Blessed Savior for making him an outcast. Times he'd have renounced all hope of eternal salvation just for a chance to play with the other boys or steal a kiss from their voluptuous sisters. For twelve long years he'd gone without friends, without so much as a single smile from the beautiful, godless girls of Durwood. He'd endured the indifference of the adults, his own uncles and aunts and cousins who'd turned their faces from the light to embrace Satan, and even resisted his own father's dogged attempts to turn him into a sinner, make him one of them.

"Folks," he'll say, "there were times I was so doggone lonely I would of spit on the blessed cross if they'd asked me to, but they didn't want nothing to do with me. And when Momma would find me crying she'd say, 'Son, can't you take a little pain for Jesus' sake? Don't you remember what He suffered for you?'"

That's the cue for the instruments to come in. A few tremulous notes from Farley's mandolin, followed by Brad's fiddle and Willy's soft guitar, and Gordie closes his eyes and sings:

> *One cross plus three nails*
> *Equals for - or - given*
> *Just do the math and you'll see*
> *One cross plus three nails*
> *Equals for - or – or - given*
> *That's what Jesus did*
> *For you and –for me*

The catch in his voice before the words *for me* never fails to squeeze a few sobs from the audience, and Gordie's proud to have written the song himself. But recently his fondness for it has acquired a bitter taste, because he has a growing suspicion that *One Cross* is the only reason he's still part of Sealed in the Spirit. The way Willy and the Cochrans play those instruments, it's like they came into this world holding them in their hands, whereas when Gordie picks up a guitar it's the same as when he thinks about putting his arm around a girl – his mind goes blank and his whole body freezes up.

In the beginning this deficiency didn't seem to matter, but in the last year or so Sealed in the Spirit's popularity has skyrocketed, and right now they're booked several months in advance at churches in Lenoir, Hickory, even as far away as Statesville. Gordie's been noticing the look that passes between Brad and Farley whenever he hits a sour note in *Softly and Tenderly* or *Power in the Blood*. Those looks are giving him a bad feeling. The group is the most important thing in the world to him, the only thing that makes his life worth living. And that's why Jesus sent Buck Pawling.

Here's how it happens. Gordie's helping Buck choose a new pair of wingtips, listening to him talk about all the real estate deals he's got going. There's a lot of money around, a lot of people itching to spend it; this part of the state is an unexploited paradise, vacation homes going up so fast in the area that the building suppliers can't keep up –

"Why, a guy I know cleared his land for development and got $400,000 for the trees alone. Lemme try those two-tones, old son."

Gordie slips the shoe onto Buck's outstretched foot. "Four hundred thousand dollars for *trees*?"

"You bet, old son. Hardwood's sky-high right now. Custom kitchen cabinets, fancy floors – heck, wood siding's even coming back, although personally I think you're better off with vinyl, less upkeep. But trees take a long time to grow. So the profit margins – naw, these pinch a little, let's go back to the Rockports. Yeah, I like these. What's this color called?"

"Chili," Gordie says. "I got some big old trees."

"Yeah?" Buck pops his gum and squints down his leg at the Rockport. Gordie can see he's not listening.

"I mean really big trees. Really big and really old."

"Yeah? Out in your front yard?"

"Nope, way back up in the mountains where I was raised. There's five or six thousand acres up there. Momma always said they belonged to my daddy. He passed a while back, so I guess they're mine now."

All at once he has Buck's attention. "Five or six th – heck you say! How much forested?"

"Pretty much all of it. Mostly oaks, I think."

Buck whistles. Pacing back and forth in his new shoes, he outlines a deal. For a small percentage he'll hire a forestry consultant to estimate the value of the timber, find the most competitive bid, take care of the contract, all the complicated stuff. All Gordie will need to do is keep an eye on the logging process once it begins.

"For this kind of project it's just smart to have boots on the ground, old son. Not my boots – I don't wanta get em dirty, ha ha. You just keep in touch with the logging company, make sure everything goes nice and smooth, and I can promise you a deal that'll make you rich rich rich."

Inside Gordie's head, an angel band begins to sing. At last he'll be able to unload this stupid job and embark on the life he was meant for, spreading God's glory, bringing souls to Jesus through song. Much as Momma hated the Noon Woods and condemned them as a temple of Satan, those acres of evil trees are going to finally do some good in the world. They're going to finance Sealed in the Spirit's crucial first CD. As producer, Gordie won't have to worry about being dumped from the group. He pictures the cover, everybody arranged so it won't be obvious he's not holding an instrument. Would it be better to put *One Cross* as the first cut or the last?

But first the logging has to happen. And crucial as the CD is, there are other reasons for bringing down the Noon Woods. They're the dark and twisted heart of his father's people, the core of all their heathenish ways. He thinks back to those dismal childhood Sundays reciting scripture on the steps of the Hardware & General, Momma sitting on the bench behind him in her best dress while he preaches salvation to everyone who passes by. The grownups hide their grins, the kids point and snicker; even the rustle of leaves overhead sounds like smothered laughter.

"They make fun of me, Momma. They call me the Peewee Preacher."

"They're godless heathens, honey. Demons clothed in flesh, every one. They're going to burn in hell for their sins, while we shall be counted among the blessed." She stands at the sink, washing dishes. "The multitudes mocked the Lord Jesus too, son. They *smote* Him on the head and did *spit* upon Him before they *nailed* Him to the cross. For us, Gordie. For you and me."

"But – "

Momma throws her sponge in the sink and pulls him to her with soapy hands, putting her face close to his.

"Listen, son. When He prayed in agony in the garden, His *sweat* was as *great drops of blood* falling to the ground. *Great drops of blood*, Gordie! And then His tormentors *stripped* Him and *scourged* Him and *crucified* Him – "

She stops, out of breath, and Gordie gazes at her in fascination. When Momma talks about the sufferings of Jesus, her eyes go weirdly bright, little red spots appear in her cheeks and her lips get wet and shiny.

He wishes he could be the one to bring that look to her face.

Abruptly she pushes him away. "The Lord Jesus died in *agony*, Gordie, that we might be cleansed of sin. He was *nailed* to a cross that we might be washed in His *blood*. Can't you take a little name calling for His sake?"

Gordie doesn't answer. How can he explain that it's not the name calling that bothers him? On the contrary, the name calling is nothing. No amount of name calling can produce that special feeling, the one he gets from the secret game he calls Crucifixion, where he pretends he's Jesus tormented and mocked by the crowd – scourged and spit on, driven to his knees beneath a hail of insults and blows. The jeering mob and the punishing hands are pretend, but the suffering is as real as he can make it; he flings himself on the ground and rubs his face in the dirt, bangs his head against a tree until his ears ring. Sometimes he even presses his palm against the point of a nail sticking out of the clothesline post behind the house, biting his tongue against the pain while he waits for the feeling of being lifted up on wings of fire.

But the game is a secret. Even though he knows deep down that Momma understands, he also knows it's not something that can ever be spoken of.

(He's walking out of the Hardware & General, licking a cherry Popsicle. Momma's across the street at Reese's getting groceries. She doesn't want him underfoot while she shops, so she's given him some money for a treat from the big freezer at the back of Uncle CW's store, reminding him after he makes his purchase to *go straight back to the car and wait, I don't want you spending time with those people Gordie do you hear me, they are all heathens every last one of them.* His uncle always tells him to just take what he wants, no need to pay, but Gordie leaves money on the counter because *we don't accept gifts from the ungodly, everything they touch is tainted and don't you forget it.*

The sugary burn of the Popsicle on his tongue absorbs him so completely that he doesn't see the crowd of boys until they're right in front of him. Jared Gorton, Spence Sayles, Harley Cole, Tyne Durwood, Darrell Reese and his little brother

Hub.

Looky there, it's the Peewee Preacher, Jared says.

They all snicker. Someone shoves Gordie from behind, and he glances back to see Conlee Cole grinning like a monkey.

Wassamatter Preacher? Doncha wanna give us a sermon? We wanna hear a sermon.

Gordie opens his mouth to yell for help – his uncle is right there inside the Hardware & General, and there's Mister Vernon smoking a cigarette outside May's Café next door – and then shuts it without making a sound

The other boys hustle him down the narrow alley between May's and the hardware store. As Conlee shoves him toward a cluster of trash cans beneath a tree he drops his Popsicle, and his squeak of dismay as it lands in the dirt makes them all laugh.

Then they let him go.

No one moves. No one's touching him. He could run away, but he doesn't. Momma's voice flits through his head.

Spit upon. Stripped. Smited. Tormented. Scourged. Mocked. Crucified.

Jared points to the trash cans. *Okay Peewee. Climb on up and let's hear you preach.*)

" – chance to settle down a little." Vance's voice yanks Gordie back to the present.

"Wha?"

"Just saying you might want to think about postponing the job a while, given what happened back there. Seems like tempers are running pretty high. Maybe folks need a chance to cool off before you bring a crew in."

Gordie shakes his head. "It's all legal. I can get the law in there if I have to."

Vance shrugs. "Okay, your call. You decided whether you want to clearcut or just thin?"

Far back in Gordie's memory, pale demon eyes gleam among green shadows. A whispering chill runs across his skin. It's high time the Noon Woods were filled with the buzz of chainsaws and the crash of falling trees. Haven't ungodly things happened there – things the witch balls were supposed to help protect them from, so secret and terrible that even hinting at them made Momma's voice shake and those little red spots pop out on her cheeks?

"Clearcut," he says.

◆ ◆ ◆

Dusk is falling by the time the bonfire roars to life in Abundance's parking lot. Flames leap from the mountain of scrap wood into the deep violet sky, bringing cheers from the spectators. Somebody passes Nick a Mason jar and he takes a sip, enduring the burn in his throat in anticipation of the glow in his belly. At least this time he knows what to expect – unlike his first gulp of moonshine, taken earlier without so much as a precautionary sniff. He'd barely managed to transform his gag reflex into an agonized wheeze that won a roar of laughter from the other men, a hail of approving fists beating his back.

How many hours ago was that? The oak leaf crown has slipped over one eye and he fumbles it back into place, aware that he's very drunk. And why not? He's King of the Greenwood. Strictly speaking, of course, the title is his by default, but that's a little secret between him and the real winner, who's nowhere to be seen.

Nick wishes him well. Steeped in liquor and fellowship, he wishes everyone well. The Midsummer festivities have transported them all back to a mythic golden past in which the Goddess is top dog and patriarchy hasn't yet ruined the world. Is it only luck that landed him here in Durwood – or, as Morgan suggested, the hand of the Lady Herself?

The tang of roast pork lingers in his mouth; May Vernon has supplemented Abundance's health-conscious offerings with a tray of her legendary barbeque, and he's already devoured two helpings. Children with cartoon cat faces pop out of the shadows and disappear back into them; Tamara, over in the face painting booth, is doing a booming business – as is Vivian, decked out in turban and shawl in the fortune-telling tent while Chad, the yoga teacher, administers shiatsu to half the town. Although Morgan made only a token effort to publicize this event outside Durwood, Nick can imagine future Oak Festivals as a benign pagan influence casting an ever widening net.

A few more swallows of moonshine and another plate of barbeque later, he finds himself trying to explain to his Queen of the Greenwood the symbolic meaning of their roles.

"The King's a nature shpirit, shee. Jack in the (hc) Green. It'sh all about fer(hc)shility."

"Fer*what*?" The corners of her eyes crinkle when she smiles. Without question she's the most beautiful woman he's ever seen, like beyond hot. Beneath the feathery crown of willow leaves, a mass of bright hair surrounds her laughing face and spills over her shoulders, catching light from the paper lanterns strung among the booths. He sways on his feet, seeing the colors dance.

"Fer. Fer – ti – tility." The word seems to stick to his tongue. "Bounty of the harvesht and hunt. The priesht and prieshtesh perform a rish . . . rishual marriage shymbolishing the pact be (hc) tween nashure and shumanity."

"Come again?" Even her laugh is sexy. She's told him her name is Sally, and somebody else mentioned she's the local midwife, but those facts belong to an entirely different reality. Here and now, her only identity is Queen of the Greenwood.

And he's King. And he wants her; he can't recall ever wanting anyone so much. Ritual marriage seems the logical next step. His room is right there above the store and he tries to lead her in that direction, but somehow her hand slips from his.

When he looks around, she's gone.

"Hey," he says, peering through the crowded shadows. "Hey, where'd you go?"

He searches among the brightly decorated booths, exchanging greetings and pats on the back with everyone he meets. Colored lanterns bob in his vision. Where is she? Away from the booths it's darker; when he stops to admire the hazy stars overhead, a giggling cat-child careens into him and almost knocks him down. Behind a booth he sees two shadows in proximity; one abruptly stalks away and he recognizes Chad, the yoga teacher. The other figure takes a few steps after him – an older woman who's clearly had too much to drink. She looks upset. In his benevolent mood Nick is about to offer comfort when he hears a man's voice say, "One spark from a chainsaw and them woods'll go right up. Only a fool'd try to log in this drought."

A dozen figures cluster beneath a nearby tree. Nick drifts closer, hearing someone say, "Well, Gordie Fuckin Durwood's nothin if not a fool."

"Yeah, but ain't no loggin company gonna risk a forest fire."

"Try and log the Noon Woods, fire's gonna be the leasta their troubles," another voice says. By now Nick can make out faces: CW Durwood from the hardware store, Pete Vernon from May's Café, some of the young men who joined the race at the last minute.

"What I hear, he means to start next week, drought or no," Pete's saying. "We can't just set by and watch. We gotta do somethin."

"Like what?" one of the young men says.

"Like maybe the old 3-S treatment."

Dark branches toss restlessly over their heads. CW lifts a hand. "Now, boys, let's take it easy. Likely the whole thing'll – "

Sighting a flash of fiery hair near the fortune telling booth, Nick stumbles off in pursuit. Too late; he's already lost her. But there's Morgan in a huddle with some of the other business owners, snatches of their discussion growing audible as he approaches.

" – human chain," Russ is saying. "If they can't get their equipment up the road, they can't log."

"I know somebody at WKHY in Hickory," Tamara says. "If there's a face-off, it'd be good to have a camera crew there."

Star nods. "I'll design a tee we can sell. Start a fund in case we need to hire a lawyer."

"We can all carry the shirts at our businesses," Morgan says. "And have petitions at our cash registers for people to sign. If we – "

"Nick!" Into his vision swims the face he's been seeking; warm fingers seize his. "Come on and dance!"

She pulls him toward the firelight, into the compass of lively music and the rhythm of clapping hands. Here's Morgan's dream of unity come true, Ben Upshaw and Jason Anders jamming with the local musicians as if they've been playing together all their lives. People are already dancing and Sally pulls him into the fray, where laughing faces whirl around him, ruddy with firelight. He's clumsy but it doesn't matter; nothing matters but the exuberant fellowship and the play of flames on penny-bright hair. When he stumbles over his own feet, hands reach out to steady him. The music creates its own dominion, one tune giving way to the next as the dancers grow flushed and out of breath and the whooping, clapping spectators egg them on to match the instruments' frenzied pace.

At last Nick retreats panting to the sidelines and lets the sound wash over him. A few minutes later Sally joins him. He gives her a sideways glance; the dancing has thinned the alcohol fog in his head and he dimly remembers trying to drag her off to his room. "Hi," he mumbles.

"Tuckered out?" She doesn't seem offended; she's watching the dancers, nodding in time to the music.

"Just catching my breath." A wild flourish from the fiddle gets his attention and he marvels at the fiddler's youth; he's maybe fourteen at the most. "Wow, that kid's really talented."

"Yeah, Skip's a real child of the wood."

"A what?"

She smiles. "That's what we say round here when somebody's got a gift. Supposed to mean they was conceived in the Noon Woods. Mighta been true once, but not anymore. Now it's just somethin folks say."

Nick's reminded of CW's vehement words at the race this afternoon. *Them woods don't belong to you, nor nobody else neither.* "What's so special about those woods, anyway?"

"Oh . . . They just been around a long time, is all. There's a lotta old stories." She's looking down, firelight catching her lashes. "Cherokee legend says if a hunter went too deep in the woods, the forest spirits'd steal his soul. Even if he found his way home again, he'd be nothin but an empty shell, no good to himself or anybody else."

Nick's spine tingles pleasurably. "You ever meet them? The forest spirits?"

"I'll tell you what . . . there's times when I'll be out huntin herbs and I'll feel like there's somethin keeping an eye on me. Not meanin harm nor nothin. Just watchin."

"Like a forest spirit?"

"Might could call it that. My granny used to tell us kids a story about Roan Durwood and his bargain with the white doe."

"Tell me." He's eager to keep her by his side, talking in that wonderful mountain twang.

"Well . . . Roan was my five-greats grandpaw. Story goes, he was passin through the mountains and stopped to make camp for the night in the Noon Woods. Fell asleep and woke to see a pure white doe dancin by herself, all silver in the moonlight, to the most beautiful music he'd ever heard. He pretended to be asleep, and when dawn came he seen her go through a secret door in one of the trees, back to the Bright Land where she come from.

"Roan waited, and the next night she was back. He couldn't keep his eyes off her, and before he knew it he was dancin with her in the moonlight. They danced for hours, and sometimes he was a stag and she was a doe, and sometimes he was a man and she was a maiden.

"But when dawn came and she tried to go back through the door in the tree, he sprang in front of her and blocked the way. Said: 'What will you give to see your home again?'

"Well, the white doe was in a takin. She offered him riches – what she said was gold and jewels, but all he saw was a pile of red berries on a yellow leaf – and he laughed. So she asked for a single drop of his blood, and in return she told him how to call the wind and rain, and how to take the shape of a stag deer so he could run with her in the forest any time he chose. And she promised no harm should ever come to him or his, for as long as the woods stood tall."

It's clear she's repeating the familiar words of a beloved tale, and Nick wants to kiss her. Instead he reaches out and brushes a stray curl from her cheek. "So . . . is that hereditary, that thing about turning yourself into an animal?"

She laughs. "Can't nobody I know do it, that's sure."

"Will you take me there?"

"The Noon Woods?" She looks surprised. "What for?"

"To meet the white doe."

She's frowning; does she think he's making fun of her? He hastens to explain. "Listen, Sally. What I mean is, there are certain places on the planet where it seems like there's an unusually high concentration of the earth's energy. Those are the places that ancient cultures chose for their sacred sites. From what you're saying, it sounds like the Noon Woods might be one of them – a natural power site. And if it is . . . " A warm chill goes through him. "If it is, in theory it should be possible to use that power to stop the logging."

She's staring at him. "Stop the – ?"

"Why not?"

"Stop it how?"

"Well, uh – " He's fumbling for words when a breeze stirs the crown on his head and he hears the leaves whisper the answer in his ear. "We – we could do a ritual."

"A – ?"

"A magical ritual. Magic works by causing change on the astral plane. If you make a change in the astral, sooner or later it'll manifest on the physical." He'd really liked the sound of that line when he'd come across it in his reading, but she's looking blank. He tries a different approach.

"Look, somebody once said that magic doesn't contradict nature, it just contradicts *what we know* about nature. So just because our current science doesn't recognize the existence of power sites, it doesn't mean the power isn't there. All we'd have to do is focus it with the right ritual, and – "

A sudden chorus of shouts drowns him out. "May! May! We need us a song!"

There's scattered applause as May Vernon emerges from the crowd, patting her bun into place, and crosses the firelit circle toward the musicians. After a brief conference Skip strikes a few plaintive notes on his fiddle, and the crowd quiets as she begins to sing.

The minor melody is hauntingly beautiful, the singer's voice true and sweet, but Nick's only half listening, distracted by the notion that seems to have come to him unbidden. Can the power of the natural world really be used to stop the logging? Why not? In a place where people live so close to the earth, where a pagan tradition already exists, where the community's founder is rumored to have wielded unusual powers, it seems enticingly possible.

As if in answer, the words of the song pierce his thoughts:

O they went to the wood, where the oaken tree stood
To cut down the tree, the oaken tree.
But the oak gave a groan for to summon his own,
And the trees closed about, and they never got out
Of the wood, the wonderful wood.

Goosebumps pucker his skin. The Goddess approves of his idea; could it be any more obvious? The wonderful wood. The phrase seems to reverberate endlessly in the fire-flecked darkness; then the musicians swing into a rollicking dance tune and people jump whooping to their feet. As the dancers whirl in a wild jig, a hand bumps Nick's elbow and there's one of the local boys, offering him the Mason jar. He wraps his fingers around it, tilts his head back and lets the fire run down his throat.

❋ 5 ❋

Beyond the turreted castle walls, extravagant bands of flamingo pink streak the sky. The wooden gates stand open, revealing a deserted courtyard. It looks like the perfect moment, but he knows the guards can't be far off. He needs to move fast.

Hidden inside this stone fortress – unless his informant in the seaside tavern was lying – is the Scroll of Al-Qabiri, the second of three magical manuscripts he needs to acquire in order to advance to the rank of Zelator and gain access to the fifth level. He's already stolen the Benvenuto Codex from the goblin monks at the Temple of the Obelisk. If he can get the Al-Qabiri, the only thing between him and Zelator will be the fabled Porphyry Tablet.

He crosses the courtyard and mounts stone steps to the iron-studded doors of the keep. Noiselessly they swing inward, revealing a cavernous hall lit by torches in wall brackets. Still no guards. This is way too easy. He thinks of the stranger in the tavern, no more than a gleam of eyes within the shadow of a hood. Has he walked into a trap? The doors whisper shut behind him. On either side of the entrance hall, an arched opening leads to a dim staircase. He heads for the one on the left. According to his informant, the scroll is kept in a chamber at the top.

He's starting up the steps when an insistent message from his body intrudes, a fiery tickle he can't ignore. There's something crawling on the back of his wrist. As he slaps at it, out of the torchlight at the top of the stairs erupts a huge figure wielding a mace. Distracted by the itch, he's slow to react; before he can swing his sword, his assailant is upon him. There's a blinding flash, then darkness.

◆◆◆

Loud knocking yanks Nick from his sodden sleep. At first he doesn't know where he is; then he remembers: Durwood, his sleeping quarters above Morgan's store. The knocking comes again. He rolls off the futon and staggers to the door.

Outside it's dark, stars visible in the sky. The shadowy figure on his threshold speaks.

"Mornin! I'm fixin to head out to the Noon Woods, if you still want to come."

Nick blinks stupidly, steadying himself on the doorframe. He knows that voice. Noon Woods . . . Through the pounding in his head, yesterday begins to seep back. The race, the crown of leaves shoved into his hand –

And the threatened logging. Now he remembers asking Sally to show him the patch of doomed trees. Remembers the story of Roan Durwood's encounter with the magical doe and his own intuition that the place might be some kind of energy vortex where a ritual can be staged to awaken the forest to its own defense. Even a roaring hangover can't dull his sense that it's an awesome idea: old pagans and new, uniting to stop the destruction.

"Uh . . . you're going now?" He's slept in his clothes, he probably smells, and his tongue tastes like a stale sock, but yesterday's ritual roles still cling. Awakened by a beautiful woman with an invitation to an enchanted forest – he rubs his chin stubble. "Okay, I'm game. Let's go."

The luminous face of his clock shows ten past five; he should easily make it back in time to open the store. As he shuts the door behind him, another fragment from last night surfaces – a commotion in the crowd, Ben Upshaw's panicky face, Sally disappearing from his side.

"Hey, did Molly have her baby last night? Or did I dream that?"

"Had a little girl about an hour ago. Gonna call her Laurel."

For somebody who's been up all night delivering a baby, she's buzzing with energy, while he – well, the thought of spending an entire day living in his body makes him want to curl up and die.

During the drive he dozes off and is jolted awake by the rocking of the truck. They're climbing a steep track that's not much more than a tree-lined ditch; half exposed roots jut at eye-level from the crumbling earth on either side and branches form a thick mesh far overhead. Grabbing the dashboard for stability, Nick sees Sally smile and releases his grip, determined to show a semblance of masculine cool. At the top of the hill they turn left through a break in the trees, following a grassy swath that leads to an old log cabin.

Sally pulls up beside the battered Jeep parked outside. "We can walk from here."

She reaches behind the seat and retrieves what looks like a picnic basket. The mere thought of food turns Nick's stomach; he fervently hopes she hasn't brought a picnic breakfast – but she's already out of the car, and he has to hurry to catch up.

Ahead of them, the ground slopes downhill to disappear into morning mist so dense it reduces Sally's figure to a ghostly outline. Plunging after her, he feels the soft pale cloud envelop him, soaking his clothes and hair. He hasn't gone more than a dozen steps before his dew-drenched sneakers start producing a rhythmic squish, squish like a comic metronome. A cracked echo from yesterday's festival flits through his aching brain:

She walked through the corn leading down to the river
Her hair shone like gold in the hot morning sun
She took all the love that a poor boy could give her
And left me to die like a fox on the run

And a wounded animal at the end of its endurance is exactly what he feels like right now. Waves of nausea come and go in sync with a relentless pounding in his skull. As he slogs forward, the mist begins to glow – pink then gold, brightening relentlessly to a dazzle of white that melts his brain. He stumbles to a halt, squeezing his eyes shut.

When he opens them again, the mist has vanished and he's standing face to face with the Noon Woods.

He sucks in breath. A vast, undulating wall of living green towers over him, the massive trees thrusting out their branches as if to ward off intruders, their myriad leaves catching the morning light in a ceaseless motion that somehow translates into a stillness of the whole. How many centuries has it been here, undisturbed by Cherokee and white alike, home to the eternal cycle of birth, death, and renewal? Now some greedy idiot wants to cut it down, destroy not only the magnificent trees but one of the few remaining places where humanity can connect in harmony with the natural world. Picturing a wasteland pocked with mutilated stumps, he's filled with resolve.

Not gonna happen. No way.

Ahead of him, Sally slips into the forest and he bestirs himself to follow. Crossing the threshold between hayfield and forest, he's first aware of cool and dark and stillness, and then his eyes adjust to take in the dense green canopy of interwoven branches, the host of gray-brown trunks stretching away to disappear in shadow. Does sunlight ever penetrate this place? The stirring of leaves is like white noise and the air feels heavy; he can't seem to fill his lungs. A crackle of twigs nearby makes him jump before he realizes it's only Sally, moving off through the trees ahead.

"Hey, w – " Wait for me, he means to say, but it emerges as a distinctly unmanly squeak and he swallows the rest.

For a while the task of keeping her in sight absorbs him – the effort required to dodge aggressive branches and clamber over fallen trunks, the need not to fall behind and be proved unworthy – but little by little this agenda slips away. He finds himself noticing not the trees themselves but the broken, striated spaces in between, an infinity of suggestive shapes hidden in plain sight. Whispering silence surrounds him, unbroken except by the rasp of his breathing. All at once he realizes he hasn't been thinking at all, only moving forward while the pervasive rustle of leaves works its way into his head. Where's Sally? He stops, heart thudding. She can't be far ahead; all he has to do is call out – but even in in the grip of this sudden panic he can't bring himself to break the silence. Surely she'll notice he's no longer behind her and come back for him . . .

But if she doesn't, how the hell is he going to find his way out of here?

A stealthy noise nearby makes him jump; he lunges blindly forward, ducks under a branch – and meets the dark startled gaze of a doe. As she stares, poised against the green, he hears himself say, *Is that hereditary, that thing about turning yourself into an animal?*

And her answer: *Can't nobody I know do it, that's sure.*

"Oh yeah?" he murmurs. At the sound of his voice the doe wheels and flees, tail raised high. Without thinking he gives chase. Thought melts away; nothing exists in this moment but breathless pursuit, fueled by an unexpected surge of lust that excludes all else. A chase through weathered trunks and summer leaves, perhaps involving a pair of folk figures known as King and Queen of the Greenwood, perhaps two human beings called Sally Durwood and Nick Rusk, perhaps a startled doe and an eager stag. And then such insignificant details fade and there's only the chase itself, only the present with its shadowed green woodscape, the flash of slender legs and a glimpse of fearful, inviting eyes as she looks back, alternately concealed and revealed by the dim forest light through which he plunges headlong, oblivious of his thudding heart and heavy loins, the treacherous terrain underfoot, the branches that lash his face and snag his clothes in passing – follows the fleeing white flag of her tail that seems to promise willing surrender, if only he can catch her.

If only he can catch her. He runs within a green sphere of woven roots and branches that rolls smoothly beneath his flying hooves. Leaves whip his antlers; lust, taut to bursting, drives him forward. Seeing her falter, he gathers his strength and bridges the distance between them in a single leap, landing squarely on her back. She stumbles beneath his weight, sinking to her knees in surrender as he tightens his grip, hips already flexing and thrusting in blind urgency.

"Nick? Where'd you go?"

The world jolts on its axis. He's hunched on the ground over a rotten log, dry humping it as if it's a woman. Shocked, he flings himself away, falling in a sweating, trembling heap, trying to recall who and where he is.

A swish of foliage nearby. "Nick? You okay?"

The sight of her face brings it all back in a rush: Sally, the Noon Woods. He was running – why? – and he fell. He picks himself up, finds he has an erection and bends over, pretending to brush leaves from his clothes.

"I'm okay. Guess I tripped." His lungs feel like boulders, each breath a nugget painfully chiseled free. The sight of a soggy, fungus-specked log nearby makes his erection shrivel.

"Come on," she's saying. "We're almost there."

Almost where? She's breathing fast, as if she's been running too. Beyond her, an eerie radiance sifts through the crooked darkness of the trees. As he moves forward it seems to pulse, swelling and brightening in rhythm with the beating of his heart.

It's coming from a clearing deep in the woods. The open patch of sky comes as a shock to senses that have already accepted the utter sovereignty of the trees. He stops at the edge, blinking at the hazy spokes of early sunlight that illuminate the ruined giant that stands alone at the center.

"Holy shit," Atop the massive trunk, instead of a leafy crown, there's a splintered mess dominated by two twisted shards, one long, one stubby. Its leafless branches are frozen in wild gesticulation, the lower ones hung with a variety of odd objects – he sees tattered wreaths of flowers, faded bits of cloth, a chrome hood ornament from a car, a Barbie doll, a string of beads and buttons.

"It's called Roan's Oak," Sally says. "Granny Dee said back in the old days it was the center of everything. Our ancestors came here to get married and came back to get buried. But not anymore. Most folks nowadays have never even been here, and the ones that have – they only come when they want something real bad."

Roan's Oak. A sensation like a low-grade electrical current begins at the base of Nick's spine and creeps outward. He's read about wish trees. The trinkets hanging from the branches are offerings, acknowledgements of the tree's spiritual power, the essence of folk magic. This evidence of a living tradition entrances him – yet when Sally steps into the clearing he finds himself hanging back, stricken by an inexplicable reluctance. What's the matter with him? This tree was once the spiritual center of the community, and even in death it obviously still serves a purpose.

He notices the roots, huge and twisted, like as mythic serpents. That's a positive image, signifying wisdom and power. He tries to focus on it as he starts forward, only to be overcome again by nausea. Sally hasn't noticed; she's set her picnic basket down beneath the tree and is bending over it. The thought of food only heightens Nick's nausea. His gaze, desperately avoiding the basket, lands instead on a deep cleft in the weathered trunk. There's something wedged into it – a sizeable stone mottled with pale green lichen. It's obviously been there a while, long enough for the crumbling bark to overgrow its edges.

Curiosity overcoming his queasiness, he moves closer and runs his fingers over the surface. In the early morning chill it feels oddly warm.

"What's this?"

She glances up. "Been there long's anybody can recall. Granny Dee always said Roan himself put it there."

"What for?"

"She said Roan never really died. Said the faery doe invited him to come and live with her in the Bright Land, so he went through the door in the oak and closed it behind him. Kids still say a verse about it."

"A verse?"

She chants softly:

"Roan, Roan, open the door,
"My tears are salt and my heart is sore.
"Roan, return and reach out your hand
"And open the door to the Bright Land."

The words revolve slowly in the shafts of filtered sunlight. Sally smiles. "We used to jump rope to it."

Staring at the stone, Nick scarcely hears her. A door in the tree, leading to the

Bright Land, the Land of Faery, the Otherworld – a wealth of different names for the universal concept of a parallel dimension, a spirit world invisibly interwoven with the material one. His heart is pounding.

Sally's hand is on his arm. "You okay?"

"Just a little hung over." He takes a deep breath. Of course the doorway's not a literal one; Roan Durwood hadn't actually squeezed his way into the cleft in the oak to travel to the Otherworld. But the tree somehow acts as an amplifier, a means of enhancing the otherworld signal. The tree is the hub, the center of the forest's latent power, connecting it to a reservoir of energy unrecognized by modern science but known and harnessed by ancient civilizations. And apparently recognized as such by one Roan Durwood.

"Listen, Sally, this makes total sense." He's talking too fast, but all at once it seems so clear. "Roan was a shaman, a traveler between the worlds of matter and spirit. A shaman has the ability to connect to an aspect of reality that's not accessible to normal consciousness. And this tree – it's got some kind of energy that pumps up that inaccessible aspect, that other dimension, gives it a little extra juice that boosts the signal. Actions and events that would normally be impossible, like controlling the weather, or projecting your consciousness into the body of an animal – those things became possible here. That's what Roan was doing. And then, over time, the connection somehow got lost or broken."

She looks dubious. "Okay . . . but what's all that got to do with stoppin the loggers?"

"Everything! The power's still here. All we have to do is plug into it, the way you'd plug an electrical cord into an outlet."

"How?"

Nick opens his mouth and then shuts it. This is not the moment to confess that he's been a pagan for less than a year, that although he's attended close to a dozen rituals, he's never led one. But he's read a ton of books on the subject, enough to know that it's just a matter of following the proper steps. How hard can it be?

"Given the situation, I think we should go for some kind of protection spell. Invoke the spirit of the place, make an offering – "

"To the tree? I got one right here."

She flips back the picnic basket's hinged lid. Taken by surprise, Nick is not enlightened by a glimpse of the contents – what appears to be a slimy coil of grayish rope mottled with darker spots. But as he leans closer an odor reaches him, sour and coppery. The smell of blood. He looks again, sees a threadwork of dark veins in the glistening mass –

She's brought . . . oh god . . . is that the umbilical cord of Molly Upshaw's newborn baby?

The clearing begins to dip and reel with a slow, sickening motion that he belatedly understands is inside his own head. He bends over and takes deep breaths. By the time he's recovered enough to stand upright, Sally has fastened the cord to a branch, where it swings slowly back and forth.

By an enormous effort of will, Nick doesn't vomit. Through the roaring in his ears he hears her say, "Granny Dee used to do this for every baby born in Durwood, to honor Roan's blood bargain with the doe. I used to think it was just old fashioned foolishness, but now . . . well, might be it's time we started doin it again."

Nick swallows hard. The offering he was envisioning, something along the lines of the wish tokens already hanging on the tree, is reduced to simpering farce by this (oh god is something dripping from it?) stark tribute of human flesh and blood. His hastily averted gaze collides unexpectedly with Sally's, and in that instant he sees again the startled eyes of the doe turning to flee. The doe. Slender haunches flickering through the trees, white tail raised high . . .

She's standing so close that he can see the individual freckles in the hollow of her throat. His nausea vanishes; he knows her offering is the right one. That blood is right, blood is powerful, and the only substance as powerful as blood is semen.

King and Queen of the Greenwood. Together they can work the spell here and now, reawaken the ancient power present in the tree. A swelling heat suffuses his groin. In her eyes he sees a reflection of dappled shade, a bottomless forest pool into which he plunges without warning, simultaneously falling and rising, hurtling at light speed through an infinite swirl of gold and green.

Their union will form the power's seed. He grips her shoulders with shaking hands, feeling the pressure of her breasts against his chest as she moves closer. And then the rising wind brings the smell of blood and, at the edge of his vision, the dark drifting of the cord.

The magic flees. Turning his head away just in time, Nick vomits among the oak's coiled roots.

❊ 6 ❊

Welcome, Warrior, to the Font of Renewal. Here you may rest and gather strength before embarking upon your next quest.

"Fuck that," Tyner Durwood says. The back of his wrist still itches like a bastard. He stops scratching long enough to search for signs of a spider bite, but finds none. Against the reddened skin his tattoo looks brand new, the oak leaves and acorns as bright and fresh as the night he and Jared got carved at that traveling fair down in Cherokee, two teenage hillbillies pledging their undying friendship in beer and matching ink. The same friendship that now lies dead and buried in the heart of the Noon Woods. Tyne fumbles for the moonshine jar beside his monitor. Empty.

"Fuck."

Rolling his chair back from the computer, he flings open the door of his study to admit the morning's air and light. A crow on the kitchen garden fence squawks and flaps away, banking as it negotiates the treetops' green chasms. Tyne watches it go. After nine years he's learned not to long for that soaring freedom, learned to make do with cyperspace instead.

This new game's really got its hooks into him. At the click of a mouse he's transformed from a cripple living in a glorified henhouse into Quert, a warrior skilled in weaponry and magical arts, already a third of the way to the exalted grade of Zelator and one badass dude. Megapixel maidens find him irresistible; goblin babies self-destruct at the sound of his name. At the moment he's dead, having managed to get himself killed on the verge of obtaining the Scroll of al-Qabiri; but in the game death is a temporary inconvenience, and he can afford the time it will take to regain the lost ground. It's not like he has anything else to do.

Two cows regard him from the other side of the pasture fence; a towhee calls in the pine woods that cover the hillside. The haze above the treetops promises another day without rain, the sun already busy firing up its forge beneath the cool of the mountain morning.

At the edge of the pine woods, feathery boughs shake and part to reveal Liz's big hat. Tyne lifts a hand and she returns the wave. Since her arrival a few months ago, an unlikely friendship has formed between them – unlikely because ever since the accident the only company he can stand is Sally's and CW's. Liz is different. Born in Durwood but gone before he was born, she knows the community but has no memories of him when he wasn't a cripple. Somehow that works for him. And from things she's let drop during the nights they've spent sharing a jar of moonshine in his study, he's gathered she has her own disabling wounds. Now, watching the force with which she wields her walking stick as she skirts the fence around the kitchen garden, he can tell something's wrong.

"What's up, sunshine? Septic tank overflow again?"

"Not funny." She points the stick at him. "We've got a problem, Tyne."

"Just tell Uncle Tyne your troubles, sweetheart. He'll make it all better."

She lowers the stick. "This logging thing – "

"What?"

"Sally and CW didn't tell you?"

"Tell me what?"

Liz is watching the tip of her stick prod the ground. "Your cousin Gordie was in town yesterday, talking about logging in the Noon Woods."

Tyne goes still. "So?"

"So we have to do something."

"Like what?" He finds himself short of breath and sucks in air. "Why should I give a shit about them fuckin woods?"

"Tyne – "

"Tell you what, Liz. Let ole Gordie cut down the Noon Woods and build a ballroom, and us two'll go dancin. You and me. Deal?"

She looks up, skewering him with those pale witchy eyes. "You know, it's scary how good you are at being an asshole when you try."

Tyne winks at her. "Practice. That's my secret."

Once she's gone, he grabs his push rims and sends his chair rattling along the wooden walkway that connects his study to the house. The kitchen is empty, but coffee's perking on the stove. Pa's already gone into town; Sally must be home.

Going in search of her, Tyne discovers a stranger sprawled on the sofa in the front parlor, a young guy around his own age, clothes smeared with dirt and leaves. He rolls closer and observes a sweating, unshaven baby face topped by a tangle of dark hair. The whisper of wheelchair tires doesn't penetrate the stranger's stupor; he lies with eyes closed, groaning softly.

"Who the hell are you?" Tyne says.

Baby Face's eyes open, struggle to focus.

"Uh . . . I'm Nick."

"You look like shit, Nick."

"I'm okay. I just . . . Sally and I were out at Roan's Oak, and I got sick." He licks his lips. "I just needed to lie down for a while."

"Roan's Oak?" Tyne says as Sally comes briskly into the room.

"Feelin better, Nick? I see you met my baby brother. Mornin, Tyne."

"Mornin. What were y'all doing at Roan's Oak?"

"Nick, you said you had to be back when? It's close to nine."

"Shit." Nick struggles into a sitting position, looking like a reanimated corpse. "I'm supposed to open the store. Wait, it's Sunday, right? Sundays we don't open till ten."

"Still, we better get goin."

"Yeah, okay. Can I use your bathroom?"

She directs him down the hall before heading for the kitchen. Tyner follows to find her pouring a cup of coffee; she gestures with the pot.

"Want some?"

"What's goin on, Sally?"

"Hm?"

"Who's he? And what were you thinkin, takin him to Roan's Oak?"

The way she rolls her eyes says he's being a pest. "He's Morgan Edwards's nephew from down in Raleigh, got himself a summer job at her store. Heard some talk about the Noon Woods and wanted to see for himself. I needed to go to the oak, so I took him along."

"An outsider."

"Yeah, Tyne. An outsider. I showed him our *deeeep, daaaark* secret."

"So what happened? He looks like shit."

Sally raises an eyebrow. She hates it when he swears. Six years his senior, she's the closest thing he's known to a mother; theirs died giving him birth. She gulps her coffee and looks at her watch.

"We gotta be goin. Morgan's gonna be mad if he's late."

Blocking her retreat with his chair: "Tell me what happened at Roan's Oak."

"Tyne, for cryin out loud. 'Happened'?"

"You're actin like somethin happened."

Both hands on her hips now. "I ain't actin any way at all!"

"Does Jared know you took this guy there?"

Color rises in his sister's cheeks. "It's no business of Jared's what I do. Nor yours neither."

He stares at her in silence. Sally sighs.

"Look, Gordie was in town yesterday, sayin he's gonna log the Noon Woods."

"Liz told me."

"Word is he's already gone and hired a crew. Everbody's talkin big about stoppin him, but nobody's sayin exactly how they plan on doin it. Except Nick."

"An outsider."

"He wants to help, Tyne. He thinks the Noon Woods are some kind of natural power site, like the ones where folks built their temples in ancient times. He wants to do a magic ritual there, to protect the trees."

"A what?" he says, and she flinches.

"Look, I know it's crazy, but we need the Bunny Dancers on our side in this. They know people, they got pull. If a magic ritual is what it takes to get em on board, if Nick can come up with somethin that gets everbody workin together – well, maybe we can stop this thing before it gets outta hand. I reckon it's worth a try."

When she's gone, Tyne sits in the kitchen watching the sun inch across the worn floorboards. Logging in the Noon Woods. A magical ritual to protect the trees. He doesn't know whether to laugh or cry.

His tattoo is itching to beat the band.

As the sun reaches its zenith, light fills the clearing at the heart of the Noon Woods, exposing without mercy the oak's decaying, lichen-speckled limbs.

Along with the other odd tokens that festoon the branches, the umbilical cord of Durwood's newest inhabitant hangs suspended in the windless air. High above, framed in a circle of leafy treetops, the sun pours its warmth earthward. As degree by degree the temperature rises, the clotted blood in the cord warms until it returns to liquid form, releasing a soft patter of droplets onto the roots below.

☆ 7 ☆

It's two days before Nick fully recovers from his introduction to moonshine – two days during which his memories of the Midsummer Festival and its aftermath commingle and crossbreed until only one stands out with any clarity: the image of Sally Durwood attaching a human umbilical cord to the dead tree known as Roan's Oak.

Just thinking of it gives him goosebumps. Grisly, oh god yes. But powerful. That token of flesh and blood has blown away all his previous notions about pagan practices and given him a whole new take on the subject. Contrary to what the majority of New Age books and websites preach, true paganism isn't gentle or PC. It's earthy, gritty, rooted in body fluids and instinct and death – everything that symbolizes the power of the natural world.

And he intends to use that power. Not dance around it like a kid around a lawn sprinkler, but ride it like a surfer taming a monster wave. What happened at the oak was spontaneous – Morgan would call it a gift from the Goddess – and he'll be the first to admit he wasn't ready for it, but it's shown him the possibilities. A ritual to stop the logging, centered around the oak and involving the whole community . . . It's a challenging debut for a newbie pagan, but what he lacks in practical experience he's gained through revelation. With the right ritual, he knows he can pull it off. When he floats the idea to Morgan, she's wildly enthusiastic.

"This could do it, Nicky! This could save the forest *and* bring Durwood together, the old and the new, in a way that really works for everybody. I'm *so* glad you got Sally on board. I knew the Festival of Oaks would be good for Durwood – and look, it's already happening!"

With her blessing he takes a day off to drive down to Lenoir, where he spends a couple of hours browsing the New Age section at the Barnes & Noble in the mall. Back in Durwood, buzzed on a pot of strong green tea, he spends most of one night plowing through *Ritual Making for Modern Pagans*, making a list of basic steps.

1. Define the purpose of the ritual.

2. Choose and consecrate the space.
3. Focus the vision.
4. Raise the energy.
5. Direct and release the energy.
6. Ground any leftover energy.
7. Evaluate the experience.

On this bare framework, with some heavy borrowing of ideas and imagery from the books he's collected over the past year, he hopes to construct something intense and dramatic that will crinkle everybody's flesh and make their hair stand on end. But it's hard not to notice that Durwood's natives seem far more concerned with the weather than the imminent logging. The extended drought forms the subject of every conversation he overhears at May's Cafe, the Hardware & General, the grocery store, and the cash register at Abundance – although the word *rain* is never spoken, as if people have stopped believing such a substance exists.

"My grampaw use to tell us bout the bad drought in '65, but I declare thisun's got it beat. Creek out backa our place's down to a trickle."

"Our corn ain't but six inches high. Oughta be three feet n more by now."

"Lucky you got corn at all. Ours dried up and blowed off."

"You hear bout Ezra and Rosie? Their well done give out."

Star's promised teeshirt, produced in half a dozen bright colors with the slogan *Save the Noon Woods* splashed across a foresty graphic, went up for sale yesterday at a number of businesses and is already being worn all over town, but not by the locals. How's Nick supposed to get them fired up when the drought is real to them and the destruction of the forest is not? By now the fellowship of the Midsummer celebration is history and he's an outsider again, with one crucial difference – now he has Sally's support. He's counting on her to rally the rest of them.

Sprawled on the futon in his sleeping quarters, surrounded by books and scattered notes, he goes through the whole thing again.

Define the purpose of the ritual. Easy. To protect the forest from the loggers.

Choose and consecrate the space. Another gimme. Roan's Oak is a natural power site.

It's Step 3, *Focus the vision*, where things get tricky. He knows spells are supposed to affect the sender as well as the object, so he doesn't want to mess with raising negative energy, either against the loggers or even Gordie Durwood. It's probably safest just to visualize the forest as an impregnable fortress guarded by nature spirits. But what exactly *is* a nature spirit? According to all the books, they're immaterial beings with no physical substance of their own, which means their appearance depends on how they're expected to look by members of a given culture. Some people see elves; some see aliens. For Roan Durwood, it was a white doe.

For the ritual, though, Nick wants an image with more muscle. He needs to visualize a powerful forest guardian – but what does such a being look like?

He rolls off the futon to pace the cavernous room. Morgan plans to put a café here at some point in the future, but for now the space is empty except for the futon where he sleeps, a battered dresser, and a bookcase in the far corner that holds Morgan's magpie collection of New Age books. Nick stops in front of it to scan the titles. His aunt is the first to admit she's no scholar of the occult, and her library consists of fluff like *Wiccan Woman's Wisdom* and *101 Spells for Happiness*. Not much of use there. He's turning away when he notices a red tassel sticking out between *To Ride a Silver Broomstick* and *Magicks for a New Age*. He grasps and pulls: out slides a slim pamphlet of the kind that sells for a few bucks at a pagan fair, the cover hand-lettered in flowery script.

Celtic Tree Ogham? The final word is unfamiliar, but the first page informs him it's pronounced *oh-am* and signifies an alphabet invented by the Druids, in which each letter is associated with a different tree. Like most ancient alphabets, the Ogham has a magical dimension.

The sacred grove of magical trees forms one of the doorways to Annwn (pronounced An-noon), the Celtic Otherworld, surprisingly near and at the same time very distant from our own. This is the Realm of Faerie, slipping out of time – hard to enter, and even harder to get out of.

Nick's hooked. Sinking to his haunches beside the bookcase, he reads on.

Among the Celts, certain trees were held in such reverence that the penalty for destroying them was death. An ancient law states: Three unbreathing things to be paid for only with breathing things: an apple tree, a hazel bush, a sacred grove.

Sacred grove. He recalls the mist dissolving to reveal the green fortress of the Noon Woods. The silence among the trees. The pulsing radiance of the clearing where Roan's Oak stands.

The booklet devotes a page or two to each tree in the Ogham, giving its Celtic name and associated magical properties. Birth and initiation for *beithe*, the birch; vision and intuition for *luis*, the rowan, and so on. The seventh letter is *duir*, the oak.

Many cultures have revered the Oak, especially those which have been struck by lightning and are seen as invested with divine power. As such, the Oak forms a doorway between the worlds of matter and spirit.

Nick thinks of the stone wedged in the blackened scar in Roan's Oak. *He went through a door in the oak to the Bright Land and closed it behind him.* Two hundred years ago, in a forest where spirits were said to dwell, a man called Roan Durwood found a way of experiencing an alternate reality, a door between worlds, and found favor with its guardian. *And she promised that no harm should come to him or his, for as long as the woods stood tall.*

But Roan is gone and his legacy lies fallow, and now his descendants are powerless to protect the sacred grove. If Gordie has his way, if the Noon Woods are destroyed, what will happen to Durwood?

This logging has to be stopped. The alternative community means well, but petitions and tee shirts aren't going to do the trick. And the tactics Nick overheard the local men discussing at the Midsummer Festival are likely to land them in jail; asking around, he's learned that the "3-S treatment" means "shoot, shovel, and shut up" – the rural solution to dogs that attack livestock.

If Roan managed to tap into the earth energy stored in the oak, there's no reason his descendants can't do the same. All they need is a guiding hand – but is he, Nick Rusk, twenty-three years old and a practicing pagan for less than a year, qualified to provide it? His revelation at the oak with Sally was spontaneous; he has no real idea what he's doing, no notion of what goes into a shamanic journey.

Focus the vision, raise the energy . . . Those are abstractions, when he needs specifics. Daunted by the prospect of going from fledgling pagan to priest-shaman in a single leap, he stares down at the page, seeing the words swim into focus.

The Oak stands for energy, inspiration and illumination. When you need the courage and strength to face great difficulties, seek out the Oak.

"You gotta be kiddin." But putting aside his book, Jared sees from Sally's face that she's not. When her mind's set on something, her eyes change color from warm forest shadow to cold river ice. They're river ice now.

For maybe the thousandth time in the years since he fell in love with her, he wonders why the hell it's not easier. But the wondering is just a pretense, a refusal to admit the hard truth that however much he loves Sally and she loves him, they want different things from life. There's a part of her he'll never understand, the part that's immovably rooted in Durwood, connected in countless ways to everything that's here.

Back when he was a kid with a crush on his best friend's big sister, this bitter fact was invisible; and it was still obscure when they made love for the first time, two awkward teenagers on a pile of feed sacks in the back room of her daddy's store. But it's pretty damn obvious now. Jared wants to leave Durwood; it's that simple. Get the hell out of a place where the present can't seem to drag itself out from under the weight of the past, where the old folks are always saying everything has to be such and such a way because that's how it's always been. Shingle your roof by the waning moon or the shingles will warp upward. Sweep dirt into the fireplace, never out the door, in case you sweep the luck out too.

And so on and so on, in a place where everybody knows that his pa has a bad back, that his ma makes the best sweet potato pie in the county, that his little sister has a temper, that when he was nine Miss Daisy Vernon whipped him for putting a dead skunk in the schoolroom woodstove. That he was one of the seven boys who ventured into the Noon Woods on the night of Tyner Durwood's accident, and that as the oldest he should have known better.

He knows the real reason he wants to leave is to escape the grief and guilt of what happened that night – to put enough distance between himself and Durwood that he can shed the pain of Tyne and him having nothing to say to each other anymore, after having been best friends their whole lives. By now they've stopped trying. When Jared visits Sally and CW, Tyne doesn't even come into the house, just stays out in that shack of his, drinking moonshine and playing on his computer.

The computer games are Tyne's escape. Jared's is to read every book he can get his hands on – history, fiction, biography, each one like a wide clean highway leading to a life where Durwood doesn't even show on the map.

But how can he go without Sally? While her grandmother was alive, he'd accepted there was no chance Sally'd leave Durwood. Granny Dee was a presence. Tall as her grown twin sons, with her corncob pipe and the man's shirt and boots she wore with her long skirts, she was a walking encyclopedia of herb lore; Durwood people firmly believed in her ability to call the rain, read a future lover's name in the curl of an apple peel, cure rheumatism with a potato in the pocket or banish warts with a notched persimmon stick.

For Granny Dee, Durwood was the center of the world, and she wasn't someone you crossed. But she's been dead three years, and in all that time Jared's efforts to convince Sally there's life outside Durwood have met with failure. He knows she feels guilty about getting her midwife certification at the center down in Lenoir instead of birthing babies the way Granny taught her, putting a knife under the bed to cut the pain in half. And guilty, too, for abandoning the old practice of offering every newborn's birthcord to Roan's Oak, secretly even wondering if her lapse is responsible for the malformed and ailing infants born since.

Not that Sally will admit to any such thing. Every time they fight about it, she has only one response: Durwood is home. And by *home* she means not just familiar names and faces, shared stories and memories and customs, but human roots intertwined with those of the encompassing forest, its cycles of growth and decay, its moods and secrets. The forest surrounds and protects the community, regulates its rhythms, dims the noise and bustle of the outside world. She doesn't think she could survive anywhere else.

"Anyhow, who'd look after Pa and Tyne?"

"Hell, we'll take em along! They can live with us."

"You really think they could survive anywhere else?"

"Why not?"

She always shakes her head.

Now she's pestering him with some cockeyed Bunny Dancer scheme to stop Gordie from logging the Noon Woods, where nine years ago a drunken prank landed his best friend in a wheelchair for life. Jared's put a lot of work into not thinking about that night, and there's only one person to blame for the fact that he's thinking about it now.

Gordie Fuckin Durwood. The Peewee Preacher, standing there on Main Street with his thumbs tucked in his belt, running his mouth about logging and lawyers. And Jared, without the slightest intention of joining the Bunny Dancers' fool race – the next thing Jared knows, he's perched in the tree at the other end of Main Street with the winner's crown in his fist and no notion how he got there. That's happened to him only once before, on the night of Tyne's accident. Trying to think about that night is like trying to haul water in a leaky bucket; by the time you get where you're going, there's nothing left. It scares him. And being scared makes him mad.

"Look," Sally's saying. "We need as many people as we can get for this thing. How's it gonna hurt you to just come and stand there?"

"It's bullshit."

"So what, long's it gets folks fired up about savin the trees?"

"I said no."

"Jared."

"Keep outta them woods. Ain't nobody got no business playin games in there."

"It ain't a game. It's a ritual."

"Call it what you want." Jared picks up his book. "Just count me out."

"Oh, *Goddess*." Morgan presses both hands to her cheeks, which are burning. "I had *no idea*."

"How could you?" Molly says. "Nobody said a word, not one word, until Annie told me yesterday. If they didn't tell us, how were we supposed to know?" She rocks the baby's basket. "I almost didn't say anything to you. But I thought if it was me, I'd rather know."

Morgan nods. Molly is her best friend here in Durwood. In spite of the fifteen year gap in age, the two of them hit it off immediately when the Upshaws arrived here and opened their craft store. Hands On went through some rough times at first, but now it offers some wonderful local crafts, like Ivy Tyner's handmade brooms and the willow-basket cradle woven by old Clark Lewis where baby Laurel now lies sleeping.

Part of the Upshaws' success, Morgan's certain, is due to their hiring Annie Sayles to help out in the store. It's smart business to have a local face behind the counter, and Annie's eager to do a good job. More than eager, in fact – positively desperate to please. Of course, as a single mom with an AWOL husband and a child living under the threat of leukemia recurrence, she has reason to be desperate. Since her husband's departure she's been struggling to survive by selling home-grown organic vegetables, and the regular paycheck from Hands On must be a welcome supplement. And of course there's the social aspect, too; this is a woman who virtually *never* stops talking. Morgan wonders what on earth made her wait until now to share this crucial piece of information about the Festival.

"What exactly did Annie say?"

"Okay, so about ten years ago some boys decided to revive the Midsummer race on their own. It was Jared, Darrell, the Cole twins – that bunch. But they didn't do it in town. They got drunk and went out into the woods in the middle of the night to climb some old tree, and one of them fell. It was Tyner Durwood."

"So that's how he – "

"Ended up in a wheelchair. Yeah." Baby Laurel whimpers and Molly rocks her. Instead of feeling sorry for the boys, people blamed them for messing around with a custom that had fizzled out on its own. Kind of like they'd, you know, trifled with the natural order of things. So when you announced the Festival of Oaks – "

"I offended *everybody* on about a *million* fronts. Oh, this is awful! Why didn't Annie say something sooner? We could have just called the whole thing off!"

"I guess she thought we knew."

"Knew? So that means she just assumed I'm the most insensitive person on the face of the earth?" Morgan rakes both hands through her hair. "Aagh. Molly, I swear to you, when CW told me about the race, he didn't say a word about Tyner. He said it was something they did when he was a boy, and then it sort of faded out during World War Two. He never even *hinted* – "

"Well, why would he?" Molly says. "I mean, we're outsiders."

"CW's not like that."

"Morgan. They all are." The baby opens her eyes and Molly rocks her until she closes them again. "How can they possibly blame us? It wasn't our fault. If it's anybody's fault, it's theirs for being so damn closety about everything. Who knows, maybe they'll learn a lesson from this."

Morgan nods, cringing from the thought of how much damage has been done.

"Morgan." Molly grabs her hand and squeezes. "They'll get over it. I shouldn't have opened my big fat mouth – Ben's always saying I have no filter. Hey, how about I make us some herbal tea?"

◆ ◆ ◆

It's night, and Tyne's standing at the foot of Roan's Oak.

In the moonlight the tree's luxuriant leaves rustle softly overhead, half masking another sound that comes and goes like an intermittent tickle in his ears, so faint it makes him wonder if he's hearing anything at all.

Woven into the sound of the leaves, it hovers at the threshold of hearing until Tyne shakes his head like a dog with a flea. Where's it coming from? The harder he tried to hear it, the more it blends into the stirring of leaves – and then, just as he's convinced it's not really there at all, it seeps across the threshold and he hears it clearly: a breathy whisper slowly growing louder, mounting gradually to a low drone. Now it's distinct enough that he can trace its source to the opening in the oak's trunk, the one blocked by the stone. He moves closer. The stone is gone, but the hole isn't empty. There's something in its place.

A human head.

As the sound shoots up the scale to an earsplitting shriek, he recognizes

Jared, mouth stretched wide in the pale blur of his face, screaming and screaming and —

Tyne wakes with a jolt, drenched in sweat.

Sunlight pours through the window of his shack, gilding the push rims of the wheelchair beside his cot. He grabs the Mason jar and takes a gulp, looking at the clock. Not yet noon; he's been asleep for less than an hour.

His routine is to stay up all night and sleep during the day, rising in time to join his father and sister at the supper table. It may be antisocial, but it keeps the worst of the dreams at bay — usually. This was a bad one. He takes another drink to purge the image of Jared's head protruding from the weathered trunk, as if the tree's trying to swallow him whole.

His tattoo begins to itch and he scratches it. Those first weeks in the hospital, Jared never left his bedside, but once he recovered enough for the two of them to look each other in the eye, things were different. It's been years since they've exchanged anything more than a hello when it can't be avoided. If Jared comes to the house for supper, Tyne stays in his study and Sally brings him out a plate.

She doesn't understand what happened to their friendship, but it isn't something Tyne can explain. The accident that permanently damaged his spinal cord at vertebra T-12 robbed him of more than mobility, more than all his assumptions about everything he was going to be and do in his life. He lost something else that night in the Noon Woods, something he balks at calling his soul but can't come up with a better name for — watched it slip through a crack in what he'd always thought was reality and vanish, leaving him with a hollow space inside into which he pours a steady stream of alcohol and fantasy games.

That was the night he was supposed to have died. He can't look into Jared's eyes without seeing it there, and he knows it's the same for Jared.

It's been easier just to let the friendship go.

Immersed in forest shadow, Nick sits absolutely still. He's trying to tune out everything but his physical sensations, to concentrate on the rough bark against his spine, the damp soil and knotty roots beneath him, the cool air touching his skin. Trying to still his busy thoughts and tune into a world where the trappings of modern industrial civilization have no meaning and instinct is the key to survival.

Ideally he'd be performing this solitary exercise at Roan's Oak, but that's not how things have worked out. He'd found the Durwood farm okay, and the walk down to the woods through the sunny hayfield filled with butterflies had been awesome. He'd been fully psyched by the idea of visiting the oak again. Of being prepared this time, being worthy.

Once inside the forest, though, he had no idea how to find the oak. Nothing seemed familiar. What looked at first glance like the obvious path petered out after a few dozen steps, and the only other possibility led him in a wide arc that eventually returned him to the forest's edge. After a while the steady whisper of leaves began to generate a kind of tickle between his shoulder blades – not fear, exactly, just a strong aversion to the idea of losing his way, wandering deeper and deeper into the dim green stillness . . . no, getting lost in the Noon Woods would definitely not be cool.

So in place of Roan's Oak he's opted for another oak near the edge of the woods, where the hayfield is visible as a comforting splash of brightness beyond the leaves. The Ogham booklet lies open on his lap.

Make physical contact with the tree by sitting with your back against the trunk. Give yourself and the tree time to tune into each other. Open yourself to the spirit of the tree without trying to control what happens. If your thoughts begin to wander, gently guide them back to the tree. Be patient. Wait for the tree to communicate.

Above his head, innumerable layers of leaves filter the light to a green glimmer. Nick closes his eyes and tries to relax against the unyielding trunk behind him, shifting his weight away from a root that's digging into his tailbone. According to the booklet, the gifts of the oak are energy, inspiration, illumination, strength, courage, and self determination. In order to lead an effective ritual, he's going to need them all.

At the top of the list – self determination.

The crisis in Durwood has given him a real sense of purpose; for the first time in his life, he has the chance to do something worthwhile. The forest needs saving, and he's ready to do whatever it takes. He's not unaware that his attraction to Sally Durwood is a factor in his resolve, but there's more to it than physical desire; he wants to prove himself worthy, show her he's someone she can respect. Show her he's a man.

The word inevitably comes to him in the familiar cadences of Judge Roland Rusk. A man does this. A man does that.

A man needs a profession, son. And there's none finer than the law.

I don't want to be a lawyer, Dad.

You're twenty-two years old, Nick. When I was your age I was already handling my own cases.

How much of his life has he spent trying to squeeze himself into some kind of prefab box to please the Judge? The family nickname makes him wince; that's how his old man has always made him feel – judged and found wanting. He's got a college degree in English and American Lit, but no notion what to do with it. After college he meant to get his own apartment but never quite got around to it, just kept living at his parents' house, working part-time at Barnes & Noble, dating various girls who never satisfied his vague expectations, drifting along without a plan for the future, until finally he gave in to the Judge's rumblings and applied to law school. All of which has led him by a circuitous path to Durwood, where he's been provided with some answers.

And some new questions as well. For instance, who exactly *was* Roan Durwood? Scouring the web for information, he's managed to find two references. The first is a news story from 1810, reporting the escape of one Owen Derwent from custody after being convicted of bewitching a Greensboro woman. The second reference dates from 1816, a couple of paragraphs from the diary of a Methodist circuit rider in the Carolina mountains, describing a certain Rowan Derwood rumored to possess magical powers learned from the local Native Americans.

Sparse as they are, the stories seem to support the notion of Roan as a magus or at least an initiate, knowledgeable enough to recognize the Noon Woods as a junction of realities, a place where unknown energies mesh. Nick's convinced that the forest isn't helpless against the logging threat; far from it. As a power vortex, it has the means to fight for its own survival.

If your thoughts begin to wander, gently guide them back to the tree.

The tree. Guiltily he tries to shut off the flow of thoughts. Squeezes his eyes shut, takes a deep breath . . .

And smells blood.

His eyes spring open. That coppery tang brings a flash of the umbilicus hanging from Roan's Oak. But the odor can't have traveled so far, can't possibly still –

Just as suddenly, it's gone. He sniffs hard but can detect no trace. Did he imagine it? He's aware of his heart pumping in his chest, of the profound silence of the woods – as if all sound is prohibited here except for the pervasive hiss of leaves that works its way into your head until you stop hearing it, not so much the absence of noise as something that actively prevents it, like a gag . . .

A gag. He thinks of the rock embedded in the oak. *Granny Dee said Roan himself put it there.* But why? What possible reason could Roan have for blocking the door, cutting Durwood off from the Otherworld?

From somewhere in the surrounding stillness comes a faint pattering like drops falling – and there it is again, the smell of blood, metallic, unmistakable, fouling the back of his throat. Sweat pops out on his skin; his gaze darts back and forth, seeking he doesn't know what.

Something drops from above, landing on the open booklet in his lap with a *crack* that makes him jump.

"Shit!"

The woods smother his voice like cotton wool. In the center seam wobbles something small and dark – an acorn. Retrieving it with unsteady fingers, Nick glances up at the branches overhead.

Wait for the tree to communicate.

An acorn. A seed, a kernel of potential, the perfect symbol for a magic spell. You summon the power, shape it, release it to do its work. Could he ask for a clearer signal? He tucks it into his jeans pocket. The blood smell has vanished again; all around him the shadowy wooded distances stretch away, legions of gray-brown trunks cloaked in green, a repeating pattern that imprints itself on his brain as he closes his eyes and tries, once more, to empty his mind.

Open yourself to the spirit of the tree.

Open your . . . self . . .

As the warmth of the earth seeps into his bones and his muscles relax, the limits of his body slowly expand until he can sense the whole tree, crown to roots. Up and out to the air and light, in and down to the dense darkness beneath, a web of interwoven branches stirring in the breeze, and the roots like a dark reflection deep in the earth – spreading, questing, endlessly seeking, irresistibly cunning, infinitely adaptable, patiently surmounting every obstacle until –

His shoulder is gripped and shaken.

His eyes open on an unknown face hovering close to his. He jerks away, banging the back of his head painfully against the tree, blinking with the shock. Pale eyes, pale hair hanging long and loose – his first panicked thought is that it's some kind of wood sprite come to warn him against trespassing. But faeries don't wear sweatshirts, and that big straw hat rings a bell from the Festival of Oaks.

I forgot to tell you she lives here. Our token celebrity.

She's holding a finger to her lips.

"Shh," says Elizabeth Wyatt.

A little later, sitting across the kitchen table in her cabin, she seems only marginally less fey. The clock above the stove reads twenty minutes to six. Nick's understanding of exactly how he got here is like a badly loaded web page, pixilated fragments embedded in chunks of blank space. He can recall going down through the field and into the woods, sitting under a tree for the meditation exercise, and then –

And then nothing. Nada. A blank.

There's a glass of clear liquid on the kitchen table in front of him. Moonshine: he can smell it. His hostess nudges it closer.

"Drink."

He takes a careful swallow, still finding it hard to believe he's sitting here with Elizabeth Wyatt. For as long as he can remember, her name has been synonymous with his favorite childhood books, read aloud to him by Morgan and then on his own so many times they eventually fell apart. *The Hundred Year Stone* series: seven enchanting, disturbing books, and then one final volume with a different artist that fell flat, a disappointing finale.

How many millions of kids have followed the adventures of the mysterious Truantina, with her owl's eyes and comet-tail hair, in her desperate search for the Hundred Year Stone? How many kids have stared at those entrancing illustrations and then met them in dreams? Here he sits in Elizabeth Wyatt's kitchen, and he hasn't even introduced himself.

"My name's Nick Rusk, Ms Wyatt. I work at Abundance. Morgan's my aunt."

"Hello, Nick Rusk. Please call me Liz."

"I have to tell you, Ms – uh, Liz, I loved your books when I was a kid."

"I only did the illustrations, you know. Valerie Garnett was the author."

"But the books would have been nothing without the pictures."

She acknowledges the praise with a vague smile. Gestures at his teeshirt. "Save the Noon Woods?"

"We're selling them to raise money, in case the town needs to hire a lawyer to stop the logging. Twenty bucks, 100% organic cotton – "

"Can I ask what you were doing there?"

"Doing – "

"In the Noon Woods. When I found you."

"Oh, was I – was I trespassing? Sorry! I thought – "

"No need to apologize. At least not to me."

He can feel his face turning red. "I just thought, I mean, since Sally Durwood took me there already – "

She's smiling, shaking her head. "Ignore me. But – do you mind telling me what you were doing?"

"Oh. I was – um, it was supposed to be a tree meditation. Sally took me to Roan's Oak the other morning, and actually I was planning to do the meditation there, but I couldn't find it, so . . . " He's talking too much; her unblinking gaze is making him nervous. "So I just . . . picked a random tree."

"And how did the meditation go?"

"Uh, it . . . I think I fell asleep."

He takes another sip of moonshine, hearing her say, "Morgan must be a wonderful aunt."

"Oh, she is. She invited me to spend the summer with her to rescue me from, uh, kind of a bad situation."

She lets it pass. "How old are you, Nick?"

"Twenty-three."

"And you grew up reading Val's books."

He nods, even though the phrase *Val's books* seems wrong; Valerie Garnett hardly ever gets mentioned even though she's the author. The books are classics by now, but it's the drawings people rave about, the Wyatt name they look for. Those faintly menacing, seductive images, lit from within by a muted glow like a shuttered lantern – elusive presences born from negative space, lurking in the pattern of the shadowy landscapes until suddenly, in a quiet corner of the picture where you hadn't been looking, you could swear you'd seen something move.

A lot like the Noon Woods.

"I must've read them about a million times. Except for the last one, the one that was illustrated by somebody else. It sucked; I don't even remember the title. Everybody thought you'd – "

He shuts up. You don't just tell someone that everybody thought they'd died.

But she hears it anyway. "Died? I guess I did, in a way."

Realizing he's staring, Nick makes himself look down, hearing her say, "It might be a good thing that you couldn't find Roan's Oak for your meditation."

"Huh?"

"How much do you know about the Noon Woods?"

"Well, Sally told me the story of Roan and the faery doe. And the door to the Bright Land."

"And I'm sure you guessed from seeing the tokens on the tree that many people in Durwood believe Roan's Oak has certain magical powers. Each of those objects represents something of value to the giver, half of a bargain like the one between Roan and the doe. You have to be willing to pay a price."

He nods, not sure where this is going.

"I grew up in Durwood," she says. "I left when I was younger than you are now, and I haven't lived here for many years. When I said I'd died, what I meant is that I lost my ability to draw, to see the world as it appears in my books – a place where everything is alive and aware and beauty can't be separated from danger. I lost the gift that gave my life meaning. When I came back a few months ago, it was to visit Roan's Oak."

Abruptly she leaves the table and goes into the great room, returning with several sheets of paper in her hand. "I left an offering. And this happened."

Drawings. She sets them on the table in front of him. The top one is done on the back of one of the flyers from the Festival of Oaks; he recognizes the color. At first glance, the smudged strokes of charcoal look like nothing more than a random conjunction of leaves and branches – and then the lines and shadings shift imperceptibly beneath his gaze and all at once he's gazing at something else entirely: a wild leafy face with shadow-cluster eyes and a ragged knothole mouth stretched in a silent howl.

His skin prickles. This is what he's been looking for: the embodiment of nature's force, endlessly seeking, ceaselessly striving, indomitable, ruthless, the perfect image for his ritual. The next drawing depicts a towering horned figure: Pan or Cernunnos, god of the greenwood. And then – again, it's like one of those faces-vases things where you simultaneously see two different images – it becomes Roan's Oak with its crown of splintery shards, ropy branches outflung in protective menace.

Green Man, says the scribble at the bottom of the page, and Nick has the sudden bizarre notion that, having slipped from the artist's imagination into this fragile incarnation of marks on paper, the spirit of the guardian won't stop here. That it's truly a traveler between the worlds. A line from the Ogham book comes back to him.

This is the Realm of Faerie, slipping out of time. Hard to enter and even harder to get out of again.

Hard to enter, but not impossible; not if you can find the doorway. Roan's Oak forms some kind of conduit to a reservoir of untapped energy, and that energy is accessible to the right approach, like an artist's imagination – or a well-constructed ritual.

He picks up the last sketch, hearing Liz say, "That one's from a dream I had."

Roan's Oak again, rendered in colored inks, black warp of branches misted with red. In this drawing the stone is gone, leaving only a black crevice that seems to suck his gaze through the surface of the paper and beyond, into swirling darkness.

When her hand on his shoulder pulls him back, he finds the drawing so close to his face that it's almost touching.

"Careful," Liz says.

◆◆◆

The waxing moon floats in the night sky above the vast reach of forest that encircles Durwood. Huddled in the midst of the trees, the town and small patches of open farmland seem insignificant and somehow irrelevant. In the wash of light entering her open window, Morgan Edwards throws off the quilt and dreams of a leaf-cloaked figure standing beside her bed.

Tyner Durwood sits at his computer, drinking moonshine and vanquishing frost giants.

Molly Upshaw rocks in her chair by an open window, feeding her baby while Ben dreams he's screwing Annie Sayles.

Liz Wyatt, hearing the witch balls stir above the steady piping of crickets, steps out onto her porch to gaze down the sloping hayfield at the massed darkness of the forest edge, where the mooncast shadows seem more substantial than the trees themselves. At the edge of her vision a dark shape darts noiselessly across the grass – Minnie on her nightly hunt.

On the old iron bed in Sally's room at the Durwood farmhouse, Jared Gorton lies with his dark head buried in the pillow, dreaming of a tree growing up through his vitals, rooting him to the earth. When Sally molds her naked body to his, he sleeps on, oblivious. They have already made love twice, the second time with an abandon that threatened to unhinge the elderly bedsprings, but she's still not satisfied. She sits up against her pillow and, gazing into the moon-silvered mirror across the room, pleasures herself beneath the faded quilt.

Streaming through the second floor window at Abundance, the moonlight coats the acorn on the floor beside Nick's futon. It fell out of his pocket as he was undressing, making him wonder briefly when and where he'd picked it up. Now he groans and shudders in response to the motion of Sally Durwood's hands, reaching orgasm in a dream that will leave no more trace in his memory than did today's tree meditation in the Noon Woods.

In the depths of those woods, a night breeze sets Laurel Upshaw's umbilical cord swaying gently among the other tokens on Roan's Oak; and just for a moment, slyly transformed by moonlight, the tree's stark silhouette is cloaked in new leaves.

9

"Robes," Tamara says. "They don't have to be fancy, but everybody should wear them; it creates an atmosphere. Definitely robes, and maybe masks."

"And we need a chant." Star's taking notes on her iPad. "Something powerful, but simple enough that people can pick it up right away."

"And at least one rehearsal, preferably two, to iron out the bumps." Vivian, who's done theater in Atlanta, is adamant on this point. "I've seen some potentially great rituals fall apart from simple lack of prep."

Listening to the discussion, Morgan can feel her confidence returning. Gun-shy following her gaffe with the Midsummer festival, she'd suggested that maybe they ought to abandon the idea of performing a ritual to save the forest. But the wonderful women wouldn't hear of it. It's not the same thing as the Midsummer race at all, they'd said – not that anyone could possibly blame Morgan for stepping on a few completely invisible toes.

Save the Noon Woods tees seem to be the group's unofficial uniform; the full color spectrum is represented around the table at the Barretts' restaurant, where at nine in the morning they have the place to themselves. While the others are reading through their copies of the ritual-in-progress, Morgan takes a moment to admire Russ and Star's renovation of what used to be a feed and seed store. Exposed brick walls, lovingly restored woodwork, refinished floors – they've done every scrap of the work themselves. It's taken the better part of two years to finish Sundial to their liking, but the place has really come together at last; ceiling fans turn lazily overhead and the liquid saxophone of Sonny Rollins plays softly over state-of-the-art speakers, accompanied by the clatter of pots and pans from the kitchen as Russ readies for the lunchtime customers.

Nick's being pretty quiet, she notices: possibly overwhelmed by the energy with which her dream sisters have embraced his project. But realistically, for something this ambitious he's going to need a lot of help.

"I asked Ben about doing the music," Molly's saying. "He'd love to."

"Great." Star makes a note. "Nick, you'll be high priest, yes? Got somebody in mind for priestess?"

"Sally says she'll do it."

"Perfect," Morgan says. Having Sally Durwood on board will provide insurance against the kind of blunder she made with the Festival of Oaks. She peers over her reading glasses at the others.

"I think we've all got a few contacts we can work to make sure there's as much participation as possible by the local people. Let's not forget this was their home before it was ours, and they have an even greater stake – "

Star, paging noisily through her copy of the ritual, cuts her off. "Nick, this oak you mention. Did you have a particular tree in mind?"

He looks surprised. "Well, sure. I mean, isn't it obvious? It's got to be Roan's Oak."

From the blank looks around the table, Morgan gathers that she's not the only one who's in the dark. "Roan – as in Roan Durwood?"

"You mean you don't know about Roan's Oak?" He looks a little smug at possessing knowledge the rest of them lack, and Morgan shoots him a warning look.

"Maybe you could fill us in,"

"Oh. Okay. It's the tree in the legend, the one where Roan met the white doe. It's, like, a gateway, a connection to the Otherworld. And it's a wish tree. People have hung all kind of offerings on it, and there's this – "

"Wait. The tree in the legend is a real tree?"

"Yeah! It's really old. And there's this – "

As the group's enthusiastic hubbub drowns him out, Star's voice dominates. "This adds so much – so much *resonance* to the section where you use the Celtic tree names to link the Noon Woods to the Druid tradition. And I'm thinking . . . what about asking the local folks to perform the part where the names of the trees are spoken aloud?"

Nick rubs the stubble on his chin. Is he growing a beard? Morgan approves; it's just the touch his young face needs. "You think they'd do it?"

"Why not? If they have an active part to play, it'll draw them into the ritual and keep them from feeling self-conscious. In fact – " a smile breaks over Star's face " – I just realized a lot of the local names actually resemble the Celtic tree names. Cole, for instance – *coll*, the hazel. Reese – *ruis*, the elder. Sayles – or Sally for that matter, your high priestess – *saille*, the willow. Lewis – *luis*, the rowan. Gorton – *gort*, ivy. And Tyner – *tinne*, holly? Kind of a stretch, but . . . And *Dur*wood, of course, the oak. So we've got a kind of human forest right on hand."

"Wow." Nick's looking dazed. Not knowing the local families, he wouldn't have made the connection, but to Morgan it seems like a wink and a nudge from the Goddess, a hint that they're heading in the right direction.

She beams at the surrounding faces. "You know what? I think this is really going to – "

Once again Star's voice overrides hers. "Let's take a few moments right now to combine energy toward our goal."

She reaches out to Nick and Molly on either side of her. Rankled by her rudeness but feeling obliged to go along, Morgan suppresses her annoyance as the six of them link hands around the table.

"Feel the life energy within you," Star intones. "Visualize it merging with the energy of those around you, joining the energy of earth and air, fire and water. . . and as our combined energy fills the circle, visualize the forest in the lap of the Goddess, safe from harm, protected by the power of the four elements."

In spite of herself Morgan can't help imagining the space within their joined hands swimming with tiny sparks of gold and violet, a phenomenon she remembers from her years with Womb&Folk. It bothers her that Star's words are able to breach her defenses so easily – and more than that, it bothers her that it bothers her. Once the circle is dissolved, she sits fiddling with her reading glasses, ignoring the chitchat as everyone is graciously dismissed by the Great Witch Queen of the Universe to go their separate ways.

"Morgan? You okay?"

Nick's leaning over her. She forces a smile. "Fine."

"You look kind of pissed off."

She wonders if she can confide in him and decides he's not old enough to know the ugly truth that his adored aunt (*I wish you were my mother,* he'd told her when he was seven) is a petty bitch.

"I'm fine. And everyone loves your ritual."

He takes the chair next to hers. "I used a bunch of different sources. Found a lot of cool stuff, like this ancient Irish law that calls for the death penalty for messing with certain trees. *Three non-breathing things paid for only with breathing things: an apple tree, a hazel bush, a sacred grove.* Isn't that awesome?"

"It is. But, um . . . you're not going to be talking about death in the ritual, are you?"

"Well, it would just be symbolic – you know, the death of the logging operation. It's one of the parts I'm still working on."

He's rolled his copy into a tube and is using it to tap out a complex rhythm on the table. There are advantages to having known him his whole life; she can see he's trying to make up his mind about something.

"Nicky, what are you up to?"

"Well . . . let's just say there are a couple of parts I didn't share with the group. Elements that will pack a lot more wallop if people don't know what to expect."

"Can you tell me?"

"I guess so . . . sure." He's bursting to tell. "You know the part where I say, 'Tonight we open once more the door between the worlds'? Well, at that point I'm going to take the stone out of the tree."

"What stone?"

"People were talking so much I didn't get a chance to tell them. The tree's been struck by lightning, and there's this hole in the trunk, supposedly connecting to the Otherworld – where the white doe came from.. But there's a stone jammed into it."

"A stone in the trunk? How weird!"

61

"According to Sally's grandmother, when Roan went to live with the doe he used the stone to block the door behind him. And it's definitely been there a long time; the bark's grown over the edges. There's some rhyme about it . . . I can't remember exactly how it goes. Something about asking Roan to come back from the Bright Land and open it again."

"The Bright Land. That gives me goosebumps."

"Me too. And since we want to reopen the door – "

Morgan claps her hands. "Yes! We take out the stone. What a perfect symbol!"

"That's what I thought too. Just – there's one thing bothering me."

"What?"

"Well . . . I mean . . . what's the stone doing there in the first place? If Roan was the one who discovered the Otherworld connection, why would he break it off? Why block the door?"

"You're taking the legend too literally," Morgan says. "The stone was there, and somehow the tree grew around it, and somebody made up a story about how it happened."

"Maybe." He's still frowning. "But I don't think so."

She gives him a quizzical glance. "Does it really matter?"

"It just bothers me. Because I keep thinking . . . what if it wasn't Roan who closed the door?"

"I'm not following."

"Just . . . It would explain so much! Have you ever been to the Noon Woods?"

"Actually, no," Morgan says. "It's not exactly off limits, but I wouldn't call it a local attraction. Before this logging thing, I hardly heard it mentioned."

"Well, there's this *atmosphere*, whatever you want to call it – this really intense stillness that feels, I don't know . . . unnatural. Like some kind of weight keeping the lid on the whole place. Keeping it tamped down."

"Keeping what tamped down?"

"The earth energy, the spirit of the forest – whatever you want to call it, that's what Roan was using to raise power. Morgan, listen – suppose people got freaked out by what he was doing? Suppose there was somebody, or even a whole faction of the community, who decided they didn't want anything to do with forces they didn't understand – who just wanted to lead ordinary everyday lives in an ordinary everyday world? Can't you just see them – narrow-minded conservatives, terrified of anything beyond their comfort zone? What if they were the ones responsible for plugging the door?"

The idea of early Durwood as anything but a harmonious pagan community gives Morgan a pang. "But why on earth would anyone – "

"Morgan. You know most people are threatened by anything outside the mainstream. They're terrified of the unknown. People like my mom and dad pretend they think Wicca's silly, but really it scares the shit out of them. Even though they spend every Sunday kissing up to an invisible bachelor in the sky."

"Okay, I'll buy fear of the unknown. But if people in the community didn't like what Roan was doing, why follow him here in the first place? And if they thought things were getting out of hand, why not just leave?"

It occurs to her that they're discussing this farfetched theory as fact, but he's always had the ability to drag her along by the force of his imagination.

"I don't know," he says. "Maybe it was some kind of cult, and Roan was the leader. Maybe they were afraid of him."

"A cult? Really? Did cults even exist back then?"

"Come on. There've always been cults."

Morgan opens her mouth and shuts it. He's right, of course, but –

"Maybe they were afraid to confront him openly," Nick's saying, "so they sabotaged the Otherworld connection instead."

"But wouldn't he have stopped them?"

"Maybe he tried. Maybe there was a power struggle and he lost." He shakes his head. "No, that doesn't make sense; he wouldn't have accepted a back seat. So maybe there was some kind of fight, and – or maybe they even killed him!"

She starts to remonstrate, but he's already off and running with the notion.

"Oh, man, it's so obvious I can't believe I missed it! They convince themselves he's a danger to the community, then murder him in secret and make it look like a disappearance – or like the story says, a desertion. 'Off he's gone to the Bright Land and left us all behind, the bastard.'

"Once they block the door in the oak, Durwood dwindles into an ordinary little town, which is exactly what they want. Humdrum lives in a humdrum world, punch a clock till you die. But now . . . the ritual is our chance to reverse the process. To open the door."

Cults, conflict, conspiracy, murder – unsettled by this lurid scenario for which there's no factual basis whatsoever (hasn't she just listened to Nick concocting it on the flimsiest possible logic?) Morgan tells herself it doesn't matter what happened then. The present is what matters. Saving the forest. She leafs through her copy of the ritual, admiring the sonorous phrases that catch her eye.

Spirit of the wildwood . . . Ancient wise ones of the sacred grove . . . Dwellers of Annwn . . .

"Nicky, what's Annwin?"

"Huh?"

"Here, where it says, 'Tonight we ask the dwellers of Annwin to join with us in fellowship once again.' What's Annwin?"

"Not Annwin," Nick says. "*An-noon.* The w is pronounced oo, like a double o. It's Welsh or something."

"What a fascinating language!"

Staring at nothing, he doesn't respond. And then: "Holy shit."

"What's the matter?"

His eyes are wide. "I just figured out something else. About the name – the Noon Woods. Morgan – noon doesn't mean midday. It's got to be a shortening of *An-noon.* The name of the Celtic Otherworld."

She tries to ignore the unpleasant flutter in her stomach.

Hal Everdale removes his gaze from the deep red glint in his wine glass to stare the length of the dining table at his wife.

"What on earth are you wearing?"

She stares back. "I think you can see it perfectly well."

Hal takes a sip. "Does your shirt really say 'Save the Noon Woods'?"

"Yes, it does."

"Mariela, for God's sake. I'm Gordon Durwood's attorney in this matter."

"I know that."

"Well, that stupid slogan runs directly contrary to my client's interests."

"Your client," Mariela says, "is an ignorant redneck who's planning to destroy a priceless natural and historical resource for no other reason than to make money."

Hal takes a deliberate swallow of Chilean Cabernet Sauvignon. "Nonetheless, he's paying me to represent him. And I'd appreciate it if you didn't actively support the other side."

"What difference does it make?" Mariela says. "It's not as if you've publicly acknowledged your association with him. No one in Durwood knows your specialty is protecting anyone who poisons and destroys the environment. People here assume we feel the way they do about the logging; no one has any idea you're helping betray them."

"And I hope it's going to stay that way."

Mariela tosses back her hair. "They won't hear it from me. But Morgan Edwards and her friends are planning to hold a magical ritual to protect the forest from the loggers, and I'm letting you know now that Chad and I will be attending."

Hal wonders how many years it's been since he's loved her and decides it's not worth calculating. "Have fun," he says.

Gordie sees the red light blinking on his answering machine as soon as he walks through the front door. In the year since Momma passed, he's gotten only three messages: one wrong number and a couple of recordings offering to consolidate his credit card debt. Normally the blinking red light would be an event, but just now it hardly registers, because this has been the worst night of his life. Close on ten years he's been singing with Willy and the Cochrans, and they were ready to ditch him just like that?

"I told you, Momma, now didn't I?" he whispers. "Didn't I say they wanted to get rid of me?"

In spite of what he's told Momma, he never really believed it would come to this. But the moment he'd walked into Farley's den tonight, he'd known it wasn't just a regular Thursday practice. Instead of the usual chat and horseplay before things got underway, the others were just sitting there tuning their instruments. A room full of the squawk and wail of strings, no one even looking up when he walked in, no one saying a word.

That noisy silence was like a chasm opening at Gordie's feet. For a while now he'd suspected things weren't right, but he'd thought there would be more warning signs – and then all of a sudden the chasm was yawning at his feet, so deep he couldn't see the bottom, and he was teetering on the brink.

"Gordie," Brad said.

He didn't really look at Gordie as he spoke; he just kept on twiddling the pegs on his mandolin, like he was making the point that he played an instrument, they all played them except for – well, that's when Gordie knew for sure. His chest felt like somebody was blowing up a balloon in there, taking all the space needed by his heart and lungs. The gospel group is the best thing that's ever happened to him, the only thing that matters in his life. He tried to make eye contact with Farley and Willy, but they were fussing over their fiddle and guitar like a couple of momma cats washing their kittens.

"We gotta talk," Brad said.

Gordie swallowed. He'd been planning to keep the CD scheme a secret until he had the money from the logging in his hand, but it was too late for that now. He was on the edge of the abyss, and Brad's next words were going to propel him over. He gathered as much of a breath as his compressed lungs would allow.

"Yeah, well, I been wanting to talk to you boys, too. You listening? Cause I got some real big news."

The answering machine light is still blinking, and now he sees the red 2 on the display. Two messages? One of them had better be Fawn Creek Logging calling with a firm date. Vance must have reported the fracas in Durwood, and now it feels like they're stalling, waiting for things to calm down. That won't do. In order to satisfy Brad and Farley and Willy, he's had to fudge the facts a little, make it sound like the logging's almost done instead of not yet started.

But at least his strategy worked. The boys are fired up; there's been no more *We gotta talk*. Still, he's cut to the quick at having to buy the privilege of staying in the group, and he'll rest easier once the logging gets going. There'll be some real foot-tapping music then – the music of chainsaws and jingling cash.

Two messages. He presses the play button and waits. The first is from the lawyer, returning his call from a couple of days ago.

"Mr. Durwood, Hal Everdale from Everdale Snead Chalmers. Regarding your question about pressing assault charges against your uncle, I'd advise against it. I understand you're upset, but this is a volatile situation and it's in our best interests not to inflame things further. Once the logging operation's finished, we can apply pressure and see if we can't get some kind of satisfaction, but for now I'm sure you'll agree that having the logging go smoothly takes precedence. Have a pleasant evening."

The bored drawl issuing from the machine makes Gordie scowl. Everdale doesn't like him and the feeling is mutual, but Buck Pawling says a good lawyer is essential and Everdale is the best. And since he owns a chunk of property up in the Durwood area, he's right on hand.

Second message. "Gordie, it's your cousin Sally. Sally Durwood."

Sally Durwood. At eleven Gordie'd had a crush on her, all the more fierce for having to remain secret, not only because she'd laugh him to scorn but because Momma was always warning him against the girls of Durwood. "Don't you ever so much as *think* of touching one of those gals, Gordie. If you do, you will *never* wash away the *stain*. They're every last one of them going to *hell*. Those pretty pink cheeks are going to be *burnt black* by the *flames of eternal damnation*."

Momma's voice in his head gives way to Sally's hillbilly cadence.

" – so I'm gonna keep it short. You need to call off this loggin thing, you hear? Folks are dead set against it, and if you don't drop it there's gonna be trouble. I know we wasn't never close, Gordie, but I don't want to see you get hurt."

Click. Not so much as a *Goodbye Gordie* or *You take care now*. He presses the button and listens to her message again. *Folks are dead set against it*. It's not hard to guess who she means. Does Sally think it's some kind of newsflash that Jared Gorton and the others hate his guts? They haven't changed one bit since they were kids, since the day they dragged him out behind May's Café.

(The trashcan is to be his pulpit.

Gordie stumbles toward it, helped on his way by a kick in the behind from Conlee Cole. No one speaks while he climbs up and finds his balance on the dented lid. When he looks down at his congregation, he sees their hands folded in mock prayer beneath grinning Satanic faces. Jared Gorton, Harley and Conlee Cole, Tyner Durwood, Spence Sayles, Darrell and Hub Reese – demons with sunburns and cowlicks and raggedy jeans. For as long as he can remember, Momma's been telling him to keep away from those boys, they're *godless hellspawn* just like their parents, just like every last person in this hateful town.

Even Daddy?

Hush, Gordie. Yes, even him.

Preach! Harley yells all of a sudden, and Gordie jumps. The others laugh. It's like the Crucifixion game, only now the jeering mob is real. Spit upon. Stripped. Smited. Tormented. Scourged. Mocked. Crucified. He thinks of Momma's eyes and lips going all shiny when she says the words.

Ye can be redeemed by the blood of Jesus, he whispers. Ye can be justified and made righteous. If ye do but accept Jesus, spirit, soul and body, Satan can hold no power over ye.

Yeeeee – haw! Jared slaps both knees. Lordy, I can feel it! I can feel the spirit!

Me too! Darrell lets out a resounding burp. Let's get us some more of that righteous shit!

A stench wafts up from the trashcan, making Gordie queasy. And there's something else, a more urgent matter. I gotta pee, he mutters.

His congregation snorts in delighted disbelief. Say WHAT?

Gotta pee.

No you ain't. You keep on preachin, we ain't saved yet. Don't you even think about quittin till we been saved!

Denied, the need grows desperate. When he grabs himself to try and pinch it off, the other boys explode into laughter. Gordie licks his lips and continues. Therefore put ye on the armor of God, that ye may stand against the Devil's wiles. For we wrestle not against flesh and blood, but against principalities, against powers, against the rulers of the darkness of this world. Normally he likes this part. Principalities, powers, rulers of the darkness – there's something grand in the way the words roll off his tongue. But now the mounting pressure in his bladder prevents him from remembering what comes next. He falls silent and licks his lips again. The blank back walls of May's and the Hardware & General stare him down; there's a muffled chuckle from the leaves overhead. How much longer can he hold it? His nose starts running and his eyes fill with tears, as if the backed up pee is trying to escape anyway it can.

Preach, the demon mob is chanting. Preach! Preach! Preach!

Gordie has a blurred glimpse of Jared's arm flying back. The next instant something hits him in the belly and he looks down just as a bright red bloodstain blossoms on the front of his shirt. There's no pain, only a creeping cold in his belly and a wobble in his knees as he realizes he's dying. – dying for Jesus! He pictures Momma sobbing beside his corpse.

Hey, looky there, the preacher done peed his britches! Preacher Peepee! Preacher Peepee!

Smited. Tormented. Mocked. Dying.

Every nerve in his body is starting to sting – harbinger of the lacerating, voluptuous fire that will soon ignite his flesh, burn away the impurities and set his spirit free. There's no pain from the bloody wound in his belly. When he probes it gently, it's cold and sticky. He sniffs his fingers, takes a tentative lick –

Cherry favor. Jared's missile was the soggy remains of his Popsicle. He's not dying after all, but it doesn't matter; nothing matters except that he's ascending in bliss, borne on white wings of flame. For the glory of the Lord is like a devouring fire, he whispers, and as the delicious fire engulfs him at last, even the faces of his pointing, hooting tormentors seem beautiful.)

"End of messages," says the canned voice.

Gordie blinks. *I don't want to see you get hurt.* He touches his bruised cheek, still tender from his uncle's bony backhand. Hurt? Hurt is knowing the other boys in the group want to replace him with somebody who plays the banjo and never sings a sour note. Hurt is working at the shoe store, having smelly feet in his face all day long when he's been put on earth to witness to the Blessed Savior's love. It's part of God's plan. And making a big career in gospel is how he's going to fulfill the plan. No matter what Brad or Farley or Willy want, no matter what Jared and the other Durwood bullies have in mind, this logging thing is fated to happen. The CD will be produced; it's the Lord's will.

Prodding his cheek, pushing and probing until the pain ignites, he whispers, *"Blessed are ye when men shall revile you and persecute you, and shall say all manner of evil against you for My Sake, for great is your reward in Heaven."*

✻ 10 ✻

Hidden among the trees at the forest edge, Jared watches and waits. One of his buddies down in Lenoir has been keeping an ear out for him, and last night he got the call he's been dreading. Today, right here above CW's farm, the logging of the Noon Woods is scheduled to begin.

Jared's gut churns with the sheer fucking nerve of it. Much as he might want to leave Durwood forever, he can't imagine the Noon Woods ceasing to exist. Not that he bears them any particular love; on the contrary, since the night Tyne fell – he glances at the inked design of oaks and acorns encircling his forearm. How many times since that night has he thought about having the tattoo removed? He knows he never will; it's part of him, like the forest. The trees have always been here and always will be, casting their shadow over Durwood for good or ill. But the loggers are on their way.

Beyond the trees, the hayfield shimmers in the heat of the July morning. Jared glances around him at the others who stand in the deep forest shade, waiting with him. Six of them – Darrell, Hub, Spence, the Cole twins, himself.

Six, where there ought to be seven.

There were seven of them running headlong through these woods that June night, chasing their own shouts and laughter through the moonlit darkness, seven teenage boys bursting with more energy than they knew what to do with. Returning the Midsummer race to the Noon Woods had been Tyne's idea, sparked by his granny's old songs and tales. Every kid in Durwood had a favorite among Granny Dee's stories, and Tyne's was the one about Midsummer's Eve, when every man and boy over thirteen had gathered in the Noon Woods to race through the dark to Roan's Oak.

"It was a wiiiild night." Granny liked to tell her stories just above a whisper, so the younguns had to lean close to hear. "Wasn't nobody knew what might happen, because once the King of the Greenwood was chosen, for that one long summer night his littlest wish was law. He had the blessin of the white doe, and nary a soul could deny him."

"He could do whatever he wanted?"

"That's what I'm tellin you."

To the kids that sounded mighty fine. But Granny said some folks took against the custom. After a time, the race got moved from the woods into town, and then from night to afternoon. Finally they just stopped having it at all.

To Tyne and Jared, neither of whom had ever seen the race run, it was as if something had been stolen from them. As youngsters they acted it out with their friends, the winner commanding the others to perform daring deeds. When Darrell broke his arm jumping off the roof of the Coles' woodshed, their parents put a stop to it and they had to make do with other games.

Jared was eighteen and Tyne fifteen when they returned from a drunken jaunt to Cherokee with matching oak leaf tattoos and little recollection of how they'd come to be so marked. But as Midsummer approached that year, Tyne started talking again about running the race the way it had been run in the old days – the way it was meant to be run. The other boys scoffed, uneasy at the notion of venturing into the Noon Woods, especially at night, and even Jared was reluctant. He'd finished high school by then and had a full time job at the body shop; the race seemed like kid stuff. But the notion had lodged in Tyne's head, and eventually he managed to talk the rest of them around.

Harley and Conlee decided to add to the fun by snitching a jar of moonshine from their daddy's still, and all seven of them were pretty drunk by the time they went stumbling through the trees. But even a bellyful of moonshine can't properly explain the cloud in Jared's memory obscuring whatever happened next. When he tries to remember, his thoughts turn thick as blinked milk. Whatever it was, the others must have experienced it too – because Tyne had lain near death at the foot of the tree for almost four hours, while for the rest of them it seemed only a few minutes had passed.

The doctors said even immediate treatment might not have prevented the permanent damage to Tyne's spinal cord, but for Jared that *might* lodged in his chest like a spike, stabbing him with every breath. Although he seldom left Tyne's bedside at the hospital, they never talked about that night, either then or later, and by now the bulk of unspoken words has come to block all others. As Tyne has retreated deeper into his private world, they've seen each other less and less.

"There they come yonder," Darrell says, and through the screen of leaves Jared sees a couple of trucks rolling down the slope. Suddenly he knows why he's doing this.

He's doing it for Tyne.

"Okay, let's go." As he steps out of the forest, the sunlight sends a bead of gold sliding along the barrel of his shotgun.

◆◆◆

Tapping at the screen door, Sally sounds out of breath. "Liz! CW just called from town! Loggers are on their way."

Her face is flushed beneath its tan; Liz guesses she's run all the way up the hill. "Do you want to come inside? A glass of water?"

"Naw. They're gonna be here any minute."

They stand on the porch in the hot stillness and wait. There's no wind, not even a whisper from the witch balls. Goldfinches chatter on the feeder out front; butterflies flit across the sunny field. It's hard to imagine a more peaceful place, impossible to believe the forest can be destroyed.

"Isn't this illegal or something?" Liz says at last.

Sally shrugs. "Fact is, Uncle Gordon was older'n Pa by twenty-seven minutes. So if the Noon Woods are some kinda family property . . . But you know folks round here don't think like that, never have."

Liz couldn't agree more with the local notion that anyone owning the forest is preposterous. "But legally – ? "

"Well, t he law might say different."

"But why destroy the woods? Does he need the money that badly?"

"I reckon there's more to it than that, Liz." Sally picks a splinter off the porch railing, flicks it away. "There's some bad family stuff there – most of it musta happened after you left. Was you still livin here when Gordon went and got married?"

"No. When I left Durwood, Gordon and your pa were both still tongue-tied bachelors."

"And stayed that way, too, till they was into their fifties. Then Pa married Ma, and a couple years later Gordon met Kathy down in Lenoir; she was up from Asheville visiting family friends. He didn't know nothin about women, and Kathy was real pretty. Delicate, like a piece of fancy china. Hard as china, too.

"When Gordon went and married her, folks tried to make her feel welcome here, but it was pretty clear she hated it from the get-go. To her we was all heathens, specially her own momma-in-law. Granny had a lot of country remedies, you know, and Kathy thought they was pure deviltry. And since we didn't have no church in Durwood – well, she had her proof right there.

"She musta figured she'd committed a sin by marryin Gordon, and it was her punishment to be stuck in this nest of evil. They lived here, you know – in this cabin. Moved out of the farmhouse so Kathy wouldn't have to share a roof with Granny Dee."

Sally jerks her chin at the witch balls hanging overhead. "Those uns was Kathy's, you know. Supposed to trap evil spirits inside. Granny laughed fit to die when she saw em, but I think her feelins was hurt. It made her sad for Gordon's wife to be so set against our ways. At first Kathy acted like she thought she could make a change round here. But all the s in and salvation talk didn't get her nowhere; you know how Durwood folks are."

Liz nods. "When I was a child, I was in the Hardware & General with my uncle when a visiting preacher came in spouting hellfire and damnation. My uncle and your grandpa just picked him up by his elbows and carried him outside with his feet kicking in the air."

Sally smiles a little. "Wish we coulda done that with Kathy. Folks just let her be, on account of she was Gordon's wife. Reckoned once her and Gordon started a family she'd settle down . . . but soon's Gordie could walk and talk, she set him to preachin scripture out on Main Street in a white shirt and a little black bowtie, while she sat there on the bench at the Hardware & General in her Sunday best. Once she had Gordie, she stopped even pretendin to get along with his pa. Gordon got to be an enemy in his own home, the two of them set against him.

"Kathy stuck it out here till Gordie turned twelve. His pa'd got him a huntin rifle for his birthday, hopin it was somethin they could do together. But that night when he got home, there was a note on the fridge sayin Kathy was takin Gordie back to Asheville, and not to come after em. I can remember how mad Granny was – not cause Kathy'd left, but she'd let the woodstove go out, and the house was stone cold.

"You know, Liz, it ain't like nobody's ever left Durwood before. I mean, you did it. Young folks leave all the time – it's too small, no opportunities. Why, Jared'd be gone quicker than a jug handle if I'd go with him. Sometimes they come back later on, like you. But I reckon Gordie's the first one ever to come back lookin to destroy us."

Destroy. The word is still hanging in the air when the sound of engines reaches them.

No more than a distant drone at first, going on and on and then shifting to a whine as the vehicles tackle the hill. Their approach seems to take a long time, grating and grinding noises that steadily mount until at last the machines roll into view – a flatbed truck hauling a bright yellow skidder, followed by a pickup with three men riding in the bed and a shabby camper in tow. One minute they're rattling past the cabin, the next they're jouncing down the slope of the field, leaving tracks in the hay as they head for the green mass of sunlit treetops.

Liz discovers her hands clenched into fists. The speed with which Gordie has mounted his operation seems to have caught Durwood by surprise; aside from the Save the Noon Woods shirts and a growing list of signatures on the petition at Abundance's checkout counter, the planned resistance hasn't gotten off the ground. So far there are only gestures, words, intentions to combat what has now become the solid reality of men with chainsaws.

A shout from the direction of the woods scatters her thoughts – half a dozen figures have emerged from the trees. She recognizes some of the young local men, Jared Gorton out in front gesturing for the trucks to stop. When they don't, his arms rise swiftly to shoulder height. There's a glint of sun on metal and a deafening roar as the shotgun blast bounces off the mountains and echoes back.

The men in the back of the pickup throw themselves flat; Liz and Sally flinch.

"He shot in the air," Sally says. "It's okay. He shot in the air."

But she's obviously shaken, and Liz is anything but reassured. Down in the field, the trucks have stopped. As the last reverberation from the gunshot dies away, the only sound is the flapping retreat of some startled crows.

A head pokes out of the flatbed cab. "You crazy, mister? Hell you think you're doin?"

The local men are spreading out in a ragged line in front of the woods. By now it's obvious they're all carrying shotguns.

"Just get gone." Jared has lowered his gun, but there's plenty of menace in the words that carry clearly across the still air. "Go on back where you come from, and won't nobody get hurt."

"Can't oblige you, boys. We been hired to do a job and we mean to do it. Sorry if that sets poorly with you, but don't take it out on us. Our families gotta eat."

Jared doesn't answer. A sudden gust of wind races from the direction of the woods across the field, bringing a breath of cool to the stifling air. Amid the tossing stalks of green hay the young men hold their ground, cradling their weapons. The logging crew have poked their heads up from the pickup bed, but they're keeping very still.

"Dammit," the driver says. "We ain't got time for this." His head disappears back inside the cab; the engine revs and the truck lumbers straight toward the local boys – a game of high-stakes Chicken. Liz and Sally exchange a panicky glance as Jared and the others raise their guns.

Just then something hurtles past the cabin, a flashing blur moving so fast that the police siren seems to unwind like a streamer in its wake. Halfway across the field, the county sheriff's car wallows to a stop; the doors fly open and two uniformed cops jump out, shouting and gesturing. Their appearance is enough to derail the confrontation. The flatbed stops; the Durwood men lower their guns.

"Everybody just calm the hell down! You hear? Calm! The hell! Down!"

Liz recognizes Larry Ewers, the potbellied county sheriff, waving a bullhorn in one hand and clutching the butt of his holstered pistol with the other. In spite of his injunction he seems anything but calm. Jared and others haven't budged. More cars are arriving – a second patrol car, a ratty red sedan, a silver SUV – and abruptly Sally bounds down the cabin steps and heads toward the confrontation at a run. Liz, trailing behind her, reaches the tense gathering as the new vehicles are disgorging their occupants – two more cops, the lawyer Hal Everdale, and Gordie Durwood.

Jared strides up to Gordie and jabs a finger in his face. "You little shit! You got no right to touch them trees!"

Gordie gives an elaborate shrug. "You see that fella there? That's my lawyer. He knows the law frontwards and backwards, and he says this is my land. *My land*. And that means I can do whatever I want with it!" Yanking a crumpled piece of paper from his pants pocket, he thrusts it in Jared's face. "You want to study the deed, be my guest!"

Jared bats the proffered paper from his hand. One of the deputies makes an unsuccessful grab as it flutters away; then a breeze carries it off. The deputies edge closer to Jared, whose face is red with anger.

"Listen up, Preacher Peepee. You get them loggers outta here before somebody gets hurt."

Beneath his raised voice comes the sighing of wind through infinite leaves. Liz glances at the woods. This close, the trees are so tall that they conceal the sweep of forest beyond, but she can feel it: a weighty presence joining earth and sky. Dense, green, alive with flowing currents of air and light, creeping sap and stirring leaves, the silent seeking of roots deep in the earth. A mass of clouds has gathered above the treetops.

As the wind dies away, Sally speaks. "Hush, Jared. All y'all hush. You boys need to take your guns and go on home."

Jared rounds on her. "What the hell, Sally! You see them chainsaws?"

"You start shootin and you're gone go to jail," one of the cops says. "What good's that gone do you?"

Gordie smirks. "Might get him a shower, anyway."

Sally turns her gaze on him. "You might could use one of them yourself, Gordie Durwood."

Behind her even words comes once more the rise and fall of leaves. In the sudden breathless quiet that follows that vast respiration, they all stand motionless, as if waiting. Liz sees that the clouds have thickened and darkened; now they're oozing across the sky in a bloated mass the color of a fresh bruise. As the day dims around them, one logger nudges another and points and now they're all looking up, watching the churning clouds gobble up the last patch of blue sky. Flocks of birds take to the air, the noise of beating wings lost in the wind that pours out of the forest, setting the trees in turbulent motion. Now it comes hissing across the field toward them, flattening the hay like the stroking of a huge, invisible hand. Everdale retreats into his car. The sheriff's hat blows off and he scuttles after it. The confrontation's been forgotten, the participants reduced to a bewildered knot of puny figures, clothes flapping and eyes narrowed against the wind.

There's a sudden bone-rattling clap of thunder, so loud it makes them all flinch. In that moment, only Liz notices Sally swaying back and forth in rhythm with the trees, her face framed by a blazing corona of windblown hair, her outflung arms welcoming the storm. And with a howl and a flash it's upon them, wind and lightning and torrents of rain that leave them no option but to flee. People dash in all directions – the cops to their cars, the loggers to their camper, the Durwood boys to the shelter of the woods. As Liz runs for the cabin, she glances back to see Sally turning in circles, arms outflung and face lifted to the blinding rain.

She's laughing.

◆ ◆ ◆

Unpacking boxes in Abundance's windowless storeroom, Nick's oblivious to the storm until Morgan appears in the doorway with her hair dripping and her clothes soaked through. Realizing he's staring at the shape of her breasts beneath her sopping shirt, he hastily averts his gaze.

"Uh . . . what happened to you?"

"It's raining!" She pirouettes into the room, spraying droplets like a revolving lawn sprinkler. "The loggers showed up this morning. But as soon as they got out to the Noon Woods, there was a huge storm!"

"So they can't log?"

"Not in the wind and rain. It's a – "

"Gift from the Goddess," he says. They share a complicit smile. Nick sits down on a carton and runs a hand over his new beard. This drought – how long has it lasted? A storm just now is an awfully convenient coincidence. Or is it more than that? "Who'd have figured they'd start so soon?" he says.

"Nobody except Jared Gorton, who only told his buddies. CW said they confronted the loggers with shotguns and there was a stand-off, but the storm came before anything really happened."

"CW was there?"

"Sally was; she called him and he called me. Nick, guess what? He wants to join in the ritual!"

"No kidding? That's great! But . . . " His jubilation ebbs. "The loggers are already here. So what happens once it stops raining?"

He sees Morgan's smile falter. Obviously it can't rain forever, and the presence of the crew, already on site, ruins their tentative plan to stage a roadblock for the media. "We've got to ride the wave," she says. "Do the ritual tonight."

"Tonight? But we haven't rehearsed it – the costumes aren't even ready! And what if it's still raining?"

"We'll get the costumes ready. And we don't need a rehearsal. We'll just call everybody and let them know there's a change of plan."

"And if it's still raining?" Nick says weakly.

"It won't be." Her confident tone says the Goddess won't allow it. She glances down at the puddle collecting beneath her on the floor, then up at him with a radiant smile. "I need to make some calls. We've got a lot to do before tonight!"

◆◆◆

Sally's still out there.

It's still raining hard, too hard for Liz to get a clear view of the lone figure in the field. It's hard to tell, but it looks as if she's stopped spinning around. Now she's just standing there beneath the downpour. Liz can't watch any longer. Opening the door, she plunges into the pummeling rain and runs across the field. Even though it's only water and she's already soaking wet, she finds herself ducking and flinching like a soldier traversing enemy fire as she gains on her mission objective – her sensible neighbor, standing motionless in the rain.

At least she's quit laughing. But when Liz touches her shoulder, there's no response. She's a charcoal sketch, hair dark with streaming water, eyes like black holes in her chalky face.

"Sally! Come inside!" And she might as well be talking to a sketch. She envisions the seasons passing while she tries to get Sally's attention: autumn leaves falling around them, snowdrifts mounding at their feet before melting to reveal spring wildflowers. And then Sally jerks like someone roused abruptly from a deep sleep, and her colorless lips move.

"Ain't the blood itself," she says. "It's what it means to you – the value of it."

That's it. Nothing else follows. The rain keeps pouring down.

"Can we go inside now?" Liz says.

Inside, she gets a fire going, seats Sally close to it, and waits. The moments pass. Finally she says, "What did you mean – what you said out there in the field?"

Sally stares into the fire.

"It was something about blood," Liz says.

A knot pops in the fire. Sally blinks. "Blood?"

"About its value. Something like that."

"Oh." A wan smile. Patchy color is returning to her face and the size of her pupils has diminished. "Just . . . when Jared and Gordie were fussin, I remembered what might of been the first time Granny took me to Roan's Oak. I was, oh, nine or ten I guess. She took this little old holly leaf and pricked my finger with it – dang if I can't still feel it – and squeezed a couple of drops of blood onto the roots. When I asked her what did a tree want with blood, she said, 'Ain't the blood itself. It's what it means to you – the value of the gift.'

"I didn't understand her then, but now I think I do. It's like the wish tokens on the tree – if you want somethin, you got to give somethin. Roan promised the white doe a single drop of blood for each year that passed, but we been cheatin on that bargain, and it's my fault. Granny used to hang every newborn's birthcord on the oak, see, and I made up my mind it was just foolishness. Then when her leg got bad and she couldn't go to the woods herself, she trusted me to do it and I didn't. And the babies – and now this thing with Gordie – " She draws a ragged breath. "I can see where I was wrong."

There's more along those lines, but Liz only half listens, letting the words flow over her. Her sketchbook is open on her knees and the pencil drags her hand across the page, drawing Sally Durwood with the wind transforming her hair into a streaming tangle of live wires, wells of dreaming light in her eyes, hands flung high to embrace the coming storm.

To the accompaniment of Sally's murmuring voice the pencil spills that wild mass of windswept hair across the page and onto the one opposite, where it becomes a mesh of feathery leaves and tangled vines rife with shadowy hollows from which peep a multitude of wild faces. Beneath the image, Liz scrawls two words.

Green Lady.

As the pencil stops, Sally falls silent and together they watch the fire, listening to the witch balls making music in the storm.

◆◆◆

"M-Morgan? It's M-Molly."

"Molly! You sound awful! What's wrong? Is it the baby?"

"The b-baby's fine. It's . . . it's B-Ben."

"Oh Goddess! Is he hurt? What happened?"

"He's not h-hurt," Molly's bruised voice says. "He . . . h-hee . . . " The syllable spirals upward into stratospheric misery. ". . . heeeeeeEEEE . . . "

Morgan clutches the phone. "He what, Mol? He what?"

"I just c-caught him k-k-k-kissing Annie Sayles!"

The facts, insofar as Morgan can piece them together through Molly's sobs, are simple. Apparently Molly was feeling isolated upstairs with Laurel. When she ventured downstairs to the shop in search of company, she found the CLOSED sign on the door. Poised to twit Ben and Annie about forgetting to turn it to the OPEN side, she waltzed in and discovered the two of them in a passionate embrace.

"Oh, Molly!" By this time Morgan's sitting on the couch in the Upshaws' apartment, passing Molly tissues and making her take sips of Tension Tamer tea. Baby Laurel, she's ascertained, is asleep in her basket. From Molly's hiccupping recital Morgan gathers that Ben has stormed off in their car.

"He didn't even say he was s-sorry! He just k-kept saying 'd-dammit, Molly,' like I'd i-ironed one of his teeshirts wrong!"

"Huh." It's news to Morgan that anyone wears ironed teeshirts, or could possibly expect anyone else to iron them. The Upshaws hail from Brooklyn, lured to Durwood by their old friend Tamara and her glowing accounts of a little place nestled among the mountains where you could leave your door unlocked at night and everybody knew your name. Molly has confessed they'd worried about it being full of Bible-thumping Evangelicals, but Tamara had waved away their fears. There wasn't even a church in Durwood; it was super pagan-friendly – practically the unofficial headquarters of the New Age!

A community unpolluted by organized religion, where their future children could play on grass instead of concrete . . . Seduced by the vision, here they are. But having heard Ben's occasional remarks about Durwood's backwardness and isolation, Morgan's not surprised to learn he's been exploring ways to stave off boredom.

Annie Sayles? She's attractive in a hungry sort of way, and it's undoubtedly just a bump in the road, a matter of her being available while Molly is *hors de combat* – but now is not the time to say so to Molly, whose sobs are steadily increasing in volume.

"Mol. Do you want me to stay awhile?"

"Would you?"

"Sure," Morgan says, thinking, Shit! The ritual! But she can't blow Molly off, not at a time like this. She'll just have to miss it; Star will be more than happy to step into her role. It isn't fair, when she really wants to participate in the ceremony, do her bit to save the forest – and give Nick her full support.

The night after the Midsummer race, she'd dreamed of an erotic encounter with a mysterious figure crowned in leaves. The details may have been cloudy, but the sensations were intense enough that she'd – well, it was the first time she'd ever reached orgasm in a dream. Lying there half awake in the delicious aftermath, she'd realized that while the ambiguous dream male had been a stranger, at the same time he'd been Nick.

Dreams are just dreams, but this one has cast a lingering aura over her feelings about Nick. She's never thought of him as a potent young male until now, and it makes her uncomfortable. Even if he returned her feelings, which he obviously doesn't, their relationship makes the notion of a sexual liaison appalling. She'd held him in her arms as a baby! Nonetheless she seems unable to shake off this new, distracting sense of him as a man and herself as a woman. Every casual touch sends her into a dither; in his presence she's hyperaware of her own body, and of the way his has changed from a gangly teenager's into a man's. She's been trying her best to blame the whole thing on some kind of premenopausal hormone cascade, but it's still disturbing. And to complicate things further, in a very real sense Nick's still her child, her pride and joy, and she wants to be there for him tonight in his debut as high priest. Now, thanks to Ben Upshaw, she has to be there for Molly instead.

Damn all men, anyway!

✳ 11 ✳

"Closed! You believe this, Momma? What in the H-E-double- toothpicks is going on around here?"

OPEN DAILY 6 AM TO 10 PM. The flyspecked cardboard sign has been taped in the window of May's Café for as long as Gordie can remember – but here it is, only a little after eight in the evening, and the place is locked up tight.

He peers into the darkened interior one last time before smacking the glass with both palms and turning away in disgust. Now what? He's so hungry his bellybutton's gnawing on his backbone, and the only other places are thirty miles away in Lenoir.

It's typical of the way this whole logging thing is going – unexpected storms blowing in from nowhere, the weather folks trying to cover their behinds by warning that the next few days may bring more of the same, the crew skedaddling back to Lenoir to wait things out – and who's been stuck with sleeping on site in their stinky camper, keeping an eye on the seventy-thousand dollar skidder in case the locals get feisty?

"I told em, Momma, I said hey, it's your doggone machine! But Jared and his boys spooked that crew pretty bad; I think they're gonna bail if they get half a chance. So I said okay, okay, I'll babysit your ole skidder."

But on an empty stomach? His best bet is to go back the camp; maybe there'll be something resembling food in the camper fridge. He digs in his pocket for his car keys. In Durwood it's unheard of to lock your car, but he's not about to take the chance of finding some token of local sentiment, a dead skunk or possum, on his front seat. That's all he needs when his car is already a piece of junk, twelve years old with a cracked rear windshield and a perpetual odor of burning transmission fluid. Once the logging money comes through, he's going to treat himself to a new one. He's already picked out a white Bronco at the Ford dealership across the street from the mall: the perfect set of wheels for a gospel star. He imagines relaxing in the all-leather interior, listening to Sealed in the Spirit's own CD on the deluxe sound system, the volume cranked all the way up on *One Cross*.

He's starting to hum it when a hand grasps his arm.

◆ ◆ ◆

Bent low to the ground, Nick edges his way backward around the clearing, dragging the knife blade through the earth. The rain has stopped, but there's still a dense cloud cover; here in the deep woods the darkness is all-encompassing.

The sound of water dripping from the trees all around serves only to accentuate the stillness. There's something primordial about the dark, a sense of floating in a cosmic void. Visualizing himself inscribing a fiery circle with his knife upon the void, Nick repeats the mantra Star suggested for this part of the ritual.

The forms pass, but the circle remains . . .
The forms pass, but the circle remains . . .
The forms pass, but the circle remains . . .

Gradually the murmured words blur to meaningless syllables, a hypnotizing drone beneath which he's aware of the soft shufflings and occasional throat clearings around him. Even though he can't see his audience and they can't see him, he keeps his movements deliberate and solemn, as befits the high priest of a magical ritual. And he *feels* like a high priest in the shaman's headdress he created this afternoon out of oak twigs and Velcro, with a few tips from the internet. The elaborate leafy robe he's wearing is a loan from Russ Barrett, left over from the Midsummer celebration. Underneath it, according to custom, Nick's completely naked. Magic depends on such details, on realigning the mind from the mundane to the supernatural.

Not that the mundane hasn't done its best to intrude, with Molly Upshaw in hysterics over catching her husband putting the moves on Annie Sayles, and Morgan having to rush to her side. Morgan is bummed, Nick knows, at missing the ritual; Star will be reading her part, but he was really counting on her being there.

And then there's Liz's reaction.
You can't do that! You can't just summon the Green Man!
But the Green Man's on our side!
Don't be an idiot. It's not that simple.

He'd felt like a slapped puppy. But it was too late to cancel; events were already in motion, and now everybody's here. He takes a deep breath and deliberately exhales the negativity. Forget it. There's only here and now. Only the ritual.

Except he hadn't realized it would be so dark. It's impossible to know if he's arrived back at his starting point, so there's no guarantee that he's actually closed the circle – and closing the circle is vital because it keeps the energy contained. An advance visit to the site would have ironed out wrinkles like this, but the speed with which the loggers descended, the unexpected storm . . . Even though he'd consented to Morgan's urging to go ahead with the ritual tonight, Nick can't help feeling unprepared, swept beyond his depth by everyone else's expectations.

Too late now. Pressure from Sally on one hand, from Morgan and her friends on the other, has brought the majority of Durwood's population together for this event. If he blows it, he can't count on them to cut him any slack; there won't be a second chance.

There. To his best guess, the circle is closed. Wiping the blade clean on the sleeve of his robe, he braces himself for the next step, trying to ignore the qualm in his belly. Daring and awesome as this part of the ritual had seemed when he'd conceived it, now that the moment has arrived he's wishing he'd taken more time to think it through. Once again, as high priest he doesn't have the option of backing out.

Approaching Roan's Oak at what he hopes is a stately pace, he stops in front of the stone embedded in the tree. By now his eyes have adjusted enough to the darkness that he's easily able to locate the candle and the box of kitchen matches tucked among the roots. His hands are shaking and it takes him three tries to light the candle, but at last he succeeds. Setting it down among the roots, he kneels and fixes his gaze on the dancing flame.

Breathe. Ground and center.

There's no turning back. Without giving himself time to think, he picks up the knife again and draws the blade quickly, firmly across the palm of his left hand.

For a second or two there's nothing – no pain, not even any blood, as if his flesh is too surprised to react – and then a white-hot burn that snatches the breath from his lungs. Staring woozily at the blood welling up in his palm, black in the candlelight, he lets it pool for a few seconds before opening his fingers and allowing it to drip onto the roots below. Space contracts to a circle of flickering flame, time to the steady patter of liquid. Overhead, the moon breaks through thinning clouds to flood the clearing – and startled from his trance by the sudden wash of phantom light, Nick looks up to see the leafy shadows alive with faces.

They ring the clearing, some in their Midsummer finery, others in hastily assembled robes of camouflage fabric, the children holding little figures of woven twigs made by Vivian late this afternoon. And even though Nick's known all along that they were there, the sight of the people of Durwood shoulder to shoulder with the trees fills him with a burgeoning awe. A voice in his mind says, *A kind of human forest right on hand*. Here they are, counting on him for protection. Isn't Morgan always saying that nothing happens by accident? He thinks of the Midsummer race, Jared Gorton shoving the King's crown into his hand, his random choice of Gorton's lover to be his queen. His flesh prickles. Has he really been brought to Durwood to save the Noon Woods?

Against the backdrop of shadowed faces, the twisted ribbon of the umbilical cord droops from a low branch. Recalling his first reaction to it, he realizes he's grown since then; now the sight brings a rush of energy. Damn, he can feel the presence of magic here, a kind of crackle in the air.

He takes a deep breath and speaks his opening lines. "We are gathered in the sacred grove, the place of flowing together, where the sacred fire burns by the well of wisdom, beneath the world tree."

A raspy smoker's cough sounds somewhere behind him. Feeling the magic recede, Nick strives to hold on to it.

"Close your eyes and find the center of your being. From that center, let your roots sink deep into the earth."

He closes his own eyes, then opens them a slit to see how things are going. Mistake: he glimpses a muddy work boot peeking from beneath someone's robe.

"From the depths of the earth, evoke your ancestors, the seed from which you spring. Feel yourself absorbing the ancient power of the earth, the power of those who have gone before you.

"Let the power flow upward through your roots, into your trunk. As the sap rises inside you, feel your arms transformed into branches. See your branches sprouting green leaves of strength and wisdom. Feel the wind blowing through your leaves."

He raises his arms and sees some of the robed figures do likewise. Slowly other arms go up around the clearing. There's some self-conscious shifting and foot-shuffling, but everyone's trying.

"Now feel the earth embracing your roots, the water flowing through you, the air stirring your branches. Feel your leaves absorbing the fiery light from the sky and connecting it to the hidden fire within the earth. Feel the fire circulating through your body, bathing your spirit in its warmth."

He pauses, counting silently. One. Two. Three.

"You have become a human tree."

When he stops speaking, the sounds of the night forest flow in. The rustle of wind through leaves, the patter of dislodged raindrops. People stand motionless, their raised arms meshing. With all his might Nick concentrates on the mental image inspired by Liz's drawing – that uncanny shape shifting between shadow and substance, between tree and human.

Spirit of the Wildwood.

Again he feels the presence of something numinous that holds him immobile while wonder blossoms inside him. Because the ritual has taken off, and now it's moving forward on its own.

◆◆◆

Liz watches the witch balls tremble along the edge of the porch roof.

The rain's stopped. The wind has died down. There's no reason for the witch balls to be moving at all, yet they're stirring ever so slightly, rubbing together with a dry whisper.

She stares up at the globes of blue-green glass. Shortly after coming to live at the cabin, she'd discovered them tucked in a dusty box under the eaves and decided to string them along the front porch roof, where some rusty hooks already existed as if for the purpose. CW had snorted when he'd seen them. They'd belonged, he said, to his sister-in-law. The threads suspended inside were meant to snare evil spirits.

Inside Liz's head there's a smoky simmer, a brushfire racing across the surface of her brain. Her right hand has become an alien rubber glove. She knows the signs. Will this be one of the times she blacks out? And if she does, will she regain consciousness or die here on the cabin floor while those fools in the woods are playing dress-up in a minefield? She's already closed the windows; now she goes back inside, shuts the door behind her, lights the lamp. While her body performs these actions, her thoughts hover around the jar of moonshine in the kitchen cabinet.

She mustn't drink tonight. Stress exacerbates the symptoms, and today she's had her share – first the confrontation with the loggers and Sally's bizarre behavior; and then, just as dusk was falling, Nick showing up at her door to announce his idiot idea.

You're doing what?

A protection spell at Roan's Oak. It'd be awesome if you came. I brought you a robe . . .

Behind him she could see people in their Midsummer costumes traipsing past her cabin, a procession of ridiculous leafy shapes heading down through the hayfield to disappear into the dusk. A shiver seized and shook her hard, like a hapless vole in Minnie's jaws.

You can't just summon the Green Man.

Hurt look on the young face. *But the Green Man's on our side!*

The notion stuns her with its sheer stupidity. By now the ritual must have begun. The fingers of her right hand refuse to hold a match, so she pinches the box between her knees and uses her left to light the fire. Going to the window, she notes that the wind is calm, the rain still holding off –

With a silent roar the pain in her head explodes, stopping her breath. She grips the edge of the table with her good hand, riding it out.

I get headaches. Bad ones.

Any other symptoms?

Blurred vision. Numbness in my right hand. Sometimes I black out.

How often would you say this happens?

Maybe a dozen times so far. Three blackouts in the last two months.

All right. Let's do some tests and see what's going on.

As the pain subsides to a smolder, she stares out the window into the darkness. She can't see the woods, but she can feel them. Massed in the hollows and on the ridges, roots entwined deep in the earth, branches joined in the air above, a multitude forming a single entity. Green Man. She's seen him countless times, watched him appear and vanish with a breath of wind or a change of light, born of suggestive junctions of branches, shaped by clusters of leaf and shadow – the mind's futile attempt to translate its sense of watchful, hovering presence into something it can grasp.

Curled on the sofa by the fire, Minnie watches her with glinting eyes.

What I have for you, Ms Wyatt, is some fundamentally good news. The scan showed you have a lesion on the surface of your brain called a meningioma.

A lesion – you mean a brain tumor? How is that good news?

Meningiomas are almost always benign. You may have had this one for years and never known it. But recently it's started to grow, and now it's pressing on your brain and causing the symptoms you described. As I said, it's right on the surface, so we can treat it with radiation, which will stop the growth and shrink the tumor. And that should be that. So you see? Good news.

Good news.

The treatments didn't hurt and lasted six weeks. But once they were over and the medical team had pronounced her cured, Liz discovered she couldn't draw anymore.

The technical skills remained. She could still render a three-dimensional object in two dimensions. But all her work was flat and sterile, devoid of the indefinable quality that had captivated the readers of the Hundred Year Stone books – her gift for revealing a world aflame with beauty and a perilous magic.

She waited for the return of those moments when the act of drawing or painting possessed her and she simply surrendered to what came. But as weeks went by, then months, she began to wonder if the tumor might have played some role in her gift. Hadn't the doctors said it might have been there undetected for years? What if that knot of rogue tissue on the surface of her brain had stimulated some obscure area that opened a door to – what? Hallucinations, or a wider spectrum of reality than humans normally experience? But those were questions she knew better than to ask the medical profession. Nor could she complain that the successful treatment had robbed her work of its soul, and so she was forced to live with the result.

Until now. The drawings she's made since her return to Durwood, since her visit to the oak – as if the spirit of the forest is tentatively reaching out, seeking ways to extend its boundaries. Listening to the stillness outside, she thinks: As long as there's no wind . . .

There's a knot inside her, a clenching of her core that a drink from the jar in the cabinet would loosen. She longs for the fiery bite of moonshine in her throat, the creeping calm along her nerves. But she mustn't give in.

Not tonight.

There's a silvery shimmer of bells, and a robed shadow emerges from the trees. A shiver runs up Nick's spine. Even though he wrote the words to the ritual and choreographed its actions, he's no longer in control of it; the ceremony of language and gesture has created its own reality, and that reality has him firmly in its grip. At this moment he's not seeing Sally Durwood, local midwife and herbalist, holding a stick hung with dime-store jinglebells. He's seeing the Queen of the Greenwood, high priestess of the rite, using the the belled staff of the Druids to invoke the spirit of the forest. The ritual is working; they've tapped into something real. However fragmented and neglected, the old magic still exists.

She stands facing the oak: *Duir*, the doorway. Now just a black hulk, a denser part of the darkness. She shakes the staff; the bells chime again.

"Spirit of the Greenwood, guide to all who seek the hidden paths, tonight your people gather once more beneath the Oak. For too long we have parted ways, but our roots are still entwined. Now, in the name of the ancient Wise Ones of the Sacred Grove, we call upon you in our time of need. Let the Trees be named!"

Enthralled as Nick is, at the back of his thoughts is the anticipation of what will happen later, when the public part of the ritual is over and people have taken their kids home. Once everyone else has gone, the priest and priestess will enact the Great Rite beneath the oak – a sexual union that will ignite the powder keg of earth energy dormant in the Noon Woods and blow open the door between the worlds.

Just thinking about it is giving him a boner. A rustle of unfolding paper recalls him to the here and now. From the shadow of the trees a voice mumbles, "*Beithe*, the birch. The, uh, seed. The beginning."

The next voice, more confident, rings on the night air. "*Luis*, the rowan. The beacon."

Now they're speeding up, the words spoken without hesitation. The pronunciations of tree names are no more than best guesses, but they're uttered with assurance. No more mumbling, no more rustling paper.

"*Fearn*, the alder. The shield. The defender."

"*Saille*, the willow. The coracle on dark water."

"*Nion*, the ash. The strong spear."

"*Huath*, the hawthorn. The prowler in the night."

"*Duir*, the oak. The shining king. The doorway."

"*Tinne*, the holly. The sacrifice."

"*Coll*, the hazel. The fair one. The grieving one."

"*Quert*, the apple. The bridge."

"*Straif*, the blackthorn. The rising smoke. The arrow's mist."

"*Gort*, the ivy. The bond."

"*Ruis*, the elder. The keeper of wisdom."

Keeper of wisdom is Nick's cue, and he feels his lips move without recognizing his own voice.

"The forms pass, but the circle remains. Tonight we renew our pact with the Greenwood, our pledge that the trees shall always stand tall. Thus decrees the ancient law: *Three non-breathing things paid for only with breathing things: an apple tree, a hazel bush, a sacred grove.*"

Wait, what? That's not what he meant to say. Much as he'd liked that piece of the ritual, Morgan had persuaded him to change it to something about preserving the sacred places of the earth. In the stress of the moment, the original version has surfaced instead.

Nothing he can do about it now; just keep going.

"Here in this sacred grove, bounded by the elements of earth, air, fire and water, we call upon the Spirit of the Greenwood to protect and shield its ancient domain. The trees are named. Let the forest awake!"

"Awake!" Repeated in a whisper from a multitude of throats. "Awake!"

The robed figures begin to move around the edge of the clearing, their shadows weaving a pattern with the shadow of tree limbs in the moonlight. "Awake!" Each time they say it, they stamp their feet. "Awake!"

The muffled thuds reverberate in Nick's chest as he turns to face the tree. Now comes the crux of the ritual, inspired by Liz's drawing of the empty hole in the oak. It's time to remove the stone and open the door to the otherworld.

The stone glints in the moonlight, and for the first time he notices the multitude of chips and scratches on its surface. Somebody had wanted to make damn sure it stayed in the tree. *Can't you just see them – self-righteous, narrow-minded, terrified of anything beyond their comfort zone?* Whoever they'd been, whatever their reason for closing the door, they'd managed to stop Roan and block the source of his power, sending Durwood into a slow decline from a nexus of otherworld energy to a poor backwoods hamlet.

Now it's time to redress the balance. Time for Durwood to make a comeback. "Awake!"

Nick grasps the edges of the stone and tugs. It doesn't budge, but he hadn't expected it to. Somebody was assigned to bring a prybar – and there it is, leaning against the trunk. Retrieving it, he wedges the tip between stone and bark and applies pressure. Not too much; it won't do for the stone to come flying out of the tree and land on his foot. On the other hand, nothing at all is happening. He puts a little more weight on his end of the prybar, then a little more. Damn, the thing is wedged tight. He pulls the bar out, reinserts it at a different point and tries again.

Liz sleeps. There was to have been only one drink, just a swallow to dull the pain and muffle the dread. But one wasn't enough, and so she took a second and then a third, and then she lost count. Now she sleeps snoring on the sofa by the fire, deaf to the rising wind.

The trees at the edge of the forest begin to stir in black, hissing swells. The wind meets no resistance as it flows up the slope of the hayfield to surround the cabin, making the witch balls tinkle and chime, reaching beneath the door to set the hearth broom swaying on its hook. The lamp has gone out; shadows of flying leaves slide over the moonlit walls in a dark dance, and still Liz sleeps while the cat hunches on the hearthstone, only her eyes moving.

Liz sleeps as the wind swoops down the chimney and revives the dying embers of the fire. Among the charred logs a single flame leaps up in a burst of golden light. Stray air currents ruffle the sketches on the table by the window, lifting and scattering them across the floor. In the light of the rekindled fire, imbued by the restless flames with movement and life, they seem more than pencil marks on paper. Minnie's ears flatten and she hisses softly.

Liz sleeps.

◆ ◆ ◆

Gordie's still a couple of miles from the logging camp when his engine dies. Manhandling the car onto the shoulder, he lets it coast to a stop. Dang. It's obviously not the battery, because the headlights are still working . . . Squinting at the instrument panel, he grunts in disbelief.

The gas gauge shows empty. Didn't he fill the tank just yesterday?

"Shitfire fuzzy," he mutters – Momma's sole indulgence in the sin of cussing. What's he supposed to do now? But he's not that far from the logging camp, and the rain has stopped, and maybe it wasn't yesterday but the day before when he got gas. He can't recollect at the moment, because he's drunk – just how drunk, he doesn't realize until he climbs out of the car and the chill of the country night hits him.

He sways on his feet, clinging to the door for support. Golly, a minute ago he had nothing more than a little buzz on, and now he can barely stand. Seems like that ole moonshine sneaks up on you.

"Yuhwuh right, Momma."

His numb lips have trouble shaping the words. She always said liquor was the Devil's prize invention. Gordie'd never had a drink in his life until she passed, and then only some spiked fruit punch at the Christmas party at the shoe store. But tonight, when Hub Reese accosted him in the street outside May's and offered him a drink of moonshine, he'd been curious to hear what one of his old tormentors had to say.

An acid hiccup escapes him. If this whole logging business wasn't turning out to be such a b-i-t-c-h, he'd of never fallen into temptation – but now he's drunk and out of gas on a dark country road, and he has to pee. As he fumbles with his fly, a glow of headlights appears in the distance. Shitfire fuzzy. He glances with loathing at the dark woods bordering the road – an unlikely refuge, but whoever's in that approaching car is unlikely to offer him anything but grief; right now he's undoubtedly the most hated man in the county. And nature's calling.

Stumbling into the trees, he unzips with a sigh of relief. They'd sat in Hub's rusty old truck that stank of dogs and motor oil for a good ten minutes, passing the moonshine jar back and forth in silence, before Hub had finally come out with what was on his mind. Turns out young Hubbard's not making enough driving for the propane company to support Miss Shelby's tastes. She's got her heart set on one of those itty-bitty satellite dishes, a clothes dryer so she won't have to hang laundry on the line, and a fancy woodstove with a glass front that lets you watch the flames. And what with the new baby and all . . .

What it comes down to is Hub offering to report any mischief the other boys are planning in exchange for a little help with his household expenses. And consenting to these terms, Gordie has to smother a big grin at the sweetness of having one of Jared Gorton's gang, even if it's just little ole Hub, come crawling.

Without warning a wave of nausea doubles him over. The moonshine burns worse on the way up than it did on the way down, scalding his nose and eyes and reducing the universe to a series of gagging spasms. When the vomiting stops he can do nothing but wait in misery for the next onslaught, gripping his knees and trying not to get puke on his shoes. When the tumult in his belly subsides at last, he zips up with unsteady hands and turns back to the road.

Or where the road ought to be. But it's not there, and the act of turning his head to locate it makes the woods start spinning like a merry-go-round. He closes his eyes and takes a dozen deep breaths. Once he feels steady enough, he opens his eyes again and turns his head very, very slowly . . .

Trees surround him on every side.

His heart begins to thump; against his will he thinks of that stupid song Granny Dee used to sing him when he was little. He can remember her visits clearly, mostly because of how much they upset Momma. Granny'd hold him on her lap and rock by the fire, crooning the old song with its endless verses. Even after all these years, the refrain sticks in his head.

O they went to the wood, where the oaken tree stood
To cut down the tree, the oaken tree.
But the oak gave a groan for to summon his own,
And the trees closed about, and they never got out
Of the wood, the wonderful wood –

A shudder grips him and he shakes it off. It's just a stupid song; trees don't move. While he was puking, he must have stumbled deeper into the woods, and now he's lost his bearings. All he has to do is –

What's that noise?

◆ ◆ ◆

The stone won't budge.

Abandoning caution, Nick throws his full weight against the bar with a determined grunt. For one giddy instant he feels movement – Success! – before he realizes it's only his bare feet slipping on the roots. The stone hasn't moved at all.

Despite the cool night air, despite the fact that he's mother-naked under his robe, his whole body is suddenly slippery with sweat. Getting the rock out of the tree is the centerpiece of the ritual, the symbolic opening of Roan's door to Annwn, the reconnection of Durwood with the Otherworld.

Tonight we open once more the door between the worlds. Tonight we ask the dwellers of Annwn to join with us in fellowship once again.

Just writing those words had given him a rush, and he's been anticipating the moment when he gets to say them – but before he can say them, he has to get the damn stone out of the damn tree. If the ritual fails to achieve its goal, it will collapse like a giant tent, leaving the participants floundering, confused, and very probably pissed off.

If the ritual fails, the magic will fail.

He digs deeper into the tree and pries for all he's worth. Nothing happens except that his sweaty palms slip on the bar and he nearly loses his balance. He casts a furtive glance around. The moon has gone back behind the clouds, as if the Goddess has withdrawn in disgust. The people of Durwood are still doing their part, circling the oak and chanting, but their unison is starting to unravel. His part is taking too long, allowing precious momentum to dissipate. Sweat pours down his face; he grunts and heaves at the bar. This has to work. It has to. It –

Warm hands cover his, stilling his struggles. Meeting the calm, smiling gaze of his high priestess, he feels like a drowning man who's just been tossed a rope. Her lips move, shaping syllables he knows.

Roan, Roan –
Open the door

The circling stops. A couple of the participants move closer to the tree; others follow, and a tighter circle forms. As they close around him, Nick hears them whispering.

Roan, Roan –
Open the door

Just a few voices at first, and then more join in, until the whole gathering is whispering as one.

Roan, Roan, open the door –
My tears are salt and my heart is sore –

The hushed words fill the clearing and rise like mist through the oak's branches.

Roan, return and reach out your hand
And open the door to the Bright Land

Nick's dimly aware that his body has dissolved. Head, hands, arms, torso, legs, feet – they're all gone, releasing his spirit to float upward on swirling vibrations of sound. This is and always has been his whole existence, this buoyant limbo in which the sound carries him like a speck on the surface of a vast void – and then he finds himself being pulled back, imprisoned once more within the limits of his body. Something strange is happening. He has hands; his hands are still gripping the prybar –

The prybar is shaking in his grip.

He lets go, but it keeps on shaking, vibrating until it works its way loose from the tree and falls with a clunk among the roots. The stone itself – is it moving? How is that possible? Nick peers closer. The stone is slowly working its way out of its niche, as if –

As if something's pushing it from behind.

By now he can see it's no longer fully embedded in the tree. His brain stutters in protest. The stone, the same one he was unable to budge with a hundred and eighty pounds against a steel prybar, is working its way out of the tree on its own.

Open the door. This is the ritual's purpose: to reconnect Durwood with the Otherworld. Nick places trembling fingers on either side of the stone. As he tugs gently, with an unexpected and unpleasant sucking sensation it comes finally, wholly free. A breath of damp, fetid air wafts from the opening.

The stone's unbelievably heavy; he doesn't so much catch it as control its fall. Concentrating on keeping it from crushing his feet, he's only peripherally aware of the commotion around him – and then, with the stone safely cradled in the roots, he hears the mutters and whispers and follows the gaze of upturned faces.

The clouds have disappeared. Encircled by leaves, the white moon floats in the night sky above the oak's wrecked crown and outflung branches. Looming above them in the otherworldly light, the tree seems to radiate an air of wary scrutiny.

Awake.

Gazing slack-jawed along with the others, Nick's peripherally aware of a faint vibration in the air, a subliminal buzz that registers not so much in his ears as along his nerves. He can't trace the source at first, and then he realizes it's coming from the cavity vacated by the stone.

◆◆◆

Gordie freezes. He could swear he heard something, there and then gone so quickly he can't even hazard a guess about what it was, but his heart is slamming against his ribs like some trapped varmint desperate to break free. And then it comes again – a kind of hum beneath the surface of the air, so deep it makes his teeth hurt.

What *is* that?

There's stealthy movement at the edge of his vision. Before he can react something smacks him in the face – not a hard blow, but it stings, and he gasps and stumbles backward. A root snags his foot. As he falls there's another blow across his chest and he lands bang on his tailbone, letting out a yelp as fire shoots up his spine. Hearing a rustle behind him; he twists around and gets a brief glimpse of a raggedy shape among the dark windblown trees. *Swish.* This time the branch knocks him forward and the blow triggers a flash of understanding. That's who was in the approaching car – that dang Jared Gorton and his crew! Looks like he's been a prize sucker, letting sweet-faced Hub distract him drunk so the others could siphon the gas out of his car, ambush him here in the woods, and beat on him to their hearts' content . . .

They smote Him on the head and stripped Him and scourged Him –

For us, Gordie. For you and me.

His moonshine-befuddled brain produces a memory of Momma's gasping voice.

Oh! Oh Precious Lord!

Stripped. Scourged.

As the blows descend, he curls into a ball and lets himself be washed clean.

"This is gonna be sweet." Unscrewing the cap from the Mason jar, Jared takes a swallow and offers it to Hub, hunched over the steering wheel.

"Hell, no, I've had enough. I shun't be drivin as it is."

"We're bound to come up on him any minute," Jared says. He knocks on the back window, eliciting whoops and laughter from the truck bed where the rest of the boys are sprawled. While Hub was distracting Gordie they were all drinking too, sharing a jar while they drained most of the gas from Gordie's tank. Once he's stranded on the dark road home they can do what needs to be done in complete privacy.

What needs to be done. Seeing the nervous grin on Hub's face, Jared knows he's worried Shelby'll have his hide if she finds out about this venture, and Jared's the first to admit his little sister can be a terror. But after today, nobody can say Gordie Fuckin Durwood ain't asked for this.

"Whoa," he says. Hub hits the brakes and the truck skids on the wet road, bringing another round of hooting and banging from the boys in the back.

"Gimme the flashlight."

Hub hands it over. Jared leans out the window and aims it down the road, where the powerful beam picks out a car on the shoulder.

"That's him yonder. Hush now. Let's come up on him quiet."

They climb out of the truck. From the bed come muffled guffaws and scuffling noises; Jared motions impatiently for the others to shut up as they start along the road. The moon appears, endowing them with spindly shadows. As they approach, they can see Gordie's car is empty. Jared opens the door and yanks the keys out of the ignition.

"Now where's that little douche got to?"

"Gotta be round here somewheres," Darrell says. "We wasn't five minutes behind him."

Conlee aims a kick at the car's battered bumper. "Well, let's getter done. Find ole GFD and kick his ass. He can't of got far, drunk as he was. Near as drunk as me."

Giggling, he staggers into the woods, and the others follow.

According to the ritual, there are some words Nick is supposed to say once the stone has been removed from the tree, but the memory of them has deserted him. Eyes moondazzled and mouth agape, he stares up at the huge horned shape that rears itself against the night sky.

All around the clearing, branches creak as the swell of leaves passes like urgent whispering from tree to tree. The wind is rising again, traveling swiftly up and down the slopes and hollows until the whole forest sways with movement. Within the black crevice vacated by the stone, the low humming becomes a breathy, fluctuating whine. Embedded in the wind but somehow distinct, it rises and falls, returns and recedes – sometimes no more than a weak warble, sometimes a whistling whisper that suggests an errant melody, luring its listeners from the familiar to a parallel realm of moonlight and shadow where thought drifts away and identity dissolves to nothingness.

The wind blows harder, forcing its way through the tree in a hollow wail that rushes over the gathering. In response they throw back their heads and erupt into howls; above the ragged chorus comes a rumble of thunder as racing clouds blot out the moon. In the sudden darkness the wind rouses the trees to frenzy, loosing a storm of leaves and setting the wish tokens gyrating on the oak's branches. The next thunderclap is directly overhead, accompanied by a blinding flash of lightning and a deluge of rain. Beneath drenching sheets of water, the folk of Durwood begin to dance, cavorting among the trees. Nick's wet robe is an encumbrance; he tears it off and lets the water pummel his naked flesh. All barriers have melted away; he's part of the greenwood, one with the rain and wind. Around the edge of the clearing the trees dance, swaying and bending, windblown shadows convulsing at their feet, while at the center of the chaos the oak stands guard. Beneath it, some of the celebrants are already coupling, pale shapes writhing in the inky darkness.

Lust shudders through him. His whole being is focused on her, the one who awaits him among the coiled roots. *Sacred tree, sacred axis, pathway between the worlds . . .*

As he moves toward her, a flash of lightning whitens the forest and his shadow shoots out in front of him to brand itself on his brain – the shape of a man with the horned head of a stag *(running, running in a world of shadowed green, pursuing a white doe whose slim flanks are dappled with sun – one with the light and shadow, one with the obstacles he leaps and dodges, one with the doe herself, hurtling headlong in the chase, two sets of hoofbeats a single rhythm like a heartbeat that drives him forward until he leaps across the gap and lands hard on her back, gripping her ribs with his forelegs so that she stumbles and together they fall, tumbling over and over, falling down and down through darkness and echoing silence to an unknown place of sunlight and trickling water where at last she twists around to face him, a human woman naked in his human arms, white skin green eyes red mouth red hair tangled with green leaves, and as their bodies join she caresses his antlers and suddenly he's falling again)*

A crack of blue-white brilliance slams Nick back into the night and the storm and the singing oak. As his body arches in explosive release the lightning flash seems to jolt through him, illuminating the tangled autumn hair and green gaze holding his – until, just at the instant that darkness returns, the beautiful face sags and collapses into the fungus-smeared fissures of a rotting log. He jerks back in horror, pulled up short by supple tendrils that encircle his wrists and arms, swarming over his shoulders and back and abrading his naked flesh as he struggles against the ropy stems, the feathery caress of leaves.

Nick screams.

✳ 12 ✳

Staggering through the woods, the boys are starting to get pissed off.

"Where is that jackass? Where in hell'd he get to?"

"Gone and got himself lost is what."

"I can't stay out here all night," Hub says. "I gotta work tomorrow."

Darrell gives him a friendly shove. "Live a little, bro. We're gonna have us some fun."

Hub walks faster and almost collides with Jared, who's stopped dead ahead, sweeping the flashlight back and forth among the trees.

"You find him?"

"No. There was – " Jared's voice trails off.

"You see somethin?" Spence says.

"Somethin white. Movin quick."

The others peer among the trees. "Don't see nothin."

"It was there just now. Right up ahead." The flashlight beam bobs as Jared moves forward. "Y'all stay here. I'm gonna check it out."

They watch the light waver among the trees, picking out knotted trunks and the gleam of wet leaves, until unexpectedly it disappears.

"What the hell?" Conlee says.

"He's just foolin around," Harley says. "Probably gonna circle back, try and scare us."

They wait. Around them the trees begin to move, branches lifting and swaying, leaves rustling and sighing. And even though they know it's only the wind, the sense of rowdy fun has vanished and they huddle together, hair whipping across their bewildered faces.

"Jared!" Harley shouts. "Jared! What the hell?"

There's no answer beyond the creak and murmur of branches all around them. And beneath the wind, a distant droning.

A grassy plain spreads before him, hazy mountains visible in the distance.

Tyne stops to check his weapons. He's been here before; the plain's peaceful appearance is a deception. Black openings can appear in the air without warning, and what emerges from them is never friendly.

Right on cue, a dark speck appears in front of him and balloons into a gaping hole. There's no time for thought, only reaction. Enormous wings thrash at his face and he swings his sword – cutting, thrusting, flinching from the accompanying cacophony of earsplitting shrieks until at last the creature flops lifeless to the ground and he's able to get a good look at it.

Head and wings of an eagle, body of a lion. A griffon. Mythical beasts are the usual visitors from these alternate universes; in the past he's encountered basilisks, dragons, once even a Minotaur. Now, seeing a glint of color at the fallen monster's neck just where its feathers merge with its fur, he reaches for the jeweled collar that undoubtedly holds secret powers.

The sky flickers and goes black.

"Dammit," Tyne mutters. The lights in his study are already back on, but the power dip has rebooted his computer. He waits while it runs through its startup routine. In his absorption in the game he's tuned out everything else; now he notices it's raining and blowing like hell outside.

He thinks of the ritual taking place at Roan's Oak. Just about everybody in Durwood has decided to join in, Sally'd told him as she headed out earlier; the arrival of the logging crew this morning really got people on board. Earlier this evening the storm seemed to be tapering off, turning to mostly wind, but now the water's coming down in buckets again. The people taking part in the ritual are going to get wet. And if that's the worst that happens, they'll be lucky. Listening to the drumming on the henhouse roof, Tyne thinks about the hole in the oak – like the holes in the game, a door to another world.

His tattoo is itching, less a burn than a maddening tickle he can't keep from scratching. Examining the inked pattern, he sees nothing that could explain the itch: no rash, no insect bite, only the luxuriant green of the curling oak leaves with their russet acorns. He takes a drink of moonshine and logs into the game.

Welcome, Warrior, to the Temple of Renewal.

That's when he hears it – a thin strand of sound carried on the wind, woven into the swift stream of the air, wavering and fluttering, pulsing and beckoning, rhythmic in its very randomness – an insidious invitation that seeps into his head and stills his fingers on the keyboard as he listens to the distant voice of Roan's Oak.

◆ ◆ ◆

Sweeping the flashlight back and forth, Jared moves cautiously through the trees. There – a pale streak skimming the edge of the beam, gone too quick to identify. He stops, poised on the balls of his feet. Makes another slow sweep with the flashlight.

Nothing now. He forces himself to breathe evenly, resisting his sense that this has all happened before. He's not in the Noon Woods now; these trees are part of the younger forest surrounding the old one, maples and poplars and locusts that have sprung up on abandoned farmland. But Tyne's accident left him with a lasting aversion to woods and darkness, and he curses Gordie Fuckin Durwood for being the reason he's here now.

Behind him a twig cracks. Jared whips around, aiming the flashlight like a gun, and feels his jaw drop.

Standing in the beam is a pure white doe. Her shimmering coat reflects the light back into his eyes; he puts up a hand to shade them, and in that instant he remembers what happened the night Tyne fell.

I saw a white doe. And I followed her.

There she stands. For a heartbeat she remains motionless, as if speared by the flashlight's beam, before bounding into the darkness.

He plunges after her. Behind him, voices call, "Jared! Jared!" but the syllables mean nothing, and when they die out it's like a weight dropping away. Funny how obsessed he's been with leaving Durwood, when freedom has been this close all along.

Now the white doe is all that exists. Past and future fall away, leaving only the present in which he runs headlong through the shadowy woods, lost in the chase. He's dropped the flashlight somewhere but it doesn't matter; the trees open a path for him, lifting their branches to let him through.

Ahead, the white shape shines like a beacon in the dark, a flash of long legs and slender haunches, eyes like dark pools in her delicate face when she looks back to see if he's still following. Those backward glances seem to drag his heart right out of his chest. He runs in a dream, oblivious to the sudden rumble of thunder overhead, flashes of lightning flickering through the forest canopy, sodden leaves shedding their freight of water on his head. He's deaf to the plaintive wailing carried on the rising wind, unconscious of the rough terrain underfoot, until a root catches his foot and sends him stumbling forward, flailing for balance and

falling

falling

falling

◆ ◆ ◆

All through the night, storms sweep over Durwood. Beneath the surging wind the air thickens with the whisper of rain soaking parched fields and woods, the trickle and gurgle of running water as dry creeks return to life. Rain beats on the roofs and window panes of the houses beneath the dripping oaks, saturating the sleepers' dreams until they sink under their own weight. Rain rinses the dusty streets and vehicles, collects in puddles and seeps into cracked sidewalks, awakens withered roots and parched seeds. Across the patchy yards and barren gardens a mist of green springs up, eager shoots emerging from wet earth to lengthen and swarm over fences, walls, gateposts, birdbaths. Glistening foliage creeps over porch steps, along walkways, up rainspouts. On the arm of the wooden bench outside the Hardware & General, a single sunflower seed lodge in a knothole sprouts and unfurls two tiny, perfect leaves. In the town and all across the surrounding woods and farms, every tree from the smallest sapling to the mightiest patriarch lifts its leaves to welcome the wind-driven rain. And on the ancient oak deep in the Noon Woods, rosy bumps erupt on twigs that have long seemed dead.

It's close to dawn when Tyne Durwood hears the farmhouse door slam. All night he's been parked at the computer, snuffing monsters and piling up bling, trying to keep his mind off whatever's happening in the Noon Woods.

The sound reaches him during a lull in the wind. He rolls to the door of his study and opens it on the rain-soaked view of the kitchen garden and the house beyond. Now the only sound is the steady drumming of raindrops on the shed roof, but he knows what he heard. He wheels out of his study and down the walkway toward the house, soaked to the skin by the time he reaches the shelter of the porch. He's expecting to find Pa and Sally in the kitchen, but the windows are dark. Maybe they went straight up to bed.

Lingering on the porch out of the unrelenting downpour, he hears a whisper in his ear. It's a trick CW showed Sally and him as kids – how a word spoken at the right spot near the front of the house can travel along the ceiling of the wraparound porch and sound right in your ear all the way at the back, as if the speaker's standing right beside you.

In spite of the rain's racket, he hears it now.

Please, Alma.

Honey, please.

The hair rises on the back of Tyne's neck. Alma was his mother's name.

His thoughts have stalled, but his hands are on the push-rims of his chair, wheeling him along the porch. Rounding the front corner, he brings the chair to a silent halt. There's a shadow in the tall parlor window, no more than a hazy outline behind the dim glass, suggestive of two people standing in a close embrace.

He hears his father whisper, "Please, honey. Please forgive me. You know it was always only you."

If there's a response, it's lost in the hiss of rain on leaves. The shadows in the window shift as if nestling closer. Tyne's skin prickles as he imagines a slim woman with curly hair whose smile, if he could see it now, would be the same as the one in the photograph that hangs on the parlor wall. His pa begins to hum a waltz. Together they sway to the quavering rhythm, sealed in their own world, and in that interval Tyne seems to glimpse a host of lost possibilities, might-have-beens for his father, his sister, himself. His throat tightens and he turns away, ashamed of intruding on this impossible moment.

Above the drenched trees, the sky is beginning to brighten. As the darkness retreats, objects take on substance; edges harden; shadows seep away. And between one breath and the next, the dawn reveals his father standing at the window, cradling the lacy parlor curtain in his arms.

The transformation stops Tyne's breath. He watches CW clutch the flimsy fabric, frantically searching its folds.

"Alma! Sweetheart, please! Don't leave me again! Honey, don't – "

Tyne's eyes are stinging. He bows his head.

"Please believe me, honey, please understand." The old man is choking on his words. "It was always only you. You know that, don't you, Alma? Always. "

Tyne can't listen anymore. Wrenching his chair around, he concentrates on putting distance between himself and the shattered voice that relentlessly pursues him, murmuring in his ear as he flees, falling silent only when he escapes from the porch into the rain. He's so intent on reaching the sanctuary of his study that he almost collides with Sally, standing on the walkway gazing out over the kitchen garden.

She doesn't even turn to look at him. "Corn's comin right back from the drought," she says. "Runner beans, too. They sure do love this rain."

Tyne speaks through the tightness in his throat. "What's the matter with Pa?"

But she doesn't seem to hear, nor to feel the raindrops that soak her hair and trickle down her face. Inside the house, the phone rings and he waits for her to run and answer it; he knows she's been worried about Lissy Lewis, whose baby is due any day. But she just keeps on staring dreamily at the rows of wet plants.

"Phone's ringin," Tyne says.

"Mmm."

"Might be Lissy," he reminds her. "Might be her time."

Her head turns toward the house so slowly that he wonders if she heard what he said.

"Sally!"

"Hm?"

"What the hell's the matter with you?"

Even the profanity doesn't earn her usual frown. The phone's stopped ringing. With an impatient jerk, Tyne rolls closer and grabs her wrist.

"I asked you what's wrong with Pa. What happened last night?"

"Last night?"

He tightens his grip. "At the ritual."

Glimmering drops fringe her lashes and trace their way down her cheeks. Her gaze skates over him, back to the garden. "Nothin much. We stood in a circle. People called out the names of the trees."

Tyne waits, but that's it. "And then what?"

"And then Nick pried the rock out of Roan's Oak."

"And then?"

"It started rainin, and we all got wet." Gently she frees her wrist. "Quit frettin, Tyne. Things are gonna be okay now."

"What's that supposed to mean?"

She doesn't answer. It's like she's listening for something, waiting for something that renders his presence a distraction.

"Hey!" he says, and she puts a hand on the back of his neck as if to calm him. After a moment the warm, slender fingers begin to knead his muscles, coaxing away the tension – and in spite of himself he can feel his thoughts beginning to slow their frantic circling, lulled by the luxury of a woman's touch.

Back before the accident, when he'd been dating Rosie Lewis, things had reached the stage where she'd let him put his hand inside her shirt while they kissed. But when she came to see him in the hospital he'd been cold to her, afraid she'd come out of pity, and a few years later she'd married Ezra Vernon. Since then, Sally's the only woman who ever touches him. He's never made love to a woman and now he never will, but it doesn't stop him from thinking about it. And if his sister's face sometimes flickers in his head at those times, he scrupulously keeps such moments separate from the rest of his existence.

Now, just as her caressing fingers threaten to breach that crucial barrier, pleasure turns to pain. "Ow! Dammit, Sally, what the hell?"

Her nails have sunk themselves into his flesh, deep enough to draw blood.

Jared wakes on a cushion of soft moss, coins of sunlight trembling on his skin. Above him stands a beautiful woman all in white, her long hair woven with green leaves, her eyes like forest pools.

Both the place and the woman are familiar, yet he can't think how. The effort of trying to solve this puzzle sends a jab of pain through his skull. She's bending over him and he half rises to meet her, but instead of the kiss he's expecting, she puts her hand on his chest and presses until he sinks back down. She keeps pressing, eyes holding his, until, with a little shock, he feels her fingers penetrate his flesh and pass effortlessly through muscle and bone to close around his heart. It doesn't hurt. But he can feel her fingers burrowing deep inside him, taking root in his entrails, spreading through every part of him. It's painful and blissful at once; he closes his eyes and surrenders.

When he opens them, she's gone. In her place, a graceful white birch springs from the center of his body, pinning him to the earth. Gazing upward, he sees a multitude of faces hovering among the green branches – faces young and old, familiar and unknown, changing and multiplying with every flicker of the sunlit leaves that spread above him for as far as he can see.

The huddled lump on the futon is Nick Rusk, shivering from head to foot, the quilt pulled over his head to shut out the noise of the wind. Or what he keeps telling himself is the wind. He can't tell if the soft rushing he hears is real or only inside his head. He's colder than he's ever been in his life, convulsed by shivering. The welts on his arms, back, and buttocks burn with a constant, freezing fire. And equally burning, equally constant is the question that hammers at his brain.

What happened at the ritual?

He clenches his fists. The left one stings; uncurling his fingers, he squints at the oozing gash across the palm. He can't remember how it got there. A fragment floats across the back of his mind and he snatches at it. Green eyes, red lips, white flesh.

Slender arms closing around him, holding him tight . . .

Tight as strangling vines.

This is the realm of Faerie, slipping out of time. Hard to enter, and even harder to get out of again.

Recalling the yielding embrace of warm flesh, the tickle of leaves against his skin, the spongy give of fungus-specked rotten wood beneath him, he feels his body shudder with mingled revulsion and lust. He groans. Even with his head buried beneath the pillow, he can still hear the wind.

❖ 13 ❖

Hurrying through the downpour toward the windblown yellow awning above Sundial's entrance, Morgan thinks the Goddess must have made up Her mind to remedy the drought in a single massive dose. The resurgence of growth that's happened almost overnight has succeeded in wiping out all traces of this year's stunted spring and summer. In fact, the two seasons seem to be staging a simultaneous comeback; leaving her house this morning, she was astonished to see the dogwood tree in her front yard covered in white blossoms.

The power's been restored, but Durwood is like a ghost town, wet streets deserted beneath the dripping trees, storefronts closed up and down Main Street. Glancing into the dark interior of May's Café, Morgan is made oddly uneasy by the empty tables, the counter bereft of its customary line of broad backs, the absence of a bustling May handing out coffee and exchanging quips.

May's is never closed. Never. But the tension over the logging has thrown everything out of whack; if May and Pete participated in last night's ritual, they're probably sleeping in. And they're not the only ones – Nick still hasn't emerged from his room although it's past noon. Not that she needed his help in the store this morning; Abundance hasn't had a single customer so far today. When Molly called with an invitation to lunch, there seemed no reason not to accept.

"Just to say thanks, Morgan. You know, for being there last night in my moment of crisis. I know how much you hated missing the ritual."

"Oh . . . " Morgan lets the word trail off before asking guardedly, "How are things with Ben?"

"Well, he came back really late last night and groveled, and I forgave him. I mean, I haven't exactly been in the mood lately . . . and Annie's just so desperate, isn't she? Ben does love to feel needed. He says it was just the one kiss and he doesn't know what came over him; he doesn't even find her attractive. She didn't come to work today, but I told him – if and when she does, he's got to fire her."

The injustice of Annie losing her job just because Ben loves to feel needed makes Morgan wince, but it's none of her business and she keeps her mouth shut. It'll be fun to meet Molly at Russ and Star's restaurant and enjoy a tasty lunch to celebrate the success of the ritual. Yes, success – because regardless of what brought the storms, even if it's only coincidence (and she *knows* it's not) there's no disputing the fact that, for the time being at least, the woods are safe. The battle may not be over, but Morgan's certain the community of Durwood, old and new citizens working together, will triumph in the end. Catching sight of Molly beneath the restaurant awning, she quickens her pace.

"Sorry I'm late, Mol. Where's the baby?"

"I didn't want to bring her out in this crazy wind. She's with Ben at the store. It's not like we're getting any customers in this weather."

"Me neither. You're the first person I've seen today."

"Well, I saw somebody." Molly looks mysterious. "You'll never guess who."

"Tell me."

"Gordie Durwood. On the bench outside the Hardware & General, just sitting there in the rain – and Morgan, he looks like somebody beat the shit out of him. His clothes are filthy, he's got bruises all over his face . . . I'm guessing certain people decided to teach him a lesson."

"You mean Jared and the others?"

"Who else?"

"Huh." Morgan's a little ashamed of her satisfaction at this piece of news; but really, doesn't it serve Gordie right? She takes Molly's arm. "Let's go in. Thank Goddess they're open; I'm starving."

Entering the restaurant, they stop dead on the threshold.

"What the – ?" Molly mutters.

Morgan just stares.

Sundial's interior has been completely altered. In place of the quirky folk art that provided much of its charm, masses of brambles now cover the walls. There are damp footprints and clumps of woody debris strewn across the floor; vines swaddle the legs of the chairs and an enormous tangle of twigs bristles in the vase beside the cash register. In the middle of the room Russ stands on a ladder, attaching a conglomeration of leaves and feathers to a ceiling fan, while Star arranges a centerpiece of pine cones and muddy hunks of quartz on one of the tables.

As Morgan and Molly hover, she notices them. "Welcome, women! How do you like our new look?"

A sideways glance shows Morgan that Molly's incapable of speech. "It's, uh, really amazing," she says, noting with misgiving that other than Star's daughter Rhiannon hunched at a corner table by herself, there's no one else here. "I guess you're . . . uh . . . not really open."

Russ descends the ladder. "Sure we are; sit anywhere you like. Star, give me a hand in the kitchen?"

"Coming, hon."

As the kitchen door swings shut behind them, Molly grabs Morgan's arm. "It's like a fucking bird's nest in here! Do we have to stay?"

Morgan's still staring after Russ and Star.

"Morgan! Let's go!"

"How can we?" Morgan glances over at Rhiannon, utterly absorbed in whatever she's holding in her lap.

"Let's just go," Molly whispers. "If she asks us later, I'll make up a lie."

It's tempting; the atmosphere in the restaurant is really weird. What's going on here? But however obnoxious Star has been recently, she and Morgan go back a long way. Star and Russ were the first people to follow her to Durwood, and it feels wrong to duck out behind their backs.

"Let's just have lunch," she says. "How bad could it be?"

By unspoken agreement they take the table nearest the door, but once seated they're at a loss. There's no evidence of the usual chalkboard with the day's specials, no sign of life from the kitchen. A few damp brownish feathers drift down from above. Morgan shifts uneasily in her chair, trying to avoid the leaves tickling her ankles, and turns toward the corner table.

"Hi, Rhiannon. How are you?"

The response is barely audible. It's not like Rhiannon to be surly, but she's approaching that age. Morgan tries again. "What's that you've got there?"

"Doll." Rhiannon holds it up briefly before bending over it again.

Doll? Morgan gets only a quick glimpse. Is that one of those little twig figures Vivian was making yesterday? Some kind of symbolic forest spirits for the kids to hold in the ritual circle. She wonders why Rhiannon's still hanging onto it. Isn't she a little old for dolls?

Star emerges from the kitchen and approaches their table, bearing a loaded platter. "It's kind of pot luck today. From Russ's private stash." The words come out in a rush. "Usually this is our shopping morning, but we're both just so tired – "

"Well, Reese's isn't . . . " Isn't open anyway, Morgan's about to say, but speech deserts her as Star sets the platter on the table. Salami, ham, some dry turkey curling up at the edges, a few hunks of elderly cheese. Russ's private stash? Sundial serves a strictly vegan menu and Morgan has always assumed the Barretts are vegan as well. Catching the look of horrified hilarity on Molly's face, she quickly looks away. The two of them take small helpings and eat in silence, avoiding eye contact. Once or twice Molly stifles a giggle.

But it isn't really funny, Morgan thinks; there's something profoundly *off* about all of this – the weird décor, Rhiannon's uncharacteristic manner, the absurd meal.

Nor, when Star returns to their table to chat, is her conversation reassuring.

"The ritual gave us both this kind of supercharged sense of the natural world, you know? So we just decided to go for it. We collected a bunch of stuff after the ritual, stayed up the rest of the night and did the whole place over."

Lack of sleep would explain Star's sallow color and the deep grooves around her eyes and mouth. Her hair looks as if it hasn't been combed today, and there's a long muddy smear down the front of her skirt.

Morgan and Molly chew, nod, smile. "All night, huh? Wow."

"Yeah, so we're both totally pooped. But – " with a glassy-eyed smile and a spasmodic wave at the room around them – "Worth it, huh?"

They find themselves nodding, endorsement sucked from them against their will by something in her voice that sounds like desperation. "Are you *kidding*? Of *course*. *No question*." Once they're done lying, Morgan asks, "How did the ritual go?"

Star's eyes close. She begins to sway back and forth, a smile on her lips. "Amazing. Just . . . Oh, the colors. The colors."

They watch, mesmerized, as the smile stretches wider and wider until it wobbles and collapses. When she opens her eyes, they're swimming with tears. In the wet, hollow gaze is a look of loss beyond fathoming.

Concern shoots through Morgan, obliterating the accumulated resentment of the past few weeks. "Star?"

"It's still not right," Star whispers.

"Not – ?"

"All this." Flinging an arm at the room. "It's still . . . not . . . *right*."

She turns and makes a beeline for the kitchen. As the door swings shut behind her Molly leans across the table. "Morgan. What's all this about?"

"You mean – "

"I mean the friggin woodland diorama in here! All they need now are a couple of stuffed raccoons. She thinks this is nice?"

"Something's wrong," Morgan says.

"No kidding. Let's get out of here."

"Okay, but there's no check. How much money should we leave?"

Molly rolls her eyes. "I'm not paying for this."

Morgan leaves a twenty on the table. Outside, beneath the dripping awning, they encounter Rhiannon's little brother Gwion clutching a dark object to his chest. Morgan pauses for a closer look. Is that another of those twig dolls?

"Gwion, can I see that a minute?"

If he answers, it's lost in a splintering crash from the restaurant.

"What the – ?" Molly turns and hurries back inside, Morgan at her heels.

In Sundial's back wall, one of the windows has been shattered. Russ stands beside it holding a sledgehammer. As they watch, he swings again and the hammer thuds into the window frame, sending a spray of glass shards and chunks of lovingly refinished wood in all directions. Beneath the spasmodic drift of leaves and feathers from the ceiling, Star wanders toward them with her dazed, stretched smile.

"Guess we should put up a 'temporarily closed for renovations' sign, huh? We just – " she flinches as the hammer hits the brick wall with a bone-jarring crunch " – just decided we needed to – to do more to recapture it."

"Recapture what?" Morgan says faintly.

"How we felt during the ritual. That sense of connection with the natural world. Really let it in, you know? Do whatever it takes."

Her eyes plead for reassurance. The hunched figure across the room, wielding its hammer with demonic intensity, is unrecognizable as genial Russ, the man with a penchant for smooth jazz and a knack for the perfect risotto. There are fragments of plaster in his hair, dark patches of sweat under the arms of his shirt. With each successive blow the jagged hole in the wall widens, brick and mortar crumbling beneath the relentless assault. The twinkle of broken glass is everywhere.

Morgan's gaze meets Molly's. They've all heard Russ and Star discuss the idea of opening up the back wall at some point to create a patio for outdoor dining, but this spur-of-the-moment demolition is something else entirely, a whole order of magnitude beyond the bizarre redecoration scheme.

Really let it in, you know? Do whatever it takes.

And there it is, beyond the drifting clouds of brick dust. Nature. A tangle of wet, windblown weeds and vines and overgrown bushes, brought into somehow menacing proximity by the ragged hole in the wall. When Russ rests the hammer and turns to face them, Morgan can't help noticing he has an erection.

"There." He speaks between panting breaths. "That's better. Isn't it?"

"Much better," Star whispers.

Back at the store, Morgan brews a cup of green tea and carries it up to Nick's quarters. There's no response to her first knock, nor to her second. She hesitates only briefly before opening the door and peering in. "Nicky?"

No answer from the hump of tangled bedding on the futon.

"Nicky!"

The hump stirs. "Uhn . . . ?"

"Time to wake up." Yes, she knows rituals are a huge energy drain, especially for the high priest and priestess. But she needs answers. "I brought you some tea." She sets the cup on the floor beside the futon and waits. Nothing. She guesses the next step is to bring out her aunt voice.

"Okay, Mister. It's really time to get up." Underscoring the words with a brisk pat on the back, she's started by his violent recoil.

"Wh – what's the matter? Are you hurt?"

He mumbles into the pillow. Now Morgan sees dark stipples on the worn old quilt that covers him. "Nicky! Is that blood?" Lifting the quilt, she sucks in her breath at the sight of the oozing welts that crisscross his back. Abruptly he snatches it back and covers himself, but the afterimage of the marks stays in her mind's eye. They look like –

Like scratches made by someone's nails.

A connection lights in her brain, robbing her of breath. The ritual. He got those marks at the ritual. What was the word Star used? *Amazing.* She'd offered no details, but all at once Morgan understands. Nick and Sally – priest and priestess, enacting Wicca's Great Rite, blessing the ritual with their union. It's a perfect symbol for the joining of the old Durwood with the new, and she should be delighted; instead she's aware of a sensation like hot acid seeping through her body – not unknown, but so unexpected in this context that it takes her a long, incredulous moment to recognize it as jealousy.

You are an idiot, she tells herself. A complete and utter fool.

Ever since that damnably sexual dream, she's had to be on her guard not to embarrass both herself and Nick by betraying inappropriate feelings he obviously doesn't return. She's even managed to tell herself that by refusing to acknowledge the attraction, she's successfully starved it into submission – an exercise in self-deception now unmasked by the maelstrom raging inside her.

"Those look infected, Nicky." She congratulates herself on achieving an overlay of motherly concern. "We need to put something on them; I'll bring some antibiotic cream from home."

◆◆◆

In her cabin overlooking the Noon Woods, Liz Wyatt listens to the silence. Waking the day after the ritual to find her drawings scattered across the floor, she'd blamed the wind; the old cabin is porous as a sieve. Now Durwood has emerged from its two-day limbo of falling water and rushing wind; now the air is still, and tentative blue rifts are appearing in the clouds. In the sudden calm, Liz acknowledges the urge that's been growing since Midsummer, since she made that first drawing.

The urge to paint.

Last week, seeing a children's watercolor set at the Hardware & Supply, she'd bought it on impulse. Now she tears a fresh sheet from her sketchbook, takes half a dozen cups from the cabinet, and begins to mix her paints. The brush moves with assurance, combining, diluting, gauging hues, adding a little more blue, another dab of water as if the last time she painted was yesterday instead of sixteen years ago.

The last time she painted – she dips the brush, lets it hover above the paper. The last time she painted, it was in her own blood.

In the aftermath of her treatment, trapped in a dull, soulless world she no longer recognized, she'd turned to heavy drinking. One night she'd accidentally broken a glass and cut her fingers picking up the pieces. The bright flow of blood seemed so eager, so effortless . . . A question floated into her head and she stopped, crouching motionless while the blood pooled on the floor.

What if she couldn't draw because she was using the wrong materials?

I don't understand, Liz. If you were so depressed, why didn't you ask for help?

Val, I keep telling you. It wasn't a suicide attempt. I was . . . experimenting.

With your own blood?

Have you seen the paintings?

No. Ferguson got rid of them.

He had no right to do that.

He said they'd damage your reputation as an artist.

Which means he was afraid they'd hurt the book sales.

That's not fair. He really cares about you. They all do. I mean, look around.

This is a really nice place.

It's a nuthouse.

Well, dammit, Liz, what do you expect? You were painting with your own blood!

Four months' stay in a psychiatric facility, the next twelve and a half years teaching art classes at a local community center for a living, using a different last name to avoid questions. Thirteen years of meaningless limbo, and then the symptoms began to recur.

Ms Wyatt, I know we had success with the radiation treatment in the past. But the tumor has shown some aggressive regrowth, and we're going to need to go ahead and remove it surgically. It's already close to impinging on some crucial brain functions, and that's a matter for concern. If we don't operate, you could be looking at severe memory loss, seizures, paralysis . . .

Nod, don't argue. But enough is enough. It was time to go back to Durwood. Time to go home.

The brush descends, makes a mark, a line. Colors root and spread. She works steadily, oblivious to everything but the partnership of hand and eye, so absorbed in the process that she doesn't even hear the noise of engines laboring up the hill until all at once the grinding, squeaking racket penetrates her concentration.

Paint and paper release their grip; dread rushes in. The loggers are back. She drops the brush and runs out onto the porch just as the Fawn Creek truck rolls past, followed by a single squad car. Not far behind the two vehicles come the people of Durwood. Liz watches them pass, members of the old families trudging side by side with the newcomers who've recently made Durwood as their home. Phones must have been ringing all over town to muster such a showing. She doesn't see Nick, or Gordie Durwood either. Gordie hasn't been back to the logging camp since the rain began; maybe Fawn Creek, knowing his presence is bound to inflame the locals, has advised him to stay away. Watching people stream past the cabin, Liz remembers a news clip she once saw of an anti-logging demonstration in California – lines of protesters with linked arms blocking the road and singing, "You can't clearcut your way to Heaven."

This isn't like that. They walk quietly down through the field, gathering in a subdued clump not far from where the sheriff and his deputy lean against their squad car. The logging crew has left the truck and now forms a huddle at the forest's edge, small orange-hatted figures dwarfed by the massive trees. What looked like the promise of good weather has vanished; the earlier patches of blue sky have surrendered to low clouds that cling to the ridges like damp wool.

The four loggers shoulder their chainsaws and enter the woods while Liz is hurrying down to join the crowd. Unthinkable as it is, the crisis is finally upon them. Can anything stop it now? The return of the wind, another bout of rain . . . Already the mist is drifting down from the ridge crests to swaddle the treetops, and the air is heavy with moisture.

As the crowd begins to move toward the woods, the police officers – two of them opposing what must be close to two hundred people – move to head them off. They look jumpy. Sheriff Ewers raises his voice.

"Listen, folks, there's nothing you can do here, so why don't y'all go home and get on with your day? I'm sure y'all got better thi – "

The nasal buzz of a chainsaw drowns him out, lasting a dozen seconds before sputtering to a stop. The crowd moves restlessly.

"We can watch, can't we, Larry?" That's CW Durwood, up at the front with Morgan, Sally, and Pete Vernon. "So long's we keep out of the way?"

"Y'all seen trees cut down before, CW. Ain't nothin much to watch."

"You sayin we can't?"

"Nope. But we'll go first, and y'all better keep behind us. Get in that crew's way and I'll sure as hell be makin some arrests, if I have to cuff the whole town. We brung extra."

Another burst of buzzing issues from the woods and then dies. In the sullen silence that follows, CW turns to face the crowd. "You heard Sheriff Ewers, folks. Keep back and don't cause no trouble."

There's an answering murmur as they surge forward. Liz joins the rear stragglers. As they enter the woods she can see them looking around with something like apprehension; many of them have never set foot in the woods, only heard the stories. The massive trunks surround them, wet leaves hanging low and heavy among ragged curtains of mist. The people of Durwood walk without speaking, their progress marked only by the squelching of the sodden ground. The only logger in sight is the foreman, easy to spot in his red plaid shirt and orange helmet. Crouched over his inert saw, he glances up warily at their approach. The two officers push their way to the front.

"How's it goin?" Forced heartiness sends Ewers's voice into falsetto.

The logger's eyes flick past him at the approaching crowd. "Saw's actin up a bit. Don't like the damp."

"Pretty wet these past couple days," Ewers says. "Course, we been needin it."

He comes to a halt and the deputy follows suit, the pair of them extending their arms in a makeshift barricade behind which the crowd closes ranks. There are rustlings and a few coughs, but no one speaks while the logger continues to coax his balky saw. Off to the left Liz can make out a second orange helmet bobbing in the mist – another member of the crew, his efforts similarly unsuccessful. The others are somewhere farther off, not visible but clearly audible from the spate of curses that follows each abortive burst from the saws.

She scans the crowd. Where's Nick? It's his ritual, after all, that was supposed to prevent the logging – and whether it's the ritual, the damp, or the palpable ill will of the Durwood community, the operation seems to have come at least temporarily to a standstill. The tension in the woods is as thick as the mist, and both are steadily increasing.

The red-shirted foreman's saw suddenly coughs and catches, and he revs it half a dozen times in succession. A moment later the other saws join in, the snarl of engines echoing through the woods. Atop her father's shoulders, little Sonia Palmer claps her hands to her ears, small face crumpling.

Red Shirt turns his back on the crowd and squats beside a massive oak. As the chain bites into the wood, the noise changes to a frenzied whine and a fountain of sawdust spews from the cut, centuries of growth demolished before their eyes.

Liz turns away, seized by the overpowering sense that, aside from the watching crowd, there are other observers present. In the chance junctions of twigs and branches, revealed and just as capriciously concealed by the shifting fog, she can't help seeing insubstantial shapes and not-quite-faces, unseen watchers lurking in the mist-laden spaces among the leaves.

A murmur from the crowd alerts her, and she turns to see the tree about to fall. Everyone's looking up, straining to see the huge crown shrouded in fog. For an endless interval it seems to hang suspended; then, with a series of groans and cracks, it topples with agonizing slowness before finally landing on the forest floor. Cushioned by branches, the impact is less a crash than a series of cracks and snaps ending in an earth-shaking *whump*. Leaves and broken twigs sift down from the surrounding trees. The other saws have stopped, and a preternatural stillness ripples outward from the fallen oak. Furtive glances and uneasy movements spread through the crowd; dread is in the air, as if some key force has been pushed perilously out of balance.

Somewhere in the crowd a child begins to cry. Liz hears one of the other saws start up again, its hornet buzz piercing the heavy silence for what seems like forever before it stutters and dies and the screams begin.

"Oh Lord! Oh Jesus, what – *what?* Oh my Gaah – "

The babbled words fuse in an incoherent shriek that goes on and on and on. By now the visibility is close to zero. Liz finds herself running and stumbling among shadowy figures, blocked and thwarted by spectral trees while the air judders with the logger's raw screams.

No one can locate him. Jim Sayles and Jeff Durwood, both running toward what they think is the source, collide heavily and hear the shrill cries pass over their heads like a flock of birds. Holly Vernon distinctly hears them behind her, but when she turns, they're still behind her. Gwion Barrett, homing in on them with his sharp young senses, finds to his amazement that they're coming from a cleft in the roots of a tree. Mariela Everdale tracks them to a clump of ferns and loses them there.

For others, every knothole and crevice becomes a distorted, shrieking mouth; screams pour from the jagged spaces among the leaves, the crannies under rocks and the holes in decaying logs, surrounding them as completely as the mist-curdled air.

By the time someone finds the injured logger, his cries have faded to whimpers. He's slumped on the ground, clutching his leg just above the knee, blood streaming through his fingers to puddle on the leaves beneath. He doesn't seem aware of the people gathering around him. Two of his buddies pry his hands away from the gash; Red Shirt loops a belt around his leg above the wound and pulls it tight. As the blood slows to a trickle, Red Shirt leans close.

"What happened, Charlie? Saw kick back on you?"

Charlie doesn't answer. He's breathing in rapid gasps, eyes white-ringed and rolling in his sweating gray face. Red Shirt grips his shoulder.

"Charlie!"

"Where'd it go?" The voice is a husk.

"Where'd what go?"

Charlie lets out a dry sob. "I seen it, Bill. It was lookin at me."

"Seen what? Wha'd you see? Was it a bear?"

Charlie stares straight ahead, tears leaking down his face. Red Shirt sends a furious glance around the circle of onlookers as if blaming them.

"It *looked at* me," Charlie says in a choked whisper. "Looked right *at* me."

People glance furtively around them. A cold hand squeezes Liz's heart.

Red Shirt forces a laugh. "Man, you done gone and spooked yourself in the fog."

"He's in shock, is what," one of the other loggers says.

A commotion in the branches overhead makes Liz look up. All she can see is mist, but suddenly people are screaming and shoving. She's carried along with the crowd as a huge branch comes crashing down, landing squarely on Red Shirt, knocking him to the ground.

There's a shocked hush, then Pete Vernon's hoarse voice: "Is he killed?"

Red Shirt groans. The cops move toward him cautiously.

"He's alive," Sheriff Ewers says. "Help me get this branch off him."

No one moves. Ewers faces the crowd, red faced and breathing audibly. "Somebody give a hand with this poor bastard, or I swear I'll arrest the lot of you."

Gordie squints into the camper's grimy mirror. Here he is, back at the logging camp to guard the skidder again while Fawn Creek puts together a new crew. This bunch managed to rack up a grand total of two and a half trees before turning tail, and now the company's making noises about backing out of the deal. But they signed a contract and he's going to hold them to it. He's got to have that money.

He peers through the haze of smudged fingerprints at his reflection. There's a bruise on his chin, another one covering the left side of his mouth and part of his cheek. Fingering the plum-colored swelling, he lets out a grunt at the pain.

From the time he was six years old, ever since the day he peeked into Momma's bedroom, he's known that pain is the only thing that can truly wash away sin. But the knowledge was a secret he shared with Momma in silence; every time he'd come even close to mentioning it, she'd get all jumpy. And it was awkward, too, because if they'd ever talked about it, he would've had to admit he'd seen her naked.

Not on purpose. Lord no. She'd sent him outside to play while she cleaned the house, the way she always did. Momma's customary cleaning routine was a whirlwind of sweeping and dusting and scrubbing, her mouth set in a tight line because she hated living in a dirty old log cabin where his daddy was always forgetting to wipe his boots.

But on that unforgettable day, when he came inside for a drink of water, the house was quiet. And as he stood puzzled, listening, in the quiet he could hear Momma's voice upstairs.

Who was she talking to? Daddy had long since gone to work, and as far as Gordie knew there was nobody else in the house. Removing his shoes, he climbed the narrow staircase to investigate.

Momma's bedroom was at the top of the stairs, next to the small room where he and Daddy slept. The door was closed. She'd fallen silent now, but Gordie knew she was in there because he could hear her breathing hard, like she'd been running. One of the door's panels had warped, pulling away from the others to make a narrow opening. Crouching, pressing his nose to the crack, he squinted through it.

All he could see at first was a colored picture lying on the floor. It looked like Momma's favorite picture of Jesus on the cross, blood trickling from his wounds and a beam of light shining down on Him from a bank of stormy clouds overhead. Adjusting his position, Gordie found a wider field of view. Now he could see Momma kneeling in front of the picture.

She was buck naked.

Staggered by the sight of her bare flesh, he didn't have time to credit what he was seeing before there came the swish and whicker of a hazel switch as she hit herself across the backside, and then a throaty gasp.

"Precious Lord! Forgive this sinner!"

Gordie dropped back on his heels, his head whirling. It looked like Momma had her own version of the Crucifixion game.

By the time he reached high school, he wasn't playing the Crucifixion game anymore. He and Momma were living in Asheville; he'd joined the gospel group, and they spent every free moment practicing. Gordie had a special compartment in his mind for what he'd witnessed that day in Momma's bedroom, a kind of limbo place in which it had happened and not happened at the same time.

As they turned the glossy pages and snickered over the naked ladies who were balancing on giant seashells and hugging swans, Gordie started to feel queasy, and when Brandon and Billy poked their grubby fingers at the painted ladies' bare boobs and the forbidden place between their legs, he thought he was going to throw up. But he couldn't make himself stop looking, and then –

"Wait, go back a sec."

Brandon flipped the page back. "Oh, man!"

"Shit," Billy breathed.

The picture showed a pale young man wearing nothing but a dinky little towel around his hips. He was tied to a marble column and he had about a million arrows sticking out of him; one was even poking right through his head, between his eyes.

But it was the look on his face that riveted Gordie. The way his eyes were rolled up and his lips were drawn tight . . . He knew exactly what the young man was experiencing. It was the Feeling. *Saint Sebastian*, said the words under the picture. *By Andrea Mantegna*. With Brandon and Billy watching bug-eyed, Gordie carefully tore the page out of the book, folded it, and put it in his wallet. At home in his room, he hid it under his mattress.

"Gordie? Son, can you come here a minute?"

Momma was sitting on the couch in front of the TV. She'd been watching Oprah, whom she loved. "That colored girl's got a lot of sense," she'd say, making Gordie wince. You weren't supposed to say colored, you were supposed to say African American, but Momma didn't pay attention to any of that. She believed that during the Tower of Babel debacle, when God had decided to change people so they couldn't talk to each other and cause any more trouble, His strategy had been to turn all the good people white and all the bad ones black. But she loved Oprah, who gave her viewers advice like *Talk to your kids instead of yelling at them. Ask them if there's something they need to tell you.*

Momma patted the couch for Gordie to sit beside her. "Is there something you need to tell me?"

"Uh . . . Like what?"

"Well . . . what about girls? Is there a girl you like?"

"Huh?" What was she asking him about girls for? Girls pretty much ignored him except for Darnelle Oakley at church, who was fat and smelled like turnip greens and had once goosed him at the water cooler.

The tip of Momma's tongue was darting in and out of her mouth like it always did when she was nervous. With a convulsive movement, she thrust something at him.

"I found *this* when I was making your bed this morning."

It was Saint Sebastian. Gordie froze.

"What are you doing with this picture, Gordie?"

He didn't know what to say. He'd stolen the picture just to look at it, but the sheer scope of Saint Sebastian's suffering had given him ideas. For one thing, his near nakedness was a matter of horrible, delicious shame. For another, he had no less than thirteen (Gordie had counted them) arrows sticking in him.

Gordie'd locked the door, undressed down to his underpants and put his back to the bedpost with his hands clasped behind him, picturing himself tied to a column, people looking at his nearly naked body while arrows flew through the air to strike him one by one, each thwack followed by a rush of purifying fire.

Lord, forgive this sinner.

It wasn't enough. He tried pinching himself.

Lord, forgive –

Still not enough. He found his book bag and searched through it for his geometry compass. Back to the bedpost. He squeezed his eyes shut, pictured people staring at his nakedness and the arrows whizzing toward him, and jabbed the sharp point of the compass into the tender skin of his inner thigh.

Precious Lord!

He hadn't realized what would happen, but he'd been careful to clean up all the traces.

"Son, I asked you a question."

"Um, he's a saint, Momma. He died for Jesus."

"He's practically naked." Momma's voice was faint. "And he's a Roman Catholic. They worship the Pope."

Gordie bit his lip. He knew that no matter what Momma said, she understood perfectly about Saint Sebastian and his arrows. At the back of his mind was the smack of the hazel switch and the gasp that came after. Anyway, wasn't it written right there in the Bible for everyone to see?

For whom the Lord loveth he chasteneth, and scourgeth every son whom he receiveth.

Momma lunged forward and grabbed him in a hug that squeezed the breath out of him. Then she pushed him away, slapped his face, and burst into tears.

"I don't want you looking at pictures of – of naked men! No matter who they are! Do you hear me?"

"Y-yes'm!"

"Now go to your room!"

Gordie leaped up and scurried away. On the threshold he sneaked a look back. Momma was examining the picture, her bosom heaving like she'd run a race, her cheeks wet with tears and bright with those little red spots.

She looked beautiful.

❊ 14 ❊

Liz stares at her unfinished painting.

Two loggers injured in less than an hour. If the logging is to continue, Fawn Creek will need to muster a crew who haven't heard about what happened here today. Her brain replays the screams ricocheting off the trees, the logger's wild eyes.

It looked at me.

The skidder is still parked in the hayfield, evidence that the logging will proceed once Fawn Creek puts together a new crew. She examines the painting. At first glance it's just colors, black lines forking through a mass of coppers and browns and greens edged in purple. But if she keeps looking, there's a kind of shift happening within the stillness of the whole, shapes that emerge and then slip away again, sly as shadows. It's the same phenomenon she's experienced countless times in the Noon Woods, the interplay between brain and –

Between brain and what? *You can't just summon the Green Man.* It's just a painting, pigment on paper. But she finds herself snatching it up, tearing it in half and then into smaller pieces, tossing the fragments onto the coals of last night's fire. The earlier sketches of the oak misted in red, of Sally with windswept hair – she gathers them up but can't bring herself to destroy them. Instead she shoves them into her portfolio, reassured by the rasp of the zipper as she locks them in. Only then does she dare to look out the window at the vast expanse of forest. Every leaf on every branch hangs motionless, an unnatural stillness like a sea with waves frozen at the crest. Above the motionless vista of leafy crowns, the mist has evaporated into a glaring gunmetal sky.

It looked at me.

Dead tree or guardian spirit? On her return to Durwood, she'd made a pilgrimage to the oak to offer what she considered her best drawing, an early sketch of Truantina from the Hundred Year Stone series. Let me draw like that again. I'll do anything. Anything. Attaching it to a branch, she'd noticed how the twigs had seemed to clasp her fingers as if reluctant to let go.

Now she scarcely registers the soft bump against her shin. It comes again, more insistent this time, and she looks down at the small furry shape. "Hungry, Minnie?"

The cat blinks slanting green eyes while Liz fills her bowl. As she's returning the box of kibble to the cabinet, her fingers brush the Mason jar.

Twenty-four ounces, and more than half full. It's already in her hand. She takes a deep breath, unscrews the lid, and lifts the jar to her lips.

♦ ♦ ♦

The buzz of voices from the house is audible all the way out to Tyne's study.

It's been hours since he heard the noise of the medevac chopper hovering over the upper field. Once it headed off to the hospital in Lenoir, the crowd had drifted down the hill to congregate at the house. Sally'd come out to his study to report the logging mishaps before returning to the gathering.

Now the day's getting on toward dusk, but no one seems to be leaving.

Tyne heads over to see what's going on. The air's still so heavy that he can feel moisture settling on his hair and skin as he wheels down the walkway and onto the porch. Captured under the overhang, the noise here is a deafening haze of angry chatter in which single words and phrases are briefly distinguishable.

– sonofabitch – never thought I'd live to see the day – not gonna take this –

He brings his chair to a stop at the front corner, seeing the porch thronged with people who've overflowed the house through the open parlor doors. No one notices him parked there in the shadows; there are a dozen vehement discussions are in progress, heads nodding, hands waving in the air. Most of Durwood is here, along with a lot of people he doesn't recognize, outsiders who've arrived since he became housebound. The indignation that stamps their faces makes them all look oddly alike. Isn't this what Sally said she wanted – Durwood's old and new citizens uniting to save the Noon Woods? There she is, talking to a couple of people he doesn't know, the woman decked out in beads and a fringed shawl, the man in designer jeans and fancy boots that wouldn't last through a day's honest work. As Tyne watches, they turn to hail another woman who's heading down the porch steps.

"Morgan! Leaving already? There's still a lot to talk about! "

She looks chagrined. "I need to check on Nick. I'm kind of worried about him; the ritual really wiped him out."

Admonishments turn to farewells. Tyne watches her hurry off, car keys jingling in her hand. Nick. Isn't he the genius who came up with the bright idea of a ritual? Morgan is his aunt, the Bunny Dancer who owns the health food store. Tyne's heard Sally tease CW about being sweet on her. A nice looking woman; who could blame him? Except –

It was always only you, Alma.

A sudden racket returns his attention to the house. CW's standing in the parlor, banging on the stovepipe with the poker. When quiet spreads, he clears his throat.

"Folks, we all know what's been goin on, and we all know it's gotta stop. So let's quit fussin and talk about what needs to get done."

♦ ♦ ♦

It's full dark when Liz emerges from her stupor. Even with every sense saturated by alcohol, she knows immediately that something's not right. Her sluggish brain registers a whistling around the cabin walls, a moaning under the

114

rafters, a muffled rattle of roof shakes.

The wind's rising.

She thinks of mist curling among the trees. The injured logger's sweating gray face. *It looked at me.* A bell shrills in the kitchen, making her jump. It comes again, and she realizes it's the phone CW installed when she'd moved into the cabin. It's never rung before; she doesn't even know the number, but clearly someone does.

It rings a third time. Standing up is a challenge, walking a greater one. She lurches across the swaying, tilting darkness. Snatches the receiver from its cradle on the kitchen wall, fumbles it to her ear.

"Liz," a voice says. "Is Gordie up at the loggers' camp?"

"Is that you, Tyne?"

"It's Abe Fuckin Lincoln," says his acerbic voice. "Is Gordie up there?"

She peers out the window. In the windswept darkness, the moonlit field is ringed with clumps of moving shadow. Down near the forest's edge she can see a faint gleam.

"Looks like there's a light on in the camper."

Tyne grunts. "You need to tell him to get the hell out of there."

"Why?"

"Because there's some kinda meetin going on at our house. Bunch of folks gettin themselves geared up to do somethin. There's gonna be trouble."

"What – kind of trouble?"

"I don't know. But I do know they took that stone out of Roan's Oak the night they did their ritual. Did you hear it? That sound?"

"I was sleeping."

"Well." He knows her well enough to take her meaning, "Let's just say it'll be better if Gordie ain't there."

"I'm on my way," Liz says.

As she hangs up the phone, her eye catches on a shadowy rectangle lying on the kitchen table.

She takes a step closer. A sheet of paper. Even in the filmy moonlight, there's no doubt what it is.

But I tore it up

She remembers destroying the half finished painting, throwing it onto the smoldering coals. But here it is, or another one just like it – finished now, forceful brushstrokes running edge to edge. Even as she reaches for it with shaking fingers, she's already seeing dozens more littering the floor like windblown leaves – frenzied renderings of twigs and branches, swirling knotholes and tangled roots, a gash of shadow like a ravenous mouth.

Her fingers are black with charcoal and smeared paint.

They took that stone out of Roan's Oak.

Breath drains from her like air from a slashed tire. She turns and flees, leaving the cabin door wide.

The night is enormous, clouds scudding across an ashen sky. Wind buffets her ears and nearly blows her off her feet; she runs low to the ground through the wildly tossing hay, heading for the lit window in the distance. In the darkness and intermittent moonlight, the camper seems a hundred miles away. The force of the wind shoves her breath back down her throat while the earth bucks beneath her, sending her staggering one way and then another until the little square of light dances in her vision like a will-o'-the-wisp.

I'm still drunk, she thinks. I did that painting and all those sketches while I was drunk. But why can't I remember?

Some of the symptoms you may experience with meningioma include headaches, muscle spasms, numbness or paralysis, or memory loss.

Fighting the gusts, imagining the tumor's delicate tendrils probing her brain, she wonders why she should care what happens to Gordie Durwood. Yet her legs keep moving, carrying her erratically toward the camper. The moon disappears behind clouds and the darkness thickens. She glances over her shoulder.

Nothing's following her. Nothing's out there.

At least nothing she can see.

The moon reappears to reveal the skidder right in front of her, looming like a giant insect. Gordie's car is parked nearby, the camper just beyond. Stumbling across the tire-churned ground, she bangs her fist on the camper door.

"Hey! Open up!"

No response. Liz bangs again, jiggles the handle, feels someone turn it from the inside. The door opens a crack.

"Listen!" She has to yell over the wind. "You need to get out of here!"

It opens a few more inches and she sees a pale, scowling face. "Who are you?" says Gordie Durwood.

"I live up there!" She gestures at the cabin, picturing the figure she must cut, appearing out of the night like a phantom scarecrow. "Tyne Durwood just called me! He said there's a meeting at his house!"

He stares at her. "So?"

She stares back, aware of the restless movement of wind-tossed shadows behind her. "Let me in, huh?"

He steps back from the door. As Liz enters, a strong gust rattles the camper and sets a Coleman lamp swinging on its hook. The flimsy door slams shut behind her, reducing the noise of the wind just enough for her to gather the thoughts flying helter-skelter through her brain. She takes a breath.

"Listen, you can't stay here tonight. It's not safe."

"Safe?" From the bruises on his face, she can see someone's already put at least one beating on him.

"There are a lot of people down at CW's right now who aren't too happy with what you're doing."

His eyes narrow. "What's it to you?"

Liz sighs. "Look, I'm against the logging. But I don't have anything against you personally." It comes out "pershonally" and Gordie peers at her.

"You're drunk."

"And you need to get out of here."

He folds his arms. "That's the plan, huh? Scare me off so they can come up here and wreck the skidder?"

"Nobody cares about the damn skidder. It's you they want."

"I'm not scared of them."

"You should be," Liz says. As if to underscore her words, something hits the outside of the camper with a bang that makes them both jump. Probably just a broken branch blown by the wind, but – seeing Gordie's battered face twitch, she seizes his arm.

"Come on. We're running out of time."

He lets her pull him to the door. As they emerge from the camper into the howling wind, it's like being sucked down the gullet of some greedy monster. Liz has never seen weather like this – the sky boiling with clouds, the battered trees convulsing as if trying to tear free of the earth. She and Gordie duck and run for his car, the racket diminishing once they slam the doors. He jams the key into the ignition and turns it; as the engine catches Liz realizes she's been holding her breath. The headlights illuminate a swarm of loose leaves swirling above the windblown hay. As he puts the car in gear and starts up the slope, Liz grabs his arm.

"Not that way! If they come up the road we'll run right into them. There's an open place over there, between the pine woods and the orchard. We can go down through CW's pasture and behind his barn and pick up the road from there."

He nods and twists the steering wheel. As the car bumps forward, Liz's eyes dart from side to side. The moonlight transforms every shadow into a solid object; something's moving just beyond the headlights and she tells herself it's a rabbit in spite of the fact that it's much too big. Ahead of them, the pine woods sway and bend in the high wind, pelting the car with a hail of flying cones; she flinches as one smacks the windshield. She tries to keep her gaze from straying toward the massed blackness at the bottom of the field.

"There!" The gap between the orchard and the pine woods shows clearly in the headlights. The pines are swinging back and forth like metronomes in the wind; and as they near the gap, Liz sees one of the taller ones hang for what seems like an endless interval at the end of its arc, and realizes it's not going to swing back. In the shrieking wind it seems to topple in perfect silence and slow motion. Unable to speak, Liz hears Gordie say, "Shitfire!" as he slams on the brakes. The wheels struggle for purchase and the car slithers to a stop just as the tree lands across the hood.

Liz feels the impact in her bones. The windshield dissolves into a sagging mass of cracks. Gordie jumps out to examine the damage.

After a moment, she follows. Trees sway in the roaring wind amid air thick with flying debris. The top of the fallen pine has lodged in one of the apple trees, causing only minor damage to the car but effectively barring their way. Wading into the mesh of branches, Gordie shoves at the tree. It doesn't even budge.

"Gimme a hand here!" His shout is no more than a squeak over the noise of the wind. Feeling small and feeble, Liz burrows among the sticky branches to wedge her shoulder beneath the trunk and heave. She might as well be trying to shift a mountain. The pungent pine smell surrounds her. The tree doesn't move.

"Try rolling it!" Gordie yells. For the moment the universe has narrowed to the dimensions of their task; they shove, shake, push and pull to no avail. A wave of dizziness swamps Liz and she stumbles back to catch her breath. Pale blobs are swimming across her vision and she wonders if she's going to pass out. She blinks, but they're still there – shakes her head, but they persist, a multitude of pale shapes floating against the dark background of the trees. She blinks again. They're real, and coming closer. The last trickle of strength runs out of her muscles. Scattered among the pines are dozens of indistinct shapes that take on substance as they approach.

The people of Durwood. Through the trees they come, moving steadily among the wind-tossed branches, their faces set and purposeful. As they emerge from the woods Liz hears a pulsing, eerie wail rise above the shrieking of the wind and remembers what Tyne said.

They took that stone out of Roan's Oak.

Gordie's seen them now. He backs away and plunges down through the pasture at a stumbling run. Half a dozen of them give chase while Liz stands paralyzed. She knows them, knows May Vernon with her neat bun disheveled and loose tendrils of apricot hair swirling in the wind, knows May's grandson Skip, his face wild with glee – knows Annie Sayles and Rose Lewis and Tiny Reese, Russ and Star Barrett, the Palmers and CW Durwood and Tamara Duke and Chad Wilson and Mariela Everdale, their features reduced to gashes of shadow by the stark moonlight.

More are coming. Sawyer Reese and Jeff Durwood, Vivian McKay, Burley Tyner, Larkie and Ward and Verna Cole – all the people gathered earlier today to protest the logging, the same ones who joined in the ritual to protect the forest. Liz doesn't see Jared Gorton and his friends among them, nor does she see Nick, or Morgan. But this is Nick's doing nonetheless, the result of his meddling in matters best left alone.

But the Green Man's on our side!

Liz feels a kind of ripple on the surface of the night, as if some fleeting presence has separated briefly from the darkness before merging with it again. Burley and Pete have caught Gordie and are bringing him back. Abruptly the wind slackens, and in the relative stillness Liz can hear them all panting. Watching Gordie stumble along, head down between the two stone-faced men, she tries to spur herself to do something, then stops with the realization that whatever's going to happen, she can't stop it on her own. She needs help.

Nobody's looking in her direction; they're all crowding around Gordie. Slowly Liz moves back, a furtive step at a time. Out of the spill of brightness from the headlights, into the shadows. Keep it slow, don't attract their attention. A few more yards and she can make her way under cover of darkness to the Durwood farmhouse, where Tyne will know what to do.

A few more yards. A few more feet. A few more steps, and now it's safe to turn and slip off through the trees – but turning, she bumps into something too yielding to be a tree.

"Hey, Liz," Sally says.

◆ ◆ ◆

Parked in the open door of his study, Tyne's listening to the wind. It started kicking up something fierce about an hour ago; the old washtub on its nail by the barn door has been clanging like a gong, and a little while ago one of the clothesline poles blew down. By now the kitchen garden, littered with uprooted cornstalks and sunflowers, looks like a war zone.

In the lulls, he listens. Did Liz get to Gordie in time? About fifteen minutes ago he thought he heard shouting, but now there's nothing.

His right hand aches from gripping the arm of his chair; his left holds the moonshine jar. He drinks, waiting for the liquor to take the edge off his frustration. What's happening up there? If only he could walk . . .

(walk surrounded by in green silence, through coins of light and shadow scattered on the forest floor)

A crash behind the shed – the other clothesline pole – chases the fragment of memory away. He takes another swallow and coaxes it back.

(Their faces turn toward him, registering surprise but no pleasure as he trots into the bright clearing where the shattered tree stands. He realizes they don't want him here. When he falters to a stop, Sally runs over to put her arm around him, brushing the spiderwebs from his hair.

Granny's hands are on her hips. Child, what on earth? However'd you find us?

Followed you.

She purses her lips. Tyne's eyes stray to the tree and the basket beneath. That's Roan's Oak, ain't it? Y'all gonna have a picnic?

No.

Then what's in the basket?

Never you mind.

I'll take him back, Sally says.

No you won't. Granny's voice is harsh. I need you here.

Well, what if he gets lost?

He'll have to stay.

He's too little, Sally says.

No he ain't.

Tyne twists within the circle of Sally's arm. Don't make me go back! I wanna stay!

Sally frowns. But Granny –

Hush. Granny turns her bright, forceful gaze on him. All right, child. Reckon I can't fault you none for being curious. But we got things to do here, important things, so you gotta keep quiet and not make trouble. Can you do that?

When Tyne nods, the sharp old eyes soften. That's my boy.

Sally releases him and Tyne moves closer to the tree. He's heard the story of Roan's Oak more times than he can count, but up to now it's been no more than a tree in a fairytale. Now it's right in front of him.

It's not at all like he imagined it. He's always pictured it green and leafy, not

---
119

bare and gray and topped with huge jagged splinters. Along its bony branches hang countless colorful treasures, some of them dangling just above his head – wreaths of withered flowers, bright bits of cloth knotted with shiny buttons, a silver necklace and a red pocketknife that makes his mouth water.

He reaches up.

Tyne! Don't you touch that!

He jams his hands into his overall pockets and sidles closer to the tree, noticing something embedded in the furrowed trunk. Forgetting Granny's injunction, he exclaims out loud.

Hey! There's Roan's door!

All at once she's standing over him, so tall she blocks the sun.

Didn't I tell you hush?

Yesm.

Sally, you ready?

Yesm.

All right. Fetch me the basket. Tyne, not a word. You hear?)

Of what follows, he remembers only that Sally cried out, and that there was blood. And blood is on his mind when he returns to the present and hears, above the racketing wind, a swelling cry that can only be the oak.

◆◆◆

Once the mob enters the woods, Sally releases her grip on Liz's arm and she's able to drop back and lose herself in the darkness. Now what? Run to the Durwoods' and ask Tyne to call the police on his father and sister? By the time they arrive it will be too late; whatever's going to happen will already be over and done.

Out of indecision she trails along behind the crowd. Soon it's obvious they're heading to Roan's Oak, and she slows to allow more distance between her and the stragglers. Several times she's on the verge of turning back. Maybe, after all, it would be better to call the police . . .

But in the end she keeps going, drawn by some awful compulsion to witness whatever's coming next. The woods at night are a black abyss intermittently spanned by frail bridges of moonlight; half blindly she follows the noise of the crowd. She can't hear the wind anymore; either it's diminished or is muffled by the dense forest canopy.

Up ahead, voices rise to an excited babble; they must have reached the clearing. Closing the distance warily, Liz can see people milling back and forth in the moonlight. The open space seems theatrically bright; afraid of being seen, she retreats deeper among the trees. She can't see much, but she can hear. There are scuffling sounds, then Gordie's high-pitched voice.

"Sons of the Devil! You sacrifice to demons, you drink from the cup of demons, you sup at the table of demons and your portion shall be the lake that burns with fire and brimstone!"

"Shut up!" somebody yells, and an outbreak of shouting follows. Then

Sally's voice, with a harsh edge Liz has never heard.

"You been warned, Gordie."

"You got no business warning me! This is my property, you hear? These woods belong to me by law!"

"There's other kinds of laws." Can that caustic voice belong to May Vernon? "Laws older'n the ones your fancy lawyer knows, and penalties for breakin em. *Three unbreathing things paid for only with breathing things. An apple tree. A hazel bush. A sacred grove.*"

The answering hubbub of agreement is pierced by Gordie's shrill response.

"I am redeemed by the blood of Jesus out of the hands of Satan! I am justified and made righteous by the blood of Jesus, the blood of Jesus protects me from evil! I am a believer, and in the name of Jesus, I bind all evil spirits!"

Furious voices drown him out. Above Liz's head, leaves stir in the wind. Suddenly a flat *thwack, thwack* surmounts the voices – sticks or stones struck together, quickly joined by dozens more.

The pounding reverberates through the clearing like a giant pulse, mounting until Liz can feel it beating in her brain. She clutches a nearby tree for support, hearing beneath the relentless rhythm a trembling thread of sound that rises and sinks, rises again – and then, as the wind intensifies, jumps to a full-throated shriek.

The oak. She claps her hands over her ears, turning and turning in the dark forest, blundering into the shadowshapes of trees in a mindless attempt at escape. But escape is impossible; the sound reaches inside her head, invades her brain to unfurl as color and shape – an intricate, whorl of leaves and branches encircling a misshapen knothole like an ancient unblinking eye, spinning faster and faster until it's staring straight into her soul.

◆◆◆

Hal Everdale has never actually set foot in his wife's studio before. He considers it an expensive toy, a harmless amusement that keeps her out of trouble. His only involvement was to approve the architect's design, a structure along the lines of a Japanese teahouse situated picturesquely at the edge of a pond.

By lucky chance, there was even a willow tree growing beside the pond, trailing its branches in the water for the perfect final touch; but during the studio's construction the incompetent builders had somehow managed to damage the damn thing, and for months it's been slowly dying. Hal reminds himself to make sure its estimated replacement value has been subtracted from the contractor's final bill.

Tonight's visit to the studio is prompted by curiosity. Ever since Mariela attended that ridiculous ritual in the woods, she's been spending most of her time here, lights burning all night long. He knows she occasionally returns to the house, because he's found the refrigerator ransacked and food scattered over the kitchen counter – fragments of cheese, orange rinds, gnawed chicken legs,

Toblerone chocolate wrappers, an empty container of milk and an open jar of peanut butter that shows signs of having been scooped out by hand. His formerly fastidious wife seems to have been transformed into a bear.

Now she's gone out. Seeing the tail lights of her car disappear down the drive, he fetches a jacket – God, this weather is foul; the drought has ended with a vengeance – and heads for the studio. He hasn't gotten around to having solar lights installed along the path, but there's enough moonlight among the racing clouds for him to see his way.

Striding along the edge of the pond, shoulders hunched and jacket zipped against the wind, he wonders fleetingly where Mariela has gone, then forgets her as he reaches the studio and stops in surprise at the sight of the luxuriant willow tendrils caressing the rippled surface of the water. From being at death's door only a couple of days ago, the tree seems to have made a complete turnaround. But that pleasant surprise is erased when he enters the studio and discovers the lights aren't working.

The breaker box is all the way back at the house. He's about to leave when he notices the dark bulk filling the room.

"Jesus," he murmurs. As his vision adjusts, the thing defines itself in more detail, as if forming beneath his gaze, shaping itself out of the darkness – a gigantic sculpture of a tree, its upper branches etched against the huge white moon that nearly fills the skylight.

Hal swallows. Up to now Mariela's pieces have all been smallish, only a couple of feet tall at most, graceless snarls of soldered metal and lumpy plaster. This is different. For one thing it's huge; she must have used every scrap of her ample supplies. It towers above him, crowding the space. For another thing, unlike any of her previous pieces, it radiates a brooding energy that commands attention. The wiry branches are laden with some kind of pale fruit. Curious, he moves in for a closer look and immediately recoils. The ovoid shapes clustering along the spiky branches by the dozens, by the hundreds, are tiny human skulls.

Resisting the creeping sensation at the back of his neck, Hal is suddenly furious. The thing is freakish, sick! Mariela's done this on purpose to show her disgust at the way he makes his living – created this death-laden monstrosity to symbolize the people he's helped his corporate clients screw out of their settlements for environmental poisons. She's never had a problem spending the money he earns, but now all at once she's become a militant tree-hugger, all because she's bored and her prissy little yoga man is playing hard to get. How dare she judge him!

Outside, the gusting wind sends shadows racing over the studio's walls and ceiling. There's a tapping at one of the windows. He spins toward the sound, feeling something brush his shoulder as he turns.

The tapping comes again – urgent, purposeful. Now he sees it's only one of the willow tendrils blowing against the glass. Why is he so jumpy? Those nasty little skulls – how dare she? He's seen enough here; might as well get back to the house. Maybe a stiff Scotch will rinse away his sudden disgust with his marriage and his life.

Starting toward the door, he's jerked back so sharply that he nearly loses his balance. Again he suppresses a surge of panic. One of the wire branches has snagged the shoulder of his jacket, that's all. Carefully he tries to free it, but the awkward angle makes it hard to reache and the prongs have somehow embedded themselves impossibly deep. At last he gives up with a muttered curse. He'll have to just surrender the jacket, which is expensive and now one more offense to be chalked up to Mariela.

But the zipper refuses to budge and suddenly the collar is strangling him and he's flailing his arms in an uncontrollable effort to break free, hearing the rattle of the tiny skulls on their branches above the creak and rasp of wire limbs. In his frenzy he's oblivious to the ominous thumping of the huge top-heavy sculpture as it rocks back and forth on its stubby roots.

The crash, when it comes, echoes across the moonlit surface of the pond. Afterward, there's only the patter of little plaster skulls raining down on the studio floor.

◆ ◆ ◆

Bound to Roan's Oak, hemmed in by the yelling crowd and the primitive rhythm of pounding stones and sticks, Gordie's head is reeling. Little flickers of thought chase each other around and around, but the only one he can catch hold of is the memory of the Crucifixion game.

Stripped. Scourged. Spit upon.

In the game he could stop whenever he wanted. But this isn't a game, and as this knowledge penetrates his guts, they turn into cold mud. Are they going to kill him? But he doesn't want to die! Especially now, when he's on the verge of becoming a gospel star. In fact he's beginning to understand he doesn't want to die at all, ever, even if he has to keep on selling shoes for all eternity. Much as he loves Jesus, however firmly he longs to be Saved, he's not ready to go.

In the midst of the hullabaloo, insignificant details keep swimming through his head. His shin is throbbing where somebody kicked him; one of his shirtsleeves has been ripped clean off; and over to his right, just at the edge of his vision, there's a one-legged Barbie doll dangling from a branch. Heathenish offerings litter the ground around the tree, sodden junk that must have blown down during the storm. *Satan's children*, Momma whispers. Their distorted faces surround him, hurling abuse, and he answers them with Scripture.

"Serpents and generations of vipers! Behold, ye shall be cast into a furnace of fire!"

He sees one of them, a girl in her teens, stick out her tongue at him and flick it like a snake's. Some of the others are laughing. If they're going to kill him, they wouldn't be laughing. Would they? Just as a fragile tendril of hope begins to sprout, from behind him comes a quavering howl that locks all his muscles and makes his heart lurch in his chest.

Like a lost soul crying out from the depths of the pit, and

He can feel himself falling, a tiny distorted figure tumbling down through a billow of red and orange like one of the pictures in Momma's book showing the torments of hell, a crowd of grinning devils with pitchforks upraised waiting below. Somewhere during the long fall, he realizes two things: the grisly wailing is coming from the tree at his back, and his bladder has emptied. These facts snap him back into the nightmare clearing, surrounded by his persecutors. But every ounce of fight has drained out of him along with the pee and his knees give way and he sags limply against the rope that binds him to the oak – now hearing another sound join its hideous wailing, a high breathless moaning that he gradually, hazily understands is coming from him.

He's the one making that other sound. He tries to stop but he can't; it's being pulled out of him against his will by the tree, the devil tree that wants to swallow his soul. He can feel his consciousness beginning to stutter, slowing to a crawl and then racing forward, blurring the grimacing faces of his tormentors and causing the sound of chanting and pounding to fluctuate between faint and deafening while he struggles to keep his balance on the surface of a huge spinning drum that's moving much too fast, forcing him to scramble frantically for purchase only to slip farther and farther back until he loses his footing and falls and there's only blackness

a far off blackness and silence broken only by the sound of someone is scrubbing concrete

Scrape scrape goes the rough brush
Scrape scrape

Each scrape brings a fiery spasm of pain, a white flash around which self gradually coalesces, one fragment at a time

Scrape
Scrape

until consciousness returns to Gordie Durwood.

He still exists. The scraping he hears is his own breathing, each successive inhale and exhale like a wire brush dragged across the raw tissue of his throat. And now, as if they've been eagerly awaiting his attention, other sensations come rushing in – the burning of a hot poker across his chest, an acrid whiff of piss –

He opens his eyes. It's still dark, but this is a darkness he recognizes. He's still in the Noon Woods, still tied to the tree. Around him the forest is silent. Where are his tormentors? He groans and turns his head stiffly, looking around as best he can.

They're gone. He's alone, and by some miracle he's still alive.

He cranes his aching neck to scan the still woods around him once more. No sign of anyone. They must have decided not to kill him, and all he can think is that Jesus must have worked a miracle.

A miracle, just for him. In an uprush of gratitude, he bows his head.

"Precious Lord Jesus, forgive me for doubting even for a second that You had me under Your watchful care. Blessed Savior, I give thanks unto You for stretching out Your heavenly hand to save me from Satan's evil minions. Lord, they were gonna kill me for sure, and I pray that You will cause them to repent bitterly of their haughty and iniquitous acts, and that You will turn your wrath upon them and cause their mirth to turn to weeping and ashes and and and BlessedJesusmayeverylastoneofthemgotojailandgetassfuckedtodeathbygiantnigg ersandqueerswithAIDS."

It just spills out of him, stuff he's never allowed himself even to think before, and he's stunned by how satisfying it feels.

"Praise Thy Holy Name," he whispers. "Amen."

Just wait till he brings the cops into this. He pictures them all in cuffs, shoved into the back of a police van and sentenced for everything they've done to him, all the times they mocked him, all the times they laughed . . .

But first he has to get free, get out of these woods, go somewhere he can take a shower and put on clean clothes. He fumbles at the rope but he can't find the knot; it must be somewhere on the far side of the trunk. He reaches behind him but the mere touch of the oak's bark, dank from the recent rain, makes his skin crawl. Sweat breaks out all over his body. He needs to get out of here *now,* in case they change their minds and come back.

Somewhere off to his left, the snap of a twig breaks the surrounding stillness.

Gordie freezes, holding his breath as he squints across the moonlit clearing at the shadowy trees, searching for any hint of movement. The trees are still; even the leaves hang motionless on their branches – but there it is again, a little snap followed by a soggy crinkle like somebody creeping over wet leaves, moving stealthily from left to right around the edge of the clearing.

What is it? What's making that noise?

His heart is hammering against his ribs. All alone in the dark, bound to the demon tree, he reminds himself that he's under the Savior's protection, sheltered by the Hand of the Lord. A Bible verse pops into his head. "I will sing of Thy power," he whispers. "Yea, I will sing aloud of Thy mercy, for Thou hast been my defense and my refuge in the day of my trouble."

God's sending him a message. He licks his dry lips and tentatively begins to sing.

"There is power . . . power . . . wonderworking power . . . "

Alone in the depths of the woods, the hoarse shaking voice that emerges from his raw throat is woefully off pitch and his chest is so tight he can't draw a decent breath, but he perseveres.

"In the blood . . . of the Lamb . . ."

As his voice trails off, there's a rustle of leaves from the clearing's edge. He takes a desperate breath and continues.

"Power . . . power . . . wonderworking power . . . "

Branches begin to sway as if keeping time. Tendrils of pale mist begin to form among the knotted trunks.

" . . . in the precious . . . blood . . . of . . . the La – "

A puff of air, warm as breath, touches the back of Gordie's neck, making his throat close and every hair on his body stand on end. He tries to keep singing but he can't make a sound. He tells himself it's just the wind – and just look, he can see the matted carpet of dead leaves beginning to stir as the wind paws through them, tossing up handfuls here and there as if searching for something. The leaves lift and hover above the ground, floating aimlessly at first and then circling to form a ragged, whirling funnel in the air – what Momma used to call a leaf devil.

Transfixed, Gordie watches it spin. As it gathers momentum and moves toward the tree, all at once his voice returns in a hoarse croak.

"Get away from me! I said get away! Help me, Jesus!"

But the leaf devil keeps coming, as if enticed by his fear and revulsion. Squirming frantically against his bonds, he's suddenly engulfed by the damp stench of decay, by rotting leaves like moist, crumbling hands that caress his cheeks and fondle his hair. Just as his eyes squeeze shut in horror he sees them – dozens of demon faces peeping at him from among the leaves, each one with patchy red cheeks and a tongue that quivers between glistening lips.

" – *Nuh – nuh – no –* "

As the wind blows harder, the oak's wails join his own in a shrill, unearthly duet.

※15※

Light pries at Liz's eyelids, seeking an entry point. She opens them briefly before squeezing them shut with a groan. During that instant, two brief impressions have managed to penetrate the thick sludge that currently passes for her consciousness.

It's morning, and she's sprawled on the lumpy sofa in front of her fireplace.

She opens her eyes again and light splits her brain like a hot wedge. It takes a number of attempts to achieve a sitting position; in the process she kicks over the empty moonshine jar on the floor and hears a glassy jangle as it rolls away.

Through a watery dazzle of morning sunlight, she can see drawings scattered everywhere, a blizzard of paper littering the cabin. Images flicker in her head: branchy windblown darkness, an implacable pounding saturating the air, a pine tree falling in slow motion. Then nothing. Her heart flutters in her chest, a ragged prayer flag in a harsh wind. Was it just a dream?

Some kinda meeting going on. There's gonna be trouble.

Again the pine tree falls slowly inside her head. Her skull feels on the verge of exploding; she presses her palms to her temples and closes her eyes as details trickle back. Did a mob really come and take Gordie into the Noon Woods? It occurs to her that she doesn't have to sit here wondering; she can walk down to the edge of the orchard right now and look. If it happened, the fallen tree and the car will still be there.

It's a slow and shaky process, but eventually she makes her way outside, shielding her eyes from a sky is so blue it hurts. Blue now, but not for long. A bank of sullen clouds lurks just beyond the ridge, threatening more rain. The ground is strewn with leaves and broken branches from last night's storm. Pain beating inside her head like a rusty clapper in a cracked bell, she starts downhill toward the orchard. Another ten yards and she'll round the jut of the pine woods and see the opening to the orchard. She wills there to be no fallen tree, no car trapped beneath it. Wills everything about last night to be a dream.

But the car is there, tree lying across the hood, caught in one of the apple trees exactly as she remembers. The sight brings a vast weight down on her shoulders. She plods forward and lays a hand on the car's muddy flank in a vain last hope that it's a figment of her imagination. But it's uncompromisingly solid, and warm from the sun.

As she looks past it toward the vast leafy wall of the Noon Woods, green and rustling in the morning light, the throbbing in her head becomes a raucous percussion of wood and stone punctuated by a wild, uncanny wailing. A shiver goes through her.

Three unbreathing things paid for only with breathing things. An apple tree, a hazel bush –

A sacred grove.

◆◆◆

Sprawled in a lawn chair in her back yard, May Vernon drifts in a fitful doze. The café was due to open three hours ago, but her and Pete are both so worn out this morning, they just stayed home. Ten o'clock in the morning, and Pete still asleep – why, she's never in all their lives known him to sleep past six! They've had too many late nights and that's a fact.

She's so tired she can't hardly remember a thing about the past few days; all she knows for sure is that something bad has passed them by, something wrong has been set right. Seems like she ought to be able to recollect more than that, but right now she's just too tuckered out. Glancing across the yard, she's surprised to see her grandsons asleep on the grass under the two little apple trees Pete planted when they was born. When did the boys get here? Usually when she keeps them for Holly it's at the café, where she can send them out back to bang pots and pans. They love banging things. They're all about commotion, those boys, and it makes her uneasy to see them lying there, limp as pillows that have lost their stuffing.

Beside them on the grass are the twig dollies they got from . . . who was it again? She can't recall; isn't that silly? Every time she tries to get ahold of the memory, it slinks out from under her touch like a cat that don't want to be petted.

She tries again. Last night, wasn't it? She was with her grandsons. Pete was there too, and lots of other folks. They were . . . Where were they? She knows there was music. And dancing. All on its own, as if remembering better than she can, her foot begins to tap out a lively rhythm.

She hates seeing the boys so still.

"Donny! Ronny! Wake up, sleepyheads!"

Pete always scoffs at her for talking to them like they can understand, but it's no different from him talking to that old hound dog of his.

"You boys come on over here and give Memaw a great big kiss."

Donny stirs first, then Ronny. Slowly they rise and wander across the grass to her chair. When May puts her arms around them, their eyes look elsewhere; they never meet anybody's gaze. Never mind. She hugs them close, kissing the warm little cheeks that smell of sunshine and fresh grass.

"Applecheeks," she says.

And for one dazzling, eternal instant she's standing in the middle of an orchard, surrounded by green rolling aisles of trees that stretch away as far as she can see. She's young, the way she is in her heart, slim and supple with hair bright as fire. The apples glow in the sunlight, the most beautiful red apples she's ever seen. As she reaches out to pluck one from its branch, it comes to her that she is not only the girl in the orchard but the tree as well, not only the girl and the tree but the apple too, not only the girl and the tree and the apple but the high sweet children's voices faintly audible inside the ripe red sphere in her hand, the sound of her grandsons singing.

◆◆◆

Goddess candles. Healing crystals. Eucalyptus breath mints. Herbal soap. Handwoven bookmarks.

For the fourth time in an hour Morgan rearranges the sales counter display, wondering how many different ways there are to display five objects. No doubt it's the simplest kind of math problem, but right now she's too distracted to solve it. She's well aware that fiddling with the counter display is a substitute for what she'd really like to do, which is straighten out the mess in Durwood.

Which by every logical measure should have sorted itself out by now. The loggers have departed, and so has the bad weather. Yes, the power's still out from last night, but most of the local businesses have brought out their oil lamps (a Durwood staple) and opened their doors. There's traffic on the streets and people seem to be going about their daily business. Nonetheless, things aren't right.

In Morgan's opinion, the most telling factor is the reshuffling that's happened since the ritual. Durwood's population still consists of two groups; that hasn't changed. But instead of separating locals and newcomers, the line has shifted to divide those who participated in the ritual from those who skipped it.

Call them Group A and Group B. Group A comprises the majority of the Durwood community including the children, most of whom are still hanging onto the twig dolls handed out at the ritual. Group A . . . well, it's hard to put her finger on it. It's not so much *what* they're saying or doing as *how* they're saying and doing it – the uncharacteristically listless, preoccupied manner they share. Nick, still in bed and showing no sign of ever getting up, is in Group A.

Then there's Group B, those who didn't attend the ritual. She tallies up them up. Obviously Gordie Durwood and his despicable lawyer; doubtless Jared Gorton and his buddies. Herself, Ben and Molly Upshaw, a handful of others who were disinclined or indisposed. In this last category is Jared's mother, as Morgan discovers when the old lady shows up at the store in search of a remedy for her husband's bad back.

"You didn't go to the ritual, Ada?"

"Naw, honey, what with Earl's back and all. Shelby went, and Hubbard had somethin else he needed to do, so we kept the baby for em."

Morgan makes a mental note: Shelby, Group A; Hub, Group B.

"Bad back . . . um, let's see. Have you asked Sally what she recommends?"

"Well, she usually gives Earl a little bottle of stuff to rub on it. But I ain't seen her. Hardware & General's closed up tight."

Sally and CW. Group A.

"Let me try her at home." When Morgan picks up the phone, the dead silence on the line reminds her that of course the phones are out, along with the electricity. She sighs. "Think she's over at Jared's?"

Ada looks coy. "Ain't nobody seen Jared since a while."

"A while?"

"Oh . . . since round about Monday night."

Monday. The night of the ritual. "Ada, it's Thursday! Aren't you worried?" She can't help noticing Jared's doting mother looks anything but.

"Well, Darrell says he's down to Lenoir on business. But I got my doubts."

Morgan isn't following. "So . . . where do you think he is?"

"Layin low, most like." The sly satisfaction on Ada's face flowers into a smile of pure motherly pride. "Just in case the law's lookin to find out how Gordie Durwood come to get beat up so bad."

Now Morgan recalls Molly telling her about seeing Gordie Durwood in bad shape the day after the ritual. Jared and his buddies – that's no surprise. She still thinks Gordie deserved it. Handing Ada a jar of Tiger Balm in lieu of Sally's specialized potion, she returns the old lady's conspiratorial smile.

"Give my best to Earl, Ada – I hope this helps."

Her next visitor is Annie Sayles, pulling into the parking lot with her weekly delivery of organic vegetables. Up to now the drought has kept the yield pitifully low, so it's a wonderful surprise to see the truck bed overflowing with baskets of collards and okra, onions, pole beans, peppers, squash and tomatoes.

Morgan hurries outside. "Wow, Annie! Where did all this come from?"

"Once the rain come everthin perked right up." For once Annie isn't smiling. She rubs a hand over her face, her eyes dull and distant. "Ripened up so quick I couldn't get it all picked."

Group A, Morgan thinks. The characteristic lack of energy is glaringly obvious in Annie, who looks like an entirely different person when her face isn't animated by the desperate desire to please. Now she climbs out of the truck and stands staring at nothing, hard lines visible around her mouth and an unfamiliar set to her jaw. Spotting a familiar blond head inside the truck, Morgan goes over to the passenger window.

"Hi Susanna! How are you, honey?" When the child doesn't answer, she leans in. "Listen, I've got some of those date bars you like. Why don't you come inside and – "

Noticing what's in Susanna's lap, she forgets what she was saying. It's the first time she's seen one of those twig dolls up close, and it gives her a nasty shock. Did Vivian really make those things? What on earth was she thinking? Above the vine-wrapped twig body, this one's acorn head has split open to reveal a pale, protruding sprout that resembles a writhing tongue. Her gaze travels from the doll to Susanna's hollow cheeks, the pools of greenish shadow below her dazed eyes. The little girl's arms and legs look flimsier than the doll's, and her dress is filthy. Morgan forces a smile.

"Honey, can I see your doll a sec?"

Susanna doesn't answer. But when Morgan reaches through the window and tries to pry the thing from her grasp, she lets out an earsplitting screech.

"MINE!"

The sheer volume of the yell makes Morgan rercoil, but not before she's seen the scratches and gouges covering the child's scrawny outstretched arms, vividly reminding her of the wounds Nick brought home from the ritual. Examining the doll – oh, Goddess! – she finds the damn thing bristling with thorns. Those rusty stains on the Susanna's dress –

Annie appears beside her. "What's all that hollerin?"

Morgan brandishes the doll. "Annie, you can't let her play with this horrible thing! Look at the scratches on her arms! There's blood all over her dress!"

"Hush now," Annie tells the wailing child. "She ain't gonna steal your dolly." To Morgan: "You best give that back right now."

"But – "

"I said *right now*."

Annie with menace in her face and voice is as unnerving as Bambi baring a full set of shark's teeth. Reluctantly Morgan returns the doll.

"Annie, I really think – ow!" Just as she's relinquishing her grip a thorn sinks itself in her thumb. Annie marches around the truck and climbs in, slamming the door with a whump that rocks the vehicle on its wheels. Morgan hears herself stammer, "Wh-what about the v-veg – ?"

The roar of the engine drowns her out as the truck jerks into reverse, then shoots forward with a jolt that catapults some of the precariously balanced baskets into the air. Sucking on her bleeding thumb, which hurts like hell, Morgan sees eggplants and peppers hit the ground and bounce, ripe tomatoes explode on impact. She's so transfixed by the carnage that it's all she sees, until a shriek of brakes and a spatter of gravel make her look up just in time to see Annie narrowly avoid a head-on collision with Liz Wyatt's Jeep.

❋ 16 ❋

Within the confines of the eight-by-ten foot henhouse, the atmosphere can only be described as awkward.

Seated on the lumpy cot next to Liz, Morgan sneaks another look at Tyner Durwood. He's not exactly what she expected. All this time she's been harboring the image of a pale invalid with soulful, suffering eyes, and it turns out she was half right: he's pale. As for his eyes – well, she got only the briefest glance from them when Liz ushered her into the shack, but for *soulful and suffering*, substitute *bleary and hostile*. He hasn't looked at her again, nor has he uttered a single word. He just sits glowering in his wheelchair. He's wearing a teeshirt, tattered jeans, and pristine moccasins. His hair, the same coppery red as Sally's, is dirty and too long, and he needs a shave.

He's also drunk; the jar on the desk next to his computer obviously contains moonshine. When he picks it up, Morgan notes the tattoo that wends its way from his wrist to his elbow in an intricate pattern of oak leaves and acorns, like the one Jared Gorton has.

The *thunk* with which he sets the jar down on the desk seems to jumpstart Liz into speech.

"We need to find out what they've done with him," she says.

Morgan shifts on the cot. An hour ago, when Liz showed up at the store with some garbled tale about Gordie Durwood being kidnapped by a local mob, she hadn't known what to think. But because Liz insisted that she could trust Morgan as someone who hadn't been among the kidnappers – and because Liz kept insisting on some kind of crisis conference involving the two of them and Tyner Durwood – and because Liz seems like the kind of person who almost never insists on things – Morgan has acquiesced.

She still doesn't know what to think. Her right thumb throbs where it was punctured by Susanna Sayles's nasty little doll. "Maybe they were just trying to scare him," she says.

Liz gives her a bleak glance. "Maybe. But I went out to the oak a couple of hours ago. The rope they used to tie him to the tree is there, but he's gone."

"Maybe he went back to Asheville." It's all Morgan can think of.

"Then he must've walked there, because his car's still sitting in the field. And there's another thing. The oak – it's got a bunch of brand new leaves. Red leaves."

"Dammit, Liz!" So Tyner can talk after all. "A lotta leaves sprout red, you know that. They green up later on."

"Okay, but why is a dead tree making new leaves?"

No response; he's done with the conversation. Not wanting to dwell on whatever point Liz is trying to make about the red leaves, Morgan gives a little attention-getting cough.

"For now, can we just stick with what we know? Tell us again who was there."

"Everybody. Well, a lot of people, anyway . . . Pete, Mae, Sally, CW, Ward and Verna, Larkie, the Sayleses, the Lewises, the Reeses, Burley, Skip . . . Star, Tamara, Vivian, Chad . . . Mariela Everdale . . . "

"I'm having a really hard time picturing any of those people doing anything violent," Morgan says, and Liz shuts her eyes briefly.

"They weren't . . . themselves."

"Meaning – ?"

"I don't know how else to say it."

Not themselves. A memory of Russ and Star flickers at the back of Morgan's mind. Stick to what we know, she thinks. "So they just *took* him?"

"They took him to Roan's Oak. There was a lot of yelling, something about breaking ancient laws."

"And then what?"

"I . . . don't remember."

Liz doesn't look well. Her left eye is horribly bloodshot and her head tilts to one side. Morgan can't help wondering if maybe she's had a stroke – if this whole story is some kind of delusion. It seems more likely than the idea of their friends and neighbors doing Gordie actual harm.

From Tyner's corner comes the sound of the moonshine jar being set down hard, like a gavel signaling *Court dismissed*. It couldn't be more obvious that he considers this powwow an imposition. Some perverse impulse makes Morgan lean toward him and say sweetly, "Any ideas about what your father and sister might have done with your cousin? Because if it's anything that might constitute a crime, it would be good if we found him before the police do."

His sullen face doesn't alter, but he begins to scratch his tattooed arm ferociously, and all at once she sees a boy worried sick about his loved ones.

"I don't know what they done with him." He's glaring at the moonshine jar. "But I know they wouldn't of done nothin if you and your friends hadn't of got em all riled up with your damn ritual."

The accusation catches Morgan off guard.

"The ritual? Listen, there's no way the ritual could have – I mean, I wasn't there, but I do know exactly what the ritual consisted of, and – and I can promise you there was nothing about – anyway, that was three days ago, and – and –"

She stalls out, remembering Group A and Group B. Those who attended the ritual, those who didn't. Group A – they're different now.

Not themselves.

Tyner's finally looking at her, a cold stare she can't sustain. Her hands creep together for comfort in her lap.

"I don't . . . I just don't see how the ritual could have possibly. . . "

"Sally told Tyne they were planning to take the stone out of Roan's Oak," Liz says. "Something about symbolically opening the door to the otherworld."

"Yes, but the key word is *symbolic*. It's not like anything actually – I mean, yes, symbolic actions are powerful. But not in that sense."

No one says anything, and in the extended silence Morgan has time to consider her own words. Hasn't she spent the past decade embracing the idea that symbolic actions are powerful in *exactly* that sense – that they can and do effect real change in the real world? Group A. The people who attended the ritual. The same ones who kidnapped Gordie. She summons logic to combat the dread beginning to stir inside her.

"How could taking a stone out of a tree make anybody do something they're not normally capable of?"

No one answers. Finally Liz says, "You could ask that question. Or you could ask why someone felt it necessary to put the stone in the tree in the first place."

Tyner refuels from his jar. "Granny claimed Roan put it there. Went to the Bright Land and closed the door behind him."

"Just traipsed off and abandoned everybody?" Morgan says. "I mean, I know it's just a legend, but that doesn't make sense. Why would – wait, Nick and I talked about this. If Roan really did discover a source of earth energy in the Noon Woods, why would he just shut it down? I mean, that was his *thing*. What Nick thinks is that it might not have been Roan who closed the door – that there may have been people in the community who opposed the idea of Durwood as anything more than ordinary, who didn't want to take part in – in –"

"Something that scared them," Liz says.

"Yes. So maybe there was a showdown, some kind of coup. They kill Roan, seal the opening in the tree, spread the rumor that he's abandoned them." Hearing herself blithely float Nick's theory, Morgan reminds herself it's based solely on a few fragments of legend and the weird phenomenon of a stone stuck in a tree.

You could ask why someone felt it necessary to put the stone in the tree in the first place.

Okay, I'm asking. What was Roan doing at the oak? Something that scared people – but what? Why block the door to the Bright Land, a place described in folklore as a realm of dancing and merrymaking, the very antithesis of threatening? And then she remembers that folklore warns of a dark side as well. Visitors are told not to eat the food, not to touch the inhabitants . . . Those who violate the taboo are trapped there. Forever. Morgan thinks of the people in Group A, the ones who aren't really *there* behind their eyes. Remembers Russ wielding his sledgehammer, Star's famished smile.

"The colors."

She doesn't even know she's spoken aloud until she sees the others looking at her. She gives a self-conscious little shrug. "Something Star said. *The colors.* And then she said, *It's still not right.* This was after she and Russ had turned their beautiful restaurant into some kind of wacked-out terrarium. I don't know what she meant."

"I do," Liz says.

◆ ◆ ◆

In his room on the second floor of Abundance, Nick crouches in the corner by the bookcase, as far as he can get from the windows. Even swaddled in the quilt, he can't stop shivering. He's never been so cold. From the angle of the light outside, he can see it's late afternoon.

Afternoon . . . noon . . .

Annwn.

There's a constant rustling in his ears, so distracting he can't seem to hold a thought for more than a few seconds. At first he blamed it on the wind, but it isn't the wind. It's coming from inside him – the whisper of roots and branches ceaselessly weaving a leafy, sunlit sphere inside his head, a tangle of green growth that blooms and flourishes in a seductive, irresistible summons from roots buried in darkness. He can feel restless energy pulsing through him, transforming his bones to a fretwork of twigs and stems, his mind to a dazzle of sunlight filtered through the infinite leaves whose shadows slide through his head, across his flesh

And he jolts into awareness to find himself curled into a ball, shuddering from that intimacy of that strange caress. The walls and ceiling seem flat and unreal, a flimsy overlay on the relentless striving of green growth that surrounds him. As he lies staring up at the bookcase, the lettered spines on the lower shelves swim into focus.

Magic of the Greenwood.

Ancient Magicks for a New Age.

Secrets of Natural Magic.

Magic. It's a word that used to thrill him with delight and now induces shivers of a different kind. What's happening to him? Desperately he tries to anchor himself with facts. He's Nick Rusk, twenty-three years old. Law school dropout, pretender to the title of King of the Greenwood, newbie high priest and amateur shaman. But right now, what he feels like most is Mickey Mouse in *The Sorcerer's Apprentice.*

Among the gaudy paperbacks a single anomalous binding catches his eye. Navy blue, banded with red and gold – a lone law book that somehow escaped his purge. Pulling the quilt more tightly around him, he sits up and retrieves it, letting it fall open in his hand. Phrases float up at him from the thick blocks of print.

Burden of proof.

Directed verdict.

Consequences of discovery.

Coerced resolution of a controversy.

The measured terms seem to radiate a sense and symmetry that were lost on him this past year, when the very idea of practicing law seemed like a death sentence for his soul.

A society governed by the rule of law imposes severe limitations on the use of coercion.

His racing pulse begins to slow. This object, which caused him such misery for the better part of a year, now seems like a protective talisman – an irony he can appreciate without enjoying it. But the whisper, the rustle that isn't the wind, is still in his head, murmuring to every cell in his body. He forces his attention back to the printed page.

Indeed, the coercion available through civil litigation is actually so feeble that someone determined to resist can thwart all but the most energetic efforts to enforce a civil judgment.

The dry words hold out the promise of a definable world from which all ambiguity has been banished, all mystery expunged.

Contributory negligence.

Substantive equitable principles.

Huddled there in the corner, muttering the sonorous phrases under his breath, the young man could be a medieval magician repeating an incantation against evil spirits.

◆◆◆

Inside the henhouse, a series of beeps and whirs from Tyner's computer equipment announces the return of electrical power to Durwood.

"The colors," Liz is saying. "What your friend was trying to describe is something that language isn't framed to express. Something for which there are literally no words."

"The ineffable," Morgan says.

"Yes. We have abstract terms for the concept, but no actual words that can capture the thing itself – none designed to describe experiences that don't take place in the narrow band of reality where we normally operate. And that deficit is crucial. Because without words, we can't think clearly about those experiences, so it's easier to act as if they don't happen. Except when they do."

Flurries of keyboarding are coming from Tyner's corner, interspersed with clicks of the mouse. Late afternoon sunlight slants through the henhouse window, emblazoning a golden parallelogram on the opposite wall.

"A woman in my coven met an angel," Morgan says. "Or something she thought was an angel."

"That's the hallmark of these experiences. They're unique, tailored to each individual's expectations. But what they have in common is a quality that mystics call 'oceanic,' meaning the expansion of your sense of self, the feeling of being part of a whole. Visitors to Faery traditionally describe what happens there as music, dancing, feasting – all activities that let you escape the limits of your identity.

"When it's over, everyday existence feels like being imprisoned in a tight little box. You're crippled, like the bride who's stolen by the faeries on her wedding night and comes back seven years later unable to walk, because she's danced her feet off in Faery. The Otherworld has robbed her of her capacity to lead a normal life. In Celtic folklore it's called *the pining*."

"So when Star talks about 'the colors' – "

"She's trying to describe what happened to her without the appropriate words," Liz says. "And without words to give them weight, the details of these experiences are almost impossible to hold onto. They have no substance; they just slip away, like a dream. You can't help forgetting, but the forgetting breaks your heart. And that's what you remember. You remember the loss."

Something in her voice makes Morgan say, "Is this something you've experienced, Liz?"

"Yes. And cutting myself and painting in my own blood seemed like a ridiculously small price to pay for the chance to have it happen again." Liz takes a deep breath. "Morgan, I need to ask you – did Nick's ritual use blood?"

"Huh?"

"Nick's ritual. Did it use blood?"

"Did . . . Of course not! Well, I didn't see the final version; we were in such a rush. But I can't imagine – "

"Remember Roan's bargain with the white doe? He got certain powers in exchange for one drop of blood a year. Most legends are rooted in some fragment of fact. So why not this one?"

Morgan's lost. "What fact? What are you talking about?"

"Listen. The day the loggers first showed up, the day that bad storm blew in – Sally said something I haven't been able to get out of my mind. Something about blood, about its value."

Without turning from his computer, Tyner says, "It ain't the blood itself, it's the value of the gift."

"That was it."

"What does that mean?" Morgan says.

He shrugs. "Just something Granny Dee said."

"Said – in relation to what?"

"Don't matter."

"Tyne." There's a frayed edge to Liz's voice. "It might matter."

"Okay, okay. It was one time when Granny took Sally to the oak. I wasn't supposed to, but I followed them. Granny had a newborn's birthcord. She hung it on the tree and pricked Sally's finger with a holly leaf and squeezed out a couple drops of blood onto the roots."

"Blood on the roots? Why?"

"As a gift, I reckon."

"What was it again?" Morgan asks.

Liz looks at Tyner. He rolls his eyes.

"Ain't the blood itself, it's what it means to you. The value of the gift."

Morgan grimaces. "So are we thinking Roan was doing something at the oak that involved blood? Like some version of Santería?"

"Santería uses chickens and goats," he says. "We're talkin about human blood."

Human blood? Morgan's insides do a somersault in slow motion. Tyner's been typing and clicking all this time; now a page emerges from the printer and he hands it to her. Shakily she reads it aloud:

"Blood has been used for magical purposes for as far back as there has been any kind of human society. The most famous adepts of blood sacrifice, especially human sacrifice, were Aztec and Mayan priests and the Celtic Druids. Blood is important in magic because blood is life. It is energy, the life force at its most basic. So Demons are attracted to it. It enables them to take form. It is quite a sight to see Demons flocking to the fresh corpses of the newly killed on the battlefield – "

She breaks off. "Whoa, hold on. Demons?"

"Just finish it," Tyner says.

"A skilled magician can dramatically improve the energy of a spell by capturing the evaporating essence of a dying body. Human blood is without a doubt the most powerful agent for a magical working. While the ideal sacrifice is the best physical specimen available, there is always a risk that the power released may be too great to control. An alternative is to use a pure offering like a child, where the energy is still in its potential form."

By the time Morgan finishes, she's out of breath and her injured thumb is throbbing. Down at the bottom of the page is the name of the website where Tyner found this little gem: *www.dark-basement-of-the-soul*.

"Is this some kind of sick joke?" she says. "I thought we were dealing with mystical experience here. What do demons have to do with it?"

"It's the blood that's important," Liz says. "Blood is life force, energy. If we lose too much, we die. And otherworld beings – whether you call them demons or angels or faeries or spirits – are said to hunger for physical energy in the same way that humans hunger for spiritual sustenance."

"Listen." Tyner's found another website. "In Black Magick, which is used for destructive purposes, the minimum sacrifice required is a large amount of blood from a pure soul, enough to kill the victim, plus one chalice of blood from another pure soul."

"Okay, stop." Morgan's heard enough. *Dark basement* indeed; the name makes her think of a bunch of grimy little boys crouched under musty cellar stairs with a flashlight, egging one another on to increasingly nasty games. And this discussion seems to have gotten similarly out of hand, linking Roan Durwood's mysterious doings in the Noon Woods with an old mountain woman's cryptic remarks about blood to come up with an improbable case for human sacrifice.

She's well aware that such practices were performed by the Atzecs, the Mayans, and the Druids. Even in the Bible, Abraham doesn't seem particularly shocked when Yahweh tells him to sacrifice Isaac, even if the old bugger turns out to be only kidding. But those events belong to the ancient world, not to the America of two hundred years ago, where Thomas Jefferson was playing his violin. There's no reason to believe that Roan Durwood's activities at the oak involved blood at all, much less human blood, any more than there's reason to believe that Gordie has been harmed by –

Tyner smacks the arm of his chair, interrupting her mental flurry. "Hell, it's right here in front of us! Look at what the website says. *The best physical specimen.* Who would that be in Durwood? Who was the strongest and the fastest and the bravest? That's what Granny always said. She used those same words every time. He was the strongest and the fastest and the bravest."

There's a beat of silence before Morgan says reluctantly, "Who?"

"The King of the damn Greenwood, that's who!"

"I'm not following you."

"The best physical specimen. The ideal sacrifice!"

"Wait. Stop." Is he suggesting that the winner of the Midsummer race was sacrificed by the Durwood community? Now they've really gone off the deep end. "That's absurd," she says shakily.

"Listen. Originally they didn't run the race in town." Tyner's leaning forward, gripping the arms of his chair. "They used to run it in the Noon Woods. They raced to Roan's Oak."

The sun chooses that instant to sink behind the mountains, plunging the shack into shadow except for the bright computer screen. Morgan shivers, remembering what Molly told her about Tyner's accident.

A bunch of drunk teenage boys racing to Roan's Oak. One of them fell.

Normally at this time of day she'd be settling down in her cozy living room, considering a fire and a cup of herbal tea. Instead she's sitting in a henhouse discussing human sacrifice with Tyner Durwood, who almost died falling from the oak on Midsummer's Eve.

He was the strongest and the fastest and the bravest.

"None of that makes any sense!" She hears her voice squeak on the last word. "I mean, if winning the race meant you were going to die – why would you race in the first place, let alone try to win?"

His eyes reflect the glow from the screen. "That's why he had to be the bravest. He had to be willing to keep Roan's bargain. And his reward was that he went to the Bright Land, where everything is the opposite of here. When it's night here, it's day in the Bright Land. When it's winter here, it's summer there. And when you die in this world . . ."

"You wake in the Bright Land," Liz says. "Tir-na-n'Og, where the air smells of apple blossom and there's no such thing as time or sorrow."

Morgan's no longer listening. She's thinking about last night's apparent abduction of Gordie Durwood. Has something irrevocable happened in Durwood, some kind of unspeakable act perpetrated by ordinary people gone mad?

"But why Gordie?"

"Not the strongest or the fastest," Tyner says. "And for damn sure not the bravest. But maybe he was the best they could do."

Even in the murky light, Morgan can see he's not kidding. "Are you saying they took him to the oak as some kind of . . . offering?"

He shrugs. "Why else?"

❋17❋

Officers Jay Bessey and Darlene Talford are driving down the dark mountain road after a long day spent chasing a bad lead on the meth operation they've been trying to nail for two months.

"I'll be glad to get home," Darlene says as the lights of the valley appear below. "Wait till I tell my kids we saw a bear."

"Gonna tell em how you screamed like a little girl?"

"I didn't scream. I made a noise, is all."

"Yeah. A noise that sounded an awful lot like a scream."

She flips him off and he chuckles. The radio crackles. "This here's Ricky. Ricky calling Officers Bessey and Talford. Come in, Jay and Day."

"Hey there, Ricky. What's up?"

"Where y'all at right now?"

"Heading home."

"Need y'all to turn around, Jay. Got a missing person report up yonder in Durwood."

"Durwood?" Jay slows the car, looking for a likely spot to negotiate the turn. "Back in there where they been having those bad storms?"

"That's the place. Try and get there quick as you can, huh?" Even through the hiss of static they can hear that Ricky's rattled. "This one sounds bad."

◆◆◆

It's nearly nine PM when Morgan pulls into the parking lot at Abundance, her brain still running a loop of the bizarre discussion in Tyner's study. She's so distracted that it takes her a moment to notice that every light in the store is ablaze. With the power out, she'd completely forgotten she'd left them on. Now the place looks like Christmas, New Year's, and the Fourth of July all rolled into one. Except for Nick's quarters, which are still dark.

Guilt smites her. She'd checked on him briefly yesterday, long enough to smear some antibiotic cream on his wounds and leave him an energy bar in case he felt like eating – but she hasn't checked on him at all today. She should have been paying more attention, making sure he's okay. She tells herself he's an adult and she's been trying to give him space. But there's a niggling sense that she's been punishing him for the circumstances surrounding those scratches on his back, letting jealousy play a role in her behavior.

The guilt is approaching seismic levels as she climbs the stairs to his quarters and gives a perfunctory knock before pushing the door open to peer inside.

"Nick?" There's no answer, but in the far corner of the dark room she sees something move. "Nicky?" A flip of the light switch reveals him crouched in the corner, flinching from the sudden illumination. "What on earth are you doing?"

One hand shielding his eyes, he mumbles something that sounds like a protest, and she hits the switch to restore the dark. "Are you sick?"

"Dunno."

She picks her way across the dim room. His forehead is scalding to her touch, triggering a memory of nursing him through the flu when he was nine, his parents off on a European jaunt. Those scratches – have they gotten infected?

"Okay, come on. Get up."

"Wha . . . "

"We're going my house, where I can take proper care of you."

When she hauls him to his feet he doesn't protest, but their progress is impeded by his refusal to relinquish the quilt wrapped around him. As they make their way slowly to the door Morgan's eyes have plenty of time to adjust to the dark. The room is a pig sty, the floor littered with clothes, books – her foot skids on something and she almost loses her balance. Looking down in annoyance, she identifies the culprit, a scuffed sheet of paper, and bends down to retrieve it. The spill of moonlight from the open door is enough to show her the antiquated font at the top of the page.

Raleigh Register, June 13, 1811.

It looks like a piece of the internet research Nick's been doing on Roan Durwood. Making a mental note to read it later, she stuffs it into her jeans pocket and herds him out the door.

The two-block drive to her house takes only a few moments. Inside, Nick lurches to the guest room and collapses across the bed with a groan while Morgan hovers over him. What he really needs is one of Sally's poultices. But where is Sally? She suppresses a sense of the world flying apart and concentrates on the practical.

"Roll over, huh? I need to look at your back."

Instead he grabs her hand and holds it tightly. After a few moments, when it become apparent he's not going to let go. Morgan sits down on the bed beside him. She can't help noticing he smells bad. His icy fingers cling to hers.

"Warm," he whispers. "You're so warm."

"Nick, you have a fever. I'm sure those scratches are infected. We need to – "

Her voice trails off as he twists around and puts his head in her lap. Automatically her free hand begins to smooth his hair. He nuzzles closer, encircling her waist with both arms and pressing his face against her. He radiates a feverish heat and at the same time she can feel him shivering, his whole body thrumming like an idling engine. As she strokes his hair, letting the dark strands slide through her fingers, hyperaware of the ebb and flow of his breath against the flesh of her belly, the shivering seems to spread from him to her.

She swallows. "Nick . . . listen . . . "

"Just stay with me," comes his muffled voice. "Please."

Officer Jay Bessey pretends to be writing in his notebook, but he's really watching the husband pace back and forth.

"It doesn't make any sense," Upshaw says again, with a glance at his glassy-eyed wife, who sits on the sofa next to Darlene. "The power was out, so we took the baby out into the back yard. We put down a blanket on the grass. We both fell asleep. When we woke up, she was just – gone."

Mrs Upshaw moans; Darlene puts an arm around her and squeezes. "Don't you fret, hon. We're gonna find your baby girl."

Good, thinks Jay. Keep her outta my hair and let me concentrate on him. In Jay's experience, if a parent is involved with the disappearance of a little one, it's usually a dad. "You see anybody hanging around?" he asks.

The dad shakes his head.

"We were being watched," the mom says. "I thought I was dreaming, but now – "

"Watched? By who? You see somebody?"

"N-not exactly."

"Man or woman?"

"I don't know! I couldn't wake up! When I did, it was dark and – and when I looked in the basket – "

The last word spirals into a wail, which she muffles in Darlene's uniformed chest.

Jay purses his lips. Yeah, that last touch definitely sets this case apart from the others. In his previous cases, nobody replaced the stolen kid with a freaky doll made out of twigs. The parents said it was lying in the baby's basket, swaddled in her blanket. He has it in the squad car now. Creepy looking thing. No way it'll yield a fingerprint.

He turns back to the dad. "You sure you didn't see anybody?"

Dad's tongue darts across his lips. "Uh, no. I was completely out."

Jumpy, Jay thinks. "Who lives next door?" he asks the mom.

"Nobody. It's a business, a pottery studio that belongs to a friend of ours. Tamara."

"Any chance it was her you saw?"

"I told you, I didn't really see anything. It was more like whispering, and rustling. Like people trying not to make any noise."

"People? So you're thinking there might have been more than one?"

"Maybe . . . I don't know!" She starts to cry again. Darlene pats her shoulder.

Jay scribbles in his notebook. "Folks, anybody you can think of who might have a grudge against you? Maybe somebody you had a fight with recently?"

Dad stops pacing. "There's a local woman, Bonnie Durwood. Her own baby died, some kind of awful birth defect. I think it had a bad effect on her mentally. Last week I had Laurel with me at the grocery store, and she followed us around the whole time, and out into the street afterward. If I hadn't told her to get lost, I think she would have followed us home."

Jay starts a fresh page in his notebook. "Durwood, same as the town? What's her address?"

"What about Annie?" Mom says suddenly, and Dad winces.

"For chrissake, Mol – "

"Who's Annie?" Jay says.

"A local woman. She's been working for us at the store." Mom wipes tears from her cheeks with the back of her hand. "We had to fire her yesterday. It wasn't friendly."

"Stealing," Dad mutters. But seeing the look his wife sends him, Jay doesn't think so.

"What's her last name?"

"Sayles."

"Okay. We'll talk to her too."

◆ ◆ ◆

The phone in the kitchen is ringing, dragging Morgan out of a delicious, dreamless torpor. She opens her eyes on a dark room that's not her bedroom, bisected by light from a half open door. Where . . . ? Reaching out blindly, she encounters a bare arm that brings her fully awake. She snatches her hand away as if scorched.

Oh, good Goddess. Nick.

A comforting embrace changing into a passionate one, a shuddering child transformed into a grown and very potent man. Morgan feels her face burning. She's actually blushing; how stupid is that?

We made love. So what? Two consenting adults.

But making love is entirely the wrong phrase for that mindless, savage coupling devoid of tenderness or affection, that frenzy of animal thrusts and grunts and moans. She can recall the bed frame banging against the wall as Nick pistoned into her, the squeals with which she urged him on. With the need assuaged, the act seems deeply sordid.

The phone's still ringing. Avoiding contact with the inert figure sprawled across the bed, she yanks on her jeans and stumbles out of the guest room to the kitchen.

"Uh, Miz Edwards?" The voice at the other end of the line is unmistakably local. "This here's Hubbard Reese. Listen, I thought you'd wanna know . . . The, uh, folks at the craft store – their, uh, their baby's gone missin."

"The folks at – you mean Ben and Molly?"

"Yes, ma'am."

"Their baby's *missing*? Hub, what do you mean?"

"Ma'am, somebody's done took her. The cops was just next door to Annie's house, askin questions."

"Asking Annie questions? Why?"

"I dunno, ma'am. I just thought since they's friends of yours and all, you'd wanna know."

Hanging up the phone Morgan steadies herself on the kitchen counter, struggling to absorb Hub's news. Things are happening too fast. Laurel missing? *Somebody's done took her.* Somebody – but who?

A fretful voice drifts down the hall. "Morgan . . .?"

"I'm in the kitchen." This latest shock seems to render their sexual encounter insignificant. "Nick, listen, that was Hub. The Upshaws' baby is missing. They think someone took her."

"Huh?" He stands swaying in the door of the guestroom, hollow-eyed beneath his dirty, tangled hair, wrapped in that filthy quilt beneath which she's well aware that he's naked. Her one and only nephew, who has recently given her the most intense orgasm of her life.

She doesn't have time to think about that now.

"Didn't you hear me? Somebody took Ben and Molly's baby! We have to go over to the Upshaws'. The police are here; there's bound to be a search party. We should be out looking for Laurel right now!"

She's surprised to find tears running down her face. It's overload, a reaction to the tension surrounding the logging, this afternoon's surreal discussion with Tyner and Liz, the sex with Nick, now the horrifying news about little Laurel – all of it happening since the ritual, since the opening of the doorway.

Seeing him flinch, she makes an effort to soften her tone. "Listen, you should probably stay here and rest. I'll be home later. And then we really need to see about your back."

Leaving the house she's only peripherally aware of the night sky streaming with clouds, the pale flowering dogwood in the yard standing out against the black bulk of shrubbery. It's hard to think clearly; the baby's disappearance overrides all else. She decides to take the car. The Upshaws' apartment is only a few blocks away, but it will be quicker than walking. And if there's some kind of search operation, they'll need cars.

The dashboard clock reads ten minutes past midnight. The streets are deserted, as they always are at this time of night. Passing Sundial, she's surprised to see lights inside; the restaurant normally stops serving at nine. She slows the car to catch a glimpse of the interior, seeing movement among the twinkling lights – a crowd of people with upraised arms. It's too dim to recognize anyone, but there must be a dozen of them. And there's music – or at least a fiddle squall that's too discordant to be called a melody, a shrill thread escaping into the night air. It seems inconceivable that they don't know about the missing baby – and yet they obviously don't, because they appear to be . . . dancing. Bodies sway against a background of dark, gleaming foliage that moves restlessly in the wind.

It looks as if Russ has removed the entire back wall. *That sense of connection with the natural world.* She thinks of Star's desperate smile, eyes wet with longing. *Really let it in, you know. Do whatever it takes.*

In folklore it's called the pining.

And then she's past, the outlandish scene in the restaurant slipping behind her, leaving her with a delayed impression that the withered vines and brambles of the newly decorated interior have burst feverishly, impossibly into riotous greenery.

The police car is parked in front of Hands On. She pulls up behind it, bracing herself to face Molly and Ben. This is horrible, unthinkable. Who in Durwood would kidnap a baby? As she gets out of the car, a fragment from the discussion in the henhouse comes back to her.

You may want to use a pure offering.
Like a child.

❊18❊

In Jay Bessey's opinion, things in this strange little town are getting stranger by the minute.

This Bonnie Durwood, mentioned by the Upshaw dad as a viable suspect, proves on interview to be a virtual zombie, as does her husband. A search of their house yields no sign of the missing baby. And rousting out Annie Sayles, Jay discovers she's a zombie too, listening slack-jawed to his questions while her small daughter clings to her leg.

Then he sees that the kid's holding a creepy twig doll like the one the kidnapper left in the baby's cradle. Now he's getting somewhere.

"Ma'am? Where'd your little girl get that doll?"

"Oh . . . They done give em out at that shindig in the woods the other night. All the kids got one."

"What shindig in the woods?"

"Some rally type thing to stop the loggin. Them Bunny Dancer folks put it together."

"Bunny Dancer folks – who are they, ma'am?"

"You know, rich hippie types. Come here from Asheville and such."

"They the ones gave out the dolls?"

"I didn't see."

"Well, who all was at the rally?"

"Most everbody."

"The Upshaws? They there?"

"Didn't see em."

"They fired you from their store, huh? How come?"

The slack face doesn't change. "Husband was horny. New baby and all, wife wouldn't give him none, so he come sniffin round me."

Jay's inclined to believe her. As the night wears on, he starts to think that pretty much everybody in Durwood must be stoned. His conclusion is based on people's reactions to the news of the missing baby – most of them shake their heads and say oh my and what a shame, but their expressions of concern strike Jay as purely perfunctory. Not so much like they're hiding anything; more like their minds are somewhere else, and his questions no more than the inconsequential buzzing of a fly.

But he can't piss-test to the whole town, so he lets them be and concentrates on talking to the few people who seem normal. Among these is a young man named Darrell Reese, who blurts out that it's not just the baby who's missing. There's somebody else as well – his partner at the local service station. Jay makes a note of this fact.

Another person who seems normal is a lady named Morgan Edwards, fortyish and very easy on the eyes, whom Jay encounters when he checks in with Darlene and the Upshaws around one AM.

"Is there going to be a search party?" Mrs Edwards is brewing a pot of flowery-smelling tea for the Upshaws, who sit together on the sofa looking dazed.

"Yes ma'am, I'm working on that. I've radioed for a dog team, but it'll be a little while before they get here. Seems like we got somebody else missing too."

"Somebody else?"

"Fella name of – " Jay consults his notes. "Jared Gorton."

Planting herself squarely in front of him, steaming teapot in hand, she seems reassuringly concerned. "What can I do to help?"

"You could start," Jay says, "by telling me why most folks around here don't seem to give a damn about any of this."

Her gaze wavers. "Oh. Well. We've had a . . . a . . . situation recently."

"What kind of situation?"

"Um, well, there's been a lot of friction over some proposed logging in the local forest. A man who used to live here seems to think he has a claim on the land. He brought in a logging crew and there were a couple of nasty confrontations, and now . . . well, now he's missing."

Another one? That makes three people missing. This Jared Gorton has already made it to the top of Jay's suspect list for snatching the baby; the other guy is likely his accomplice.

"What's his name?"

"Gordie Durwood."

Jay turns to Darlene. "I'm guessing Gorton and him partnered up on this."

Mrs Edwards is shaking her head. "That's impossible."

"People can surprise you, ma'am, specially with crimes like this."

"I'm sure that's true. But Jared hates Gordie. Everybody in Durwood does, because of the logging. In fact – " She stops abruptly.

"In fact what, ma'am?"

"I can't really say, I wasn't there."

"Wasn't where?"

"Look, Officer, I don't want to repeat what's probably just gossip. Let's just say people around here have made their hostility to Gordie pretty clear."

Jay yanks out his notebook. "Ma'am, I'm gonna need you to be just a tad more specific."

◆◆◆

"That's it! That's the missin piece!" Excitement has transformed Tyner into an entirely different person; for the first time, Morgan can see a resemblance to Sally.

"I got it wrong," he's saying. "It wasn't the King of the Greenwood who was the sacrifice. He was the top dog, the man who could pick any woman he wanted. The sacrifice was the child, *their* child, conceived that night in the Noon Woods. One drop of blood a year, remember? One drop, one life. Roan was usin the kids! That's gotta be the reason they ended up shuttin him down!"

There's a knot in Morgan's belly and her head hurts. It's going on two in the morning, but having more or less stonewalled the nice police officer she couldn't just sit around at the Upshaws doing nothing. And she isn't prepared to face Nick yet, so she headed back out to the Durwoods' to see if Liz was still there.

She is. Her head is still on crooked and her left eye is red as a ripe tomato, but to Morgan she seems less spacy than earlier this evening.

"To keep Roan's bargain, they had to trade somethin of value for what they got from the Bright Land," Tyner's saying now. "And that somethin was the child."

Morgan rubs her pounding temples. "That doesn't seem possible. I mean, even if Roan wanted to do such a thing, why would the rest of them go along?"

"Maybe he told em he was sendin the kids to the Bright Land," Tyner says. "Maybe they wanted to believe him so they could keep on gettin their fix of faery dust or whatever. But I'm guessin they went along mostly because of the bargain. They were doin what they needed to do to protect Durwood. I mean, tonight – don't you think that's why somebody took the baby?"

"But if they already had Gordie – "

"Somethin of value, remember? Maybe Gordie don't measure up." He sings under his breath: "*The first doe he missed, the second he kissed, the third doe went where nobody wist, among the leaves so green-O.*"

Half whispered and half sung, the words send a shudder through Morgan. As she rubs her cold hands together, something crinkles in the pocket of her jeans. She pulls out the bedraggled paper she stumbled across, literally, in Nick's quarters.

"Oh, I forgot about this. I think it's some research Nick did on Roan. It might – might – "

Reminded of what she was doing with Nick only a few short hours ago (as far as she can remember they hadn't even kissed, just succumbed to that frenzied primal coupling) she has to stop and pull herself together before going on.

"What I'm trying to say is . . . it might shed some light. Listen.

"Raleigh Register, June 13, 1811. A convicted man escaped from custody following yesterday's Court of General Session in the Town of Greensborough. Owen Derwent gave bailiffs the slip outside the courthouse where he was found guilty of the practice of diabolic arts.

"Known locally as a conjure-man who told fortunes and sold potions,

Derwent was accused by Mr Josiah Taylor of bewitching his wife. Mr Taylor stated that Derwent put a spell on Mrs Taylor, who lost the power of human speech and could only bark like a dog after refusing to pay Derwent for a fortune she deemed unfavorable. Judge Watson sentenced the defendant to whipping and two months' imprisonment.

"The fugitive Owen Derwent is being sought by the Town of Greensborough. He is thus described: some two and twenty years of age, about five feet and eight or nine inches high, being slight made with freckled skin, gray eyes and red hair."

Owen Derwent. Not the same as Roan Durwood, but close enough? And the description – young, slight, freckles, gray eyes, red hair – could easily Tyner's.

No one comments on that. Morgan turns the printout over and scrutinizes it briefly. "Okay, this one's from the diary of a Methodist circuit rider in 1816.

"On my travels in the western mountains of Carolina I heard frequent tales of a man called Rowan Derwood, said to be in league with the Cherokee forest spirits, from whom he had learned all manner of magic such as the summoning of tempests and the ability to alter his shape to that of a stag deer. Many spoke of the strong dread they felt in the presence of this man, who seemed to them both more and less than human.

"In the fall of 1816, finding myself near to the place where this Derwood and his folk were said to dwell, I sought them out with the hope that I might perform the Lord's work among them and bring them to the Path of the Light. But the woods thereabout grew so thick and deep that I could find no sign of any human habitation, and indeed did lose my way and wander for some hours until it was near nightfall.

"When at last I again found the path, there came over me a powerful sensation of being watched. I looked back and saw what appeared to be a great stag observing me from among the trees.

"I closed my eyes and said a prayer. When I opened them, the beast had vanished."

Once she stops reading there's silence. Then Liz says, "He changed. Roan changed."

"Changed?" Morgan says.

Tyner's nodding. "She's right. Somewhere between the fortune telling in Greensboro and the time the preacher hears about him, something big happens."

"How do you mean?"

"Look, in the newspaper story he's just a hustler. But in the preacher's diary he's callin storms, he's changin his shape . . . he's moved way up the scale."

"So what made him change? What happened to him?"

"The Noon Woods happened to him. They got inside his head, pulled him into somethin way bigger than his wildest dreams – way more than he could handle and hope to stay sane. The forest took him over, turned him into a part of itself. Among the leaves so green-O."

Liz is nodding now. "Joining forces with the forest would have worked both ways – boosting Roan's power and also the power of the Noon Woods itself. The community was an energy source, like rain or sunlight, something the forest could use to survive and spread. What they got in return, those visits to the otherworld, became so important that they were willing to make any sacrifice to keep getting it. There must have been a group who understood that the bargain was destroying them. Roan had become the Green Man. They had to protect themselves."

"And they succeeded," Morgan says, "Nothing's happened since. So why now?"

"You don't stop nature," Liz says. "They managed to weaken the spirit of the forest, yes. But even two centuries later Gordie's mother could still feel its presence; that's why she hung up the witch balls. As for why it's become active again, I think Tyne's right. I think Nick's ritual supplied the kind of energy it needed to make a comeback."

Morgan's head is whirling. For nearly a decade she's called herself a witch, communed with the Goddess, blithely accepted the existence of unseen dimensions and spiritual energy. Now, for the first time, she's scared. She was the one who encouraged Nick to act on his idea, picturing a storybook outcome in which the trees were saved and everyone lived happily ever after. They'd planned the ritual with the best intentions, but if even a fraction of what she's heard tonight is true –

"So we think Laurel was kidnapped by somebody who was at the ritual? That doesn't narrow it down much."

"Does it really matter who it was?" Liz says. "We just need to find her."

Tyner turns to Morgan. "You said you talked to the cops. You tell em about the oak?"

"Um . . . no. I didn't really want to get into it."

"But they're gonna search the Noon Woods?"

"They were waiting for the bloodhounds when I left."

"Okay." He stares into space, fingers drumming the desk. "So we got a little time."

"Time to do what?"

"To put that rock back into the tree, for starters."

"Hold on," Morgan says. "Why do we – "

"Because that's what they did the first time. If it worked once – "

"Wait. Why can't we just let the cops handle this?"

He gives her a look. "You really want a bunch of folks with guns runnin round the Noon Woods right now? You need to plug that hole."

The pronoun makes Morgan flinch. "Me?"

"You and Liz. I'd love to help, but – " He gestures at his chair. "No four-wheel drive."

Morgan looks helplessly at Liz, with her wonky posture and bloodshot eye.

"Come on," Tyner says. "Anybody who can make up a ritual must know how to do a banishin spell."

He's full of surprises, this young man.

"How do you know about banishing spells?" Morgan says.

151

"I'm a gamer."

"Oh. Well, I've done a few. But it was a while ago, and I don't remember exactly what – "

"I can find you one online."

"Really?" Morgan says. "You really want us to go out to Roan's Oak, in the middle of the night, and perform a banishing spell you found on the internet?"

"It's worth a try. And Liz – take your walkin stick. Applewood's supposed to have protective properties."

They all look at the gnarled stick leaning by the door. Above the patch worn smooth by Liz's grip, the wood has been deeply grooved by the twining of some long-dead vine. Morgan counts the spirals – three – and recalls her Wiccan basics. Three is a number of power.

Tyner's staring at the staff, his fingers twitching. Liz retrieves it and hands it to him. Watching him grip it tightly, Morgan is seized by the crazed notion that he's going to use it to stand up and walk. Then he sets it aside.

"Gimme a few minutes to look up some stuff. And then you two need to head out to Roan's Oak."

Jay surveys the shadowy faces of the volunteers gathered around the squad car. He recruited the Cole brothers himself; the other two men have been mustered by Darrell Reese, business partner of the missing Jared Gorton.

He knows he's lucky to have them. Aside from being practically the only people in Durwood who actually seem to give a damn about the spate of disappearances, the young men are able-bodied and alert. Add in himself and Darlene, and the dog team once it arrives, and he's got a working search party. He looks at his watch. Past two AM; the dog handlers are taking their sweet time. He motions the locals closer.

"Okay, listen up. The baby's our priority, so once the dogs get here we're gonna do another quick sweep of the town. If we come up empty, we'll head out to those woods where y'all think your buddy is, and that other fella." He looks around at them. "Now, I know don't nobody wanna believe this, but there's a good chance the two of them are in on this thing together."

One of the young men gives a squirrelly laugh. "You got no idea how crazy that is, buddy."

"Shut up, Hub," another says.

Jay's consulting his watch again when the squad car radio crackles. "Calling Officer Bessey. You there, Jay?"

Jay yanks the door open and slides onto the seat. "Bessey here."

"Jay, it's Nate. We're about twenty miles out."

"Well, come ahead," Jay says. "We're waiting on you."

"Yeah. There's a big tree down across the road."

"Well, can't you go around it, for Chrissake?"

The radio fractures Nate's laugh. "Maybe with a dozer."

Jay's silent, calculating. Sending one of the locals to collect the dog team – a forty-mile round trip on winding country roads – will mean one less searcher for the house-to-house, and they won't get the dogs out to the woods as quick as he'd like. But he can't see any other way.

A big tree down across the road. Talk about bad timing.

"Sit tight," he tells the hissing radio. "I'm sending somebody to fetch you."

Hunched on Tyne's cot, Liz keeps trying to peer through the red haze that's all she can see out of her left. Morgan sits next to her, examining an ugly puncture wound in her thumb. Except for the occasional clicking of the mouse as Tyne searches the internet for banishing spells, the only sound is the rising wind outside. Since nightfall it's been up and down, periods of calm alternating with violent gusts.

"I got a couple spells you can try," Tyne says at last. "Here they come."

A sheet of paper emerges from the printer and Liz retrieves it. The words are a blur; she passes it to Morgan, who peers at the page.

"On a moonless or cloudy night, set a rusty iron nail upon a flat stone. With an iron hammer, strike it thrice. At each stroke, say: CLAVUS FERRUS, MALLEUS FERRUS, FERRUM REFILUM, FERRUM NOBILIS. Score the stone three times with the point of the nail. Take the stone and bury it far from your house. Keep the nail with you as a charm."

"We got nails in the barn," Tyne says.

To Liz their voices seem to float across some watery expanse, as if she's overhearing people chatting on the far side of a lake. Banish the Green Man? The notion seems laughable, futile, like trying to uproot the forest itself. The guardian is as ancient as life itself, mindlessly tenacious and infinitely adaptable, abiding in every furrow of bark and budding leaf, in the odors of earth and rot, the trickle of hidden water, the lacy pattern of black branches against the moon and the shimmering green stillness of trees massed beneath the noonday sun. The guardian is everywhere around them – and by now Liz knows he's inside her head as well, a seed germinating in the dark of her imagination, using her to seek tangible form.

What was it like for Roan Durwood when the Green Man started to gain a foothold in his mind? Did he intentionally seek the bond, or did be succumb unknowingly to a process as subtle as moss creeping over bark or rain puddling in the hollow of a leaf, slowly but irresistibly altering his thoughts, persistent as roots burrowing through soil, pushing through crevices in rock, patiently overcoming every obstacle. As the green shadows thickened inside Roan's head and the spirit of the forest infiltrated his very substance, did reason surrender to instinct, speech blur to the murmur of wind and rain, even his physical form shift and change?

"Here's the second one." Just as Tyne speaks, the wind buffets the shed so hard they feel it shake, and the lights go out.

The sudden darkness generates a brief, shocked silence, broken the next moment by Tyne saying calmly, "Wind musta downed a power line. Lamp's on top of the bookshelf on your left, Liz."

Oil lamps are an indispensable household item in Durwood, where power outages happen all the time. As Liz gropes for the familiar shape, the window's dim rectangle shows her the silhouettes of trees swaying against the night sky. She finds the lamp and passes it to Tyne.

There's the scrape of a match. The flame that blooms out of the darkness brings a sense of comfort out of all proportion to its size. "So much for the internet," Tyne says. "Print job finished, anyway."

He holds the page close to the glowing lamp chimney. "I command you, O ye demons dwelling in this place, by whatsoever power hath been given you by God and our holy Angels over this place, to abdicate all power to guard, habit and abide in this place, to leave me in peaceable possession and rule over this place, or whatsoever legion you be and of whatsoever part of the world.

"By order of the Most Holy Trinity and by the merits of the Most Holy and Blessed Virgin, as also of all the saints, I unbind you all, spirits who abide in this place, and I drive you to the deepest infernal abysses. Thus: Go, all Spirits accursed, who are condemned to the flame eternal which is prepared for you and your companions if you – "

"Stop," Morgan says.

"I ain't done."

"Oh yes you are. What *is* that?"

"It's from the Grimoire of Pope Honorius."

"I don't like it. The language is so – aggressive."

"They ain't people, you know." Tyne sounds irritated. "If you ask em nice, it's not gonna work."

Liz wishes her left eye would function and her dizziness would abate. She's worried about Morgan, who of course knows nature spirits aren't people; as a Wiccan, she must be familiar with the notion of beings from the spirit dimension. But familiarity with an abstraction is one thing, the possibility of practical confrontation another. Can she handle this?

Morgan's looking at her watch. "It's past two. Maybe we should – "

Liz lifts a hand. "Did you hear something?"

They fall silent, listening.

"Hello . . . ?" The calling voice outside blends eerily with the wind. "Hellooo . . . ?"

Morgan goes to the door and opens it a crack. "Who's there?"

"Excuse me, I – " A face, puffy and tear streaked, appears in the opening.

"Molly!"

"Morgan! I saw your car out front – "

"Come inside! Did they find the baby?"

Molly squeezes in and presses the door shut against the wind. "No. They have a search party, but the dogs got delayed. And the police are very methodical, you know, I think they feel they have to, uh, do everything by the book. I came out here because I . . . I just had a feeling."

"A feeling – ?"

Molly takes a hard breath. "That whoever took her . . . would bring her to the Noon Woods."

In the yellow lamplight the four of them share a look. Tyne says, "Here's what we gotta do."

◆◆◆

There's danger from the car that rattles through the front gate and comes to a haphazard stop inside the fence. Danger from the woman who jumps out to survey the darkened farmhouse before cupping her hands around her mouth to call above the wind.

"Hello? Hello?"

Glimpsed from the truck hidden among the trees beyond the house, her face is a pale blur in the moonlight that fades and brightens among hurrying clouds. She looks around, catches sight of the wavering lamplight from Tyne's shed and blunders toward it. After a moment the door opens to receive her, then closes again.

The danger has passed. Beneath the shadows of wind-tossed leaves the child sleeps, a dark bundle on the passenger seat. Doubt has departed, and any trace of regret; all that remains is the resolve to set things right.

It's nearly time.

❖ 19 ❖

Three of us, Morgan thinks as she hurries through the moonlit woods. Three. A number of power.

Liz is in the lead with the flashlight, the only one who knows the way, with Molly behind her and Morgan bringing up the rear. It's tempting to imagine them representing the three aspects of the Goddess: maiden, mother, crone. Morgan uses the notion to distract herself from the unpleasant reality of scrambling over rocks and roots, avoiding the black hulks of the trees, stopping periodically to disentangle branches from her hair. Maiden, mother, crone . . . Molly's the mother, of course; that's a no-brainer. And although Liz is the eldest, somewhere in her sixties, there's a decidedly girlish quality about her and Morgan doesn't think she's ever been married; whereas she, Morgan, has all those wasted years with Tim.

Nope, she thinks with surprising equanimity, I might as well face it. Liz is the maiden. I'm the crone.

The wind has died down, and in its absence their progress through the woods makes an ungodly racket – snapping twigs and swishing leaves punctuated by the audible panting of three people in a hurry. There are other sounds too, faint unidentifiable skitterings among the trees and the occasional distant hoot of an owl – but beneath all the noise is an impenetrable silence that presses like a weight on Morgan's heart. She's trying her best to stay focused on the task at hand, which is getting to the oak – trying not to think about the missing baby, or what Durwood's first settlers might have gotten up in these woods, or what may or may not have happened here as recently as last night.

She's profoundly glad not to be making this trek alone. Although she considers herself a nature lover, she's now realizing she likes nature best in small, manageable doses – a stroll through a park, a scenic autumn hike leading somewhere with walls and a roof and a glass of wine – something altogether different from this immense living entity that renders her acutely aware of her own flimsiness and insignificance. But here she is.

We need to close the door.

She considers what Liz said about the bargain between Durwood and the

Noon Woods. An exchange of physical energy for spiritual, with the oak somehow forming a conduit to some invisible dimension where life force can be traded for a taste of bliss.

In the ten years she's spent embracing Wicca, invoking the Goddess and the sacred spirits of earth, air, water and fire, she's never once questioned her beliefs until now, when the possibility of encountering such a force forms a knot in her belly. Ten years without an inkling that she's been fooling herself, believing with her brain but not with her gut. Even now she's resisting the idea, holding out for some other, more prosaic explanation. But there's a wobble in her knees, a nearly irresistible urge (as she blunders into a spider web and stops to wipe the sticky strands from her face) to turn and run for home where she can climb into bed and pretend it was all a bad dream.

She pushes the impulse away. She's here to do whatever it takes to find Molly's baby. Whatever it takes.

"Liz?" Molly's voice ahead. "How much farther?"

"Almost there."

Morgan touches the folded papers in the back pocket of her jeans. Tyner insisted she bring along the banishing spells and a backpack of supplies, and she acquiesced because she had nothing better to suggest. She can't imagine what will happen if they can't find Laurel, or what Tyner honestly expects them to do at Roan's Oak. Three women by themselves, against –

Against what?

Long after the door of his study closes behind the three women, Tyne sits staring at the reflection of the lamp chimney in his dead screen. In his thoughts he's making his way through the dark woods with them, retracing his journey of nine years ago. For as long as he can remember, he's been drawn to the hushed green domain that spreads for miles over the surrounding hills and hollows. A place where reality and legend intersect and impossible things happen.

The King of the Greenwood, now, he was the most important man in Durwood.

How come, Granny?

Because he was the fastest and the strongest and the bravest. The protector of Durwood.

Of all the games Tyne played with his friends, King of the Greenwood was his favorite. Even after the adults outlawed it as too dangerous, they kept on playing it in secret. Even when the others outgrew it, he couldn't quite let go.

"Pa, how come they quit havin the Midsummer race?"

"I don't know, son. I reckon because of the war."

"What war?"

" '41 to '45. Lot of Durwood boys went off to fight the Nazis. The ones that lived to come back, they didn't feel much like runnin races."

"But that was so long ago. Can't we start it up again?"

Pa and the other grownups showed a surprising resistance to the idea. The practice had died out on its own, they said. Best let it be.

Just a bunch of superstitious nonsense anyway.

Superstitious nonsense like sneaking into the Noon Woods to hang a wish token on Roan's Oak? Asking a tree to give you something you wanted bad enough to brave the heavy silence of the woods, the sense of something watching you from the green shadows? Nobody will admit to hanging the lockets and toys and other treasures on Roan's Oak, but they get there somehow – even an old pocket watch dangling up so high that the owner must have thrown it into the branches as hard as he could. What had he wanted bad enough to throw away time?

The lamp is smoking; Tyne trims the wick. There's a sheet of paper on the floor by his chair and he picks it up, thinking the women have left behind one of their banishing spells, but it's the old newspaper article reproduced from the Raleigh Record.

The fugitive Owen Derwent. Some two and twenty years of age, about five feet and eight or ten inches high, slight made with freckled skin, gray eyes and red hair.

Seven generations separate him from Roan, but they share the same features, the same blood, the same longing. When Roan fled the witchcraft charge in Greensborough, there were some who quietly followed him. Hidden in the mountains, cut off from the outside world, they formed their own community, marrying and burying beneath the lightning-struck oak in the Noon Woods, hanging the birthcords of their newborns from its branches, a dozen families growing together like the interwoven boughs of the forest canopy. As the generations passed, the legends emerged. It was said that here among the ancient trees Roan had found a door to the Bright Land. That on certain nights of the year the people of Durwood had danced beneath the oak in the moonlight of a hidden world.

That era ended, it was said, with Roan's departure to the Bright Land – a signal honor for a mortal man. Perhaps the subsequent sealing of the door between the worlds was a condition imposed by the white doe, capricious as any human woman. But Durwood was left with a stone embedded in a tree, a bittersweet legend repeated by old women on winter evenings by the fire, and a mournful little verse passed down through the generations, sung by mothers to their babies and chanted by children as they played.

Roan, Roan, open the door
My tears are salt and my heart is sore.
Roan, return, and reach out your hand
And open the door to the Bright Land.

Only a legend, an old folk tale. But what about the interval since the opening of the door in the oak, when the wind of another world seems to blow through Durwood?

Tyne's reaching for the moonshine jar when the lights come on; a moment later his computer screen flickers into life. The power company must have crews out working late. He waits a few minutes and tries the internet.

It's working. What was he looking for before the power went out? Some kind of guidance about how to shut down Roan's Oak, some clue –

He starts searching for answers. Clicking here, clicking there, reading a few sentences, moving on, following links, threading his way deeper.

Click. Click.

WHEN BANNISHING SPIRITS & DEMONS REMEMBER THAT U HAVE A BODY & THEY DONT. THIS GIVES U MAGICKAL LEVERAGE.

Click.

A nature spirit is linked to a place & for this reason they are very difficult to banish. Before proceeding, make certain the entity truly needs to be banished. Convincing it to leave willingly is always the better option.

Click.

This is a pretty good spell but wont work with every demon. Even when it cant actually overcome the spirit tho it can still hurt them enough to keep them at bay.

Click.

There are certain sounds and rhythms . . .

His finger, about to click, stays poised above the mouse as he reads the words again.

. . . certain sounds and rhythms, such as a healer's chant or a shaman's drum, that are known to cause a shift in human consciousness. By stimulating the non-dominant hemisphere of the brain, these sounds shift our perception of reality from the analytic left to the symbol-oriented right. The result is a radically altered experience in which individual identity is subsumed by the mythic imagery of the psyche, instinct is liberated, and time and space no longer exist. These are the characteristics of the Otherworld.

Tyne sits back in his chair, takes a deep breath. The door in the oak. Not some quaint wee door set into the trunk like something in a children's book. Not the physical opening made by the lightning strike, but a symbolic door in the brain, opened by sound.

The stone had been put in the oak to close that door. Now it's open.

Certain sounds and rhythms , , , He thinks of the unearthly quaver woven into the wind, capable of affecting him even at the distance of more than a mile. Near the oak it would be overpowering. He thinks of the women heading for the tree, armed with some flimsy snippets of magical advice pulled from random websites, completely ignorant of what will happen if the wind starts to blow.

A radically altered experience . . .

The Otherworld.

They're heading straight for it. And there's nothing he can do to warn them.

◆ ◆ ◆

On the bed in Morgan's guest room, Nick lies staring at the ceiling.

He screwed her. Right here in this bed.

Morgan.

He's always considered her attractive, but that's not the same as being attracted to her. She's his aunt, his mother's sister. His favorite family member. He's never thought of her as a sexual being until tonight, when everything about her – her warmth, her smell, the touch of her hands – kindled the irresistible urge to possess her.

The mere thought of her arouses him now. If she were to walk through the door this minute, he knows he wouldn't be able to resist having her again. He doesn't understand what's happening to him since he took part in the ritual, but in retrospect it seems incredibly stupid to have assumed he could just step into the role of shaman and travel blithely between the worlds –

Someone's knocking on the front door.

His gaze flies to the clock radio by the bed. Its display shows only a steadily blinking 12:00, evidence of a power outage at some point. It feels late, very late. But he definitely heard knocking – didn't he? He props himself on one elbow and listens. Nothing. And then

Tap tap tap

Maybe the Upshaws' baby's been found and someone can't wait to share the good news. Rolling off the bed, he wraps the quilt around him and starts down the hall.

Tap tap tap

Now it sounds less like knocking, more like raindrops hitting the porch roof. He shuffles closer and lays his ear against the door. Silence from the other side. Reluctant to open it, he holds his breath to listen,. There's nothing now. And then a whisper.

Nick

The welts on his back and buttocks are tingling.

Tap tap tap

Nick

The tingle becomes a burn. The door's not locked. People in Durwood never lock their doors. He gathers his breath, grasps the knob and turns it, easing the door ever so slightly open.

There's no one. No one on the porch, and no one in the yard, as far as he can see in the spill of brightness from the porch light. Or is there? The night is full of the intermittent tap of raindrops and the breathy greeting of wind comes like a warm exhalation.

Nick

The moon floats high in a sky of streaming clouds; the soft air carries a flowery fragrance. A stray current tugs at the quilt around him, nudging through its folds to touch his bruised flesh, and he feels his body respond.

Where is she? He knows she's here. His gaze travels over the dark street with its moon-silvered puddles, the sleeping houses shadowed by the hulks of dripping trees – seeking, seeking, returning at last to Morgan's yard.

And there she is, standing across the yard in the moonlight, waiting for him. Blindly he stumbles down the porch steps, oblivious to the nail head that catches the edge of quilt and yanks it, leaving him naked. Driven by need, he's oblivious to everything but the sight of her across the yard, fragile and slender and veiled in a froth of white blossom, the smooth fork of her supple limbs eagerly awaiting his embrace.

◆ ◆ ◆

"There," Liz says.

The three of them stop for breath at the edge of the clearing where Roan's Oak stands etched in moonlight and shadow.

Morgan's heartbeat is almost choking her. Unspeakably horrible things have happened here, right here, where they're standing now. Some detached corner of her brain notes the new leaves softening the tree's stark outline.

"So . . . it's not dead after all?"

"Not anymore," Liz says.

"Laurel?" Molly's call breaks the stillness. "Baby, Momma's here! Laurel!"

Silence closes over the words. Molly runs toward the oak and the others follow. As they approach, its gaunt shadow seems to suck the substance from the flashlight beam, reducing it to a wan pencil of light.

Molly points. "What's that?"

"The rope they used to tie Gordie."

They survey the slack coils without comment. After a moment Liz lets the flashlight's beam explore further. "There's the stone."

Cradled in the roots, the hunk of tawny rock has a faint sheen that's not moonlight. When Molly tries to push it with her foot, it doesn't budge.

"It's heavy." She glances at Morgan. "Should we try that spell?"

Morgan takes it out of her pocket and unfolds it. The paper quivers in the flashlight's beam.

On a moonless or cloudy night . . . She glances up briefly. It's not moonless, but there are plenty of clouds.

Set a rusty iron nail upon a flat stone. With an iron hammer, strike it thrice.

In her backpack are a hammer and a ten-penny nail scavenged from the Durwoods' barn. The stone isn't flat, but it's here, waiting. And it's apparently been successful in blocking the opening in the past.

At each stroke, say: CLAVUS FERRUS, MALLEUS FERRUS, FERRUM REFILUM, FERRUM NOBILIS.

Iron nail, iron hammer . . . That's about as much as Morgan can decipher; her high school Latin is even rustier than the nail. But she finds the repetition of the word *ferrus* reassuring; hasn't she read somewhere that iron is hateful to faeries and their kin?

Score the stone three times with the point of the nail. Then take the stone and bury it far from your house. Keep the nail with you as a charm.

"Okay, let's try it. We'll say the words, then we'll put the stone back in the tree, and maybe it'll work."

She looks at the others for agreement. Molly's staring into the surrounding darkness, looking and listening for some sign of Laurel, but Liz nods dubiously.

"So where's the, uh – " Here in the dark woods Morgan finds herself avoiding the word doorway, in case it might encourage – well, just in case. "Where was the stone . . . before?"

Liz swings the flashlight up to reveal a gaping hole in the trunk a little below chest height. The sight of that ragged opening gives Morgan a qualm, but the spell has to be done, and she's the logical one to do it. The others are looking to her for leadership; she can't let herself falter.

"All right. First let's try moving this thing so it's right below the hole. Then at the proper moment we can pick it up and shove it in. Ready, Liz? Mol?"

They range themselves around it, worming their fingers underneath.

"On three," Morgan says. "One . . . two . . . three!"

Given the size of the stone, the three of them should easily be able to move it, but it barely budges.

"Come on, women," Morgan says through gritted teeth. The experience of working with all-female energy brings back her coven days, those heady moments when womanpower seemed capable of accomplishing anything. "We can do this. Where there's fear, there's power. Think of everything you're afraid of. Now take the power of your fears and put it into lifting this stone. Ready? One, two – "

"THREE!" they all cry together. This time they manage to shift the stone a foot nearer the trunk before it escapes their grip, landing among the slippery roots with an impact that makes them wince.

"Good enough!" Morgan tries her best to sound positive. She shrugs off the backpack and burrows into it for her magical tools – a hammer and a nail. Holding them in her hands she has a sense of time coming to a halt, all the helterskelter moments of this interminable day slithering to a messy stop like a vehicle in deep snow, leaving her suspended over a void. Here she is with a hammer, a nail, a stone and a few Latin phrases of uncertain meaning, taking on something in which she doesn't quite believe but can't afford to dismiss. However fervently she's affirmed the existence of nature spirits and elemental beings in the past, right now she'd like nothing better than to discover it's all a load of crap.

"I think it's best if we all say the spell together."

The others nod. They squat together around the rock; Molly holds up the printed page and Liz shines the flashlight on it. Setting the point of the nail on the rock, Morgan swings the hammer and strikes.

Chink!

"Clavus ferrus! Malleus ferrus! Ferrum refilum! Ferrum nobilis!"

In the dark vastness of the woods, their voices sound thin and unconvincing.

Chink!

"Clavus ferrus! Malleus ferrus! Ferrum refilum! Ferrum nobilis!"

Above their heads the oak's new leaves tremble.

Chink!

"Clavus ferrus! Malleus ferrus! Ferrum refilum! Ferrum nobilis!"

From the depths of the black opening in the tree comes a whispery whistle that curdles the skin on their bones. Molly lets out a yelp; Morgan involuntarily drops the hammer. As the leaves subside, the eerie noise dies away.

"Score it," Liz whispers. "Three times."

With the point of the nail, Morgan scrapes a crude asterisk on the surface. The three of them seize the stone and struggle to lift it, bumping into one another as they stumble among the roots. They manage to raise it to waist height, then higher – and are within inches of shoving it into the hole when it slips from their hands and thuds to the ground, barely missing Molly's foot.

"Shit!" Morgan gasps. At that moment the tree looses a quavering whine and her knees give way, dropping her in a heap on the roots. She sees Molly crumple and clutch her head in her hands, sees Liz raise wide eyes to the creaking branches overhead.

"It's just the wind," Morgan says. But she doesn't want to hear that sound again – not now, not ever. Even though it's no longer audible, she can feel a sustained vibration compressing the air.

"Are we going to try again?" Molly's voice is shaking.

"We have to."

This time the wind comes in a rush – and while Morgan fully understands it's just a matter of air blowing through the tree, air forced through an opening on the same principle as a whistle or a flute, that doesn't prevent its nerve-shredding frequency from undoing her. It sounds like a banshee, a vengeful ghost, a damned soul. The impulse to run wells up like nausea. Fumbling for the other spell, she ducks out of the tree's quivering shadow and squints at the printed page in the moonlight.

I command you, O demons dwelling in this place . . .

A dark spot stains one corner of the paper; fresh blood is oozing from the wound in her thumb. As she opens her mouth to speak the words, the wind snatches the spell from her hand. Molly dives after it and misses. Cringing at the yammer of the wind through the tree, the three of them helplessly watch it sail away.

"Now what?" shouts Liz. She's visibly shivering, the wind suspending her long hair in pale streamers around her head.

Yes, Morgan thinks, now what? In her coven days she performed Wiccan banishing spells for purposes that now seem utterly frivolous – cleansing a friend's new apartment from the previous tenant's smoking habit, stopping a neighbor's cat from pissing in her flowerbeds. But the racket from the oak makes it impossible to concentrate; her thoughts are collapsing into rubble. Even if she can remember a spell, can she perform it under these conditions? She doesn't even have an athame.

Stop whining, she tells herself. Use the standard substitute: index and middle fingers extended to form the ritual blade. She struggles to form a silent prayer: Goddess, I know you're there. You've got to be. I can swear there are times when I've felt your presence. You know I'm not really qualified for this. Please help me, let your power flow through me. That's all I'm asking.

She beckons the others to cluster together a half dozen yards from the oak. Forming an athame with her right hand, she points it directly at the moon overhead, down in a sweeping arc to the ground, then straight out in front of her. Slowly she turns counterclockwise. Widdershins, the direction of decrease.

She comes to a stop facing the oak and surveys the dubious result. Working in the congenial atmosphere of her coven, buoyed by waves of estrogen and sisterhood, she always found it easy to visualize the protective circle as a shining barrier. Here in the dark woods, if she's created anything at all, it's flimsy as tissue paper. Liz and Molly are staring at the oak with glazed eyes. The whining wind batters their ears, bombarding them with a storm of whirling twigs and loose leaves; ringed by thrashing branches, the entire clearing seems on the verge of taking to the air and carrying them with it.

Morgan takes a deep breath and finds the words of the Wiccan banishing spell waiting in her head.

"Spirits of evil, unfriendly beings, unwanted guests, be gone!"

Less a command than a plea, barely audible over the noise from the tree. The wind pummels her, throws grit into her eyes, tears at her clothes. In some far corner of her mind she can hear Tyner saying, *If you ask em nice, it's not gonna work.* Fighting the impulse to cover her ears, she forces out the next words in a shout:

"Leave this place, leave this circle, that the Goddess and God may enter!

"Go, or be cast into the outer darkness! Go, or be drowned in the watery abyss!

"Go, or be burned in the flames! Go, or be torn by the whirlwind!

"By the power of – "

The voice of the oak jumps to a pulsating shriek that seems to pierce her skull. Jagged lines of light shoot across her vision in a quivering pattern through which she sees a ripple of movement within the flailing shadow of the tree – a dark shape of thrashing branches and windblown leaves, appearing, vanishing, reappearing with every shift of darkness and moonlight.

On some level Morgan understands that what she's seeing is the process of her brain trying to impose a recognizable form onto something for which it has no conscious frame of reference, only the buried race memory of some archaic spirit. The result is a distorted shape that fluctuates between tree and human; she glimpses a ragged face with blind, mossy hollows for eyes, a wet knothole mouth warped by a silent, insatiable hunger. Air empties from her lungs; her mind vibrates like a bell.

As she hangs suspended by a fraying thread of sanity, a shrill voice reaches her:

"Today I put on the power of Heaven, the light of the sun, the radiance of the moon, the splendor of fire, the fierceness of lightning, the swiftness of wind, the depth of the sea, the firmness of earth and the hardness of rock!"

Molly's long black hair is streaming sideways and there's a spot of bright red on each cheek. She's screaming at the top of her lungs, competing with the hullabaloo around them. They're being strafed by flying leaves as wind howls through the oak, unraveling the icy air. High in the tree, a massive branch snaps and crashes to the ground.

" – God's strength to steer me, God's power to uphold me – wisdom to guide me – hand to protect me – shield for my shelter – "

Morgan watches the nightmare shape flicker and fade and form again, made of moonlight and shadow and whatever unfathomable force exists in this forest. Is it coming closer? She stands paralyzed, knowing her circle will provide no protection. Knowing Molly's tiring, her voice a mere thread in the gale.

" . . . God's angels to guard me from the ambush of devils . . . from all who wish me ill, whether distant or close, alone or in hosts –

"Christ beside me, Christ before me, Christ behind me –

"Christ within me, Christ beneath me, Christ above me –

"Christ on my right hand, Christ on my left, Chr – "

Her voice falters as a whirl of flying debris engulfs them. Morgan can't move, can't see. She hears Liz shouting through the wind.

"Stop! It's not working! You're making it worse!"

As Molly subsides, the oak erupts in a triumphant screech.

"Run!" Liz screams.

They flee, hands clapped to their ears against that demonic sound, stumbling headlong away from the clearing to blunder through an endless dim maze of trunks and branches and clutching undergrowth, trying not to lose one another in the dark. All at once Liz, in the lead, comes to an abrupt stop. The others pile up behind her.

"Go! Go!"

"I can't! There's no way through!" They're trapped in a cul-de-sac of tangled vines. With the howls of the oak still clawing at their ears, Liz swings her walking stick, slashing a path through the dense foliage.

It fights back, tangling the stick with woody tendrils, showering them with leaf fragments, but at last the way is clear enough to run again – run as best they can, fending off shadowy obstacles that loom out of the dark, tripping on the uneven terrain, fleeing the sound that somehow keeps pace with them no matter how far they've come. At one point Morgan stumbles and lands hard on her knees and elbows. Almost before she has time to register what's happened, the others are beside her, dragging her to her feet, hustling her along.

When at last they stagger out of the trees, it takes them a few moments to realize that the woods behind them have gone silent. The stillness hurts their ears. For a while they just stand there in the hayfield on unsteady legs, regarding one another with dazed stares.

At the top of the moonlit slope, a light burns in the window of the cabin. As they start toward it Morgan seizes Liz's arm, her voice emerging in a croak.

"Did you – did you see it? That – thing?"

Liz turns, her eyes hollows of shadow. "See it? I'm the one who brought it here."

As they trek up through the field, the night's silence surrounds them, broken only by the whisper of hay marking their passage. When they reach the cabin, the front porch is littered with shards of glass that crunch under their feet, but Liz offers no explanation and the others are beyond asking.

Inside, they sit without speaking, passing the moonshine jar around until the shakes subside. At last Molly, twisting a lock of hair around one finger, says, "But what do we do now? I've got to find Laurel!"

No one answers. Finally Morgan says, "What was that, anyway – that stuff you were saying back there?"

"Huh?"

"That prayer, whatever it was."

"Oh." Molly shakes her head. "My Irish grandmother taught it to me when I was little. Saint Patrick's Breastplate. I didn't even know I remembered it."

"Saint Patrick?"

"I was raised Irish Catholic." She looks embarrassed, a conscientious pagan caught in a shameful lapse.

"Well, that *thing* didn't like it much."

"He doesn't like us trying to shut him out," Liz says. "Not again."

※20※

"I think it's my fault," Liz says quietly.

It's nearly five AM, still dark out. Exhausted, Morgan and Molly have fallen asleep by the dying fire. She's left them at the cabin to make her way down the hill toward the lit window of Tyne's study.

When she recounts what happened at the oak, he doesn't seem surprised.

"It coulda been worse. After you left I found some stuff on the web. There are certain sounds – like the one the wind makes blowing through the tree – that affect your brain, send it into some kind of altered state. We gotta plug that door again."

"It's too late, Tyne. He's too strong, thanks to my – "

"Don't be an idiot. You didn't create him; he's always been there. It was those New Age assholes got him goin again, takin the stone out of the tree." Leaning forward in his chair to lightly punch her shoulder. "This ain't on you, Liz."

"He's using my drawings the same way he used Roan. As energy. A host. But I think there's something I can do."

He regards her somberly. "Do whatever you gotta. I'd like to help, but you know about how much that's worth." Gesturing at his legs: "Looks like you're on your own."

On her way up the hill she can see the darkness beginning to soften, wooded ridges emerging in silhouette against the sky. Inside the cabin the other women are still asleep. Quietly Liz gets her portfolio case and takes it out onto the front porch to sort through the contents.

Green Man. Moving through her, traveling from imagination to pencil marks on paper – and from there, awakened by Nick's reckless ritual. In spite of what Tyne says, she's played a key part in this. *The first doe he missed, the second he kissed, the third doe went where nobody wist, among the leaves so green-O.*

Gordie, Jared, Laurel. Is this only the beginning? The perilous bargain between Durwood and the otherworld nearly destroyed the community once. Now it's on the brink of doing so again.

The dizzy spells have receded, but her left eye's still not functioning and there's a familiar vise squeezing her skull; she needs to do this while she still can. Replacing the drawings, she tucks the case under her arm, takes up her stick, and makes a brief stop by the woodshed before heading for the forest.

◆◆◆

Welcome, Warrior, to the Temple of Renewal.

Tyne grimaces. It's the third time he's died in less than an hour. His plan of using the game as a distraction isn't working; the cyberworld feels flat and flimsy next to the reality of Liz on her way to Roan's Oak.

He stares at the screen without seeing it, idly fingering the mouse, letting his mind shuffle the events of the past couple of weeks. What if it's just a case of mass hysteria, a community pushed to the edge by stress? Surely the alternative – a guardian spirit protecting the forest – is impossible.

Isn't it?

Roan, Roan, open the door –

Tyne reaches for the moonshine jar. He knows a few things about impossible. For nine years he's dismissed his memory of the night he fell from Roan's Oak as a delusion brought on by pain and shock. It seems to be the nature of such memories to fade from consciousness, bury themselves like poison splinters beneath the mind's surface.

I wasn't supposed to remember.

I wasn't supposed to survive.

That's how the Noon Woods protects itself. How it keeps its secrets. His tattoo is itching like a bastard. With a convulsive click of the mouse, he starts the game again. He's been in the Temple of Renewal so often he can perform the required actions without thinking. Receive the ministrations of the healer, ask the priest's blessing on his quest, visit the armory, pick a destination. He chooses the seaport of Ardyss and waits for the scene to load, trying to ignore his itching arm.

It's night in Ardyss. He finds himself on the quay, the harbor abristle with masts, damp cobbles shining in the moonlight. Turning his back on the tide-smell and chuckle of lapping water, he climbs the steep, crooked street. Right now he needs to be around people, even if they're only binary.

Tavern windows glow beneath a swinging sign adorned with the words *Pig & Whistle*. Opening the door, he's met by a babble of rowdy voices, the clink of pewter, snatches of drunken song. Among the grainy shadows, faces turn briefly toward him and away. As he takes a seat across from a hooded figure bent over a flagon, a digital barmaid appears. Time for some canned chitchat.

Welcome, stranger. What is your pleasure?

Ale. Will you join me?

Gladly. How are you called?

Quert.

Your name is known here, Quert.

The player's name is always known. Now she'll recite a laundry list of the trolls and monsters he's vanquished, the swag he's won, the powers he's earned.

What do they say of me?

That you flee a quest you are pledged to fulfill.

That's a new one. "What the hell?" he says aloud.

The digital girl doesn't answer; how could she? She's only a series of ones and zeroes programmed to carry on a limited, predictable conversation. But her eyes . . . Her eyes are shadowy as forest pools.

He leans back in his chair. *You flee a quest you are pledged to fulfill.* Did she really say that?

The hooded shape across from him glances up briefly. All at once the noise of merrymaking stops, leaving the room so quiet that Tyne can hear the crackling of the fire in the hearth. One of the logs bursts, releasing a shower of sparks that land hissing on the hearthstone.

The sound is like the whisper of wind through leaves.

His arm is itching like crazy and he looks down to see his tattoo changing beneath his gaze, the leaves multiplying, unfurling new lobes with lightning speed, a burst of green that races up his arm to his shoulder with a prickling sensation like feeling returning to a numb limb. Pins and needles spread across his chest and back, leaves swiftly mantling him from head to foot, swarming across the table, engulfing the furniture and the tavern guests, climbing up the walls and across the ceiling until everything is a mass of rustling green.

Everything but the figure still seated across from him. With a shock Tyne recognizes the familiar, beloved face within the hood: glinting eyes above a sharp nose, long white hair bundled back in a careless knot.

He was the fastest and the strongest and the bravest, says Granny Dee. *The protector of Durwood.*

Fastest, strongest, bravest. Those are the words that sing in Tyne's head as he runs, feeling the muscles in his legs flex and stretch to carry him swiftly forward. He's running through the Noon Woods, running with an effortless ease that seems like flying. All around him he can hear the other boys crashing through the dark woods, whooping and hollering across the night.

It's Midsummer's Eve.

When Conlee and Harley showed up with a quart jar snitched from their daddy's still, all seven of them took the opportunity to get lickered up. Tyne knows the others don't care about the race; to them it's just a way to defy the grownups and blow off some steam. But he's running to win – and in spite of the pretense at being too old for such foolishness, so is Jared. Tonight one of them will be King of the Greenwood. Surefooted in spite of the darkness and the drink, they're running the race the way it was run in Roan's day

(on the curved inner surface of a green orb rolling with no end and no beginning, a woven sphere of roots and branches and sunlit leaves suspended in time)

and he emerges from the waking dream to find himself standing beneath the oak, head mazy with moonshine. All around him the woods are still; briefly he wonders where the others are and then forgets them as he gazes up at the tree towering above him. Moonlight glistens on the tokens that hang along its branches, endowing even the most commonplace with an air of mystery.

He grasps a low limb and swings himself up.

At first it's no different than climbing any other tree. He stays close to the trunk, tests each branch before committing his weight, sets his feet firmly before reaching higher. Before long he's moved beyond the decorated branches to the bare ones above. Bare? As he climbs he becomes aware of a constant flicker at the edge of his vision, a host of invisible leaves that fade into air when he turns his head to look. Their whispering surrounds him, filling his head until everything else drifts away.

Moving steadily higher, he's conscious only of the texture of bark against his hands, the strong branches beneath his feet, the flex and release of muscles, each minute adjustment of balance, as if he has no existence apart from this moment. Higher still and he can no longer distinguish between motion and stillness, between the tree's substance and his own.

There's a rush of wind at the top. He steps up between the oak's ragged horns, grasping one in each hand as he gazes out over the vast well of dreaming forest. He's King of the Greenwood, protector of Durwood, and the rustling voice of his kingdom greets him – rough as bark and soft as moss, dark and rich as leaf mold, hard as heartwood, tender as a new leaf.

Noticing a glint of light at his feet, he crouches to find a hollow brimming with rainwater. Within its glimmering mirror, his shadowy reflection leans close; and behind it he sees, instead of shattered branches, a vast, luxuriant crown of leaves. Mingling with their rustling are old, familiar words.

And for each year that he gave a drop of his blood, for as long the woods stood tall no harm should come to him or his.

The world within the moonlit water looks close enough to touch. The wind rises.

Ain't the blood itself, says Granny Dee, and in the water's reflection he sees that the hooded figure from the tavern has appeared at his side. *Ain't the blood itself. It's what it means to you. The value of the gift.*

Her voice breaks on the word *gift*. Suddenly he understands that he's been raised and shaped entirely for this moment – that all he has to do is let himself fall. The shrouded head beside him gives a sharp little nod, the way Granny always does when he's pleased her. But when he turns, there's no one there, only the oak's splintered horns jutting into the night sky.

The value of the gift. With a last glance at the living crown of leaves in the water, Tyne slowly straightens from his crouch. All he has to do is let himself fall.

All he has to –

His footing slips on the mossy bark and his body responds with an instinctive jerk that jolts him from his trance. Convulsively his fingers clutch the tree's horns and dig in. *King of . . . Protector of . . .* The words dissolve on the wind, leaving only a fifteen year-old boy stranded at a perilous height, paralyzed by the distance between himself and the ground and knowing in spite of everything

Granny put into preparing him that he's neither king nor protector, neither strong nor brave, that he's nothing but a dreamstruck child who understands nothing of courage or sacrifice. All he wants is to feel solid earth under his feet, look into the faces of his friends and –

Without warning, the branch he's clutching crumbles in his grip and he's holding a handful of rotten wood. As he flails for balance the oak seems to give an impatient shake, tossing him off like a nuisance tolerated long enough, and faster than thought can follow he plummets downward, striking an endless succession of gnarled branches that fling him off like a broken doll, too battered and dazed to register pain, down and down and down –

Time divides, past and present twisting like root tendrils to double back on themselves, a knot with infinite strands.

In one strand he loses his grip and falls.

In another he remains crouched at the top of the ruined tree, gazing into the rainpool between the horns.

Ain't the blood itself, says Granny Dee, *it's what it means to you. The value of the gift.*

In the water he sees reflected beside him the hooded figure from the tavern.

I'm ready, he says. I'm ready now.

No need. The gift's been given.

Gift? You mean Jared? No, you can't – you have to let me take his place! I said I'm ready!

The dark shape pushes back its hood, revealing a young, thin face under a tangle of coppery hair, uncannily like his own. *Then come,* says Roan Durwood as his moonlit outline melts into a shimmer of reflected leaves..

Tyne bends over the silvery pool. In its bottomless depths, a slender white shape flees through flickering green shadow. The wind is soft as gossamer on his face as the oak's crown sways around him, leaves whispering a welcome. In the moment before time twists back upon itself once more, he feels himself float free of the known world as gently as a leaf falling from a branch, spiralling down and down and then borne up and up through buoyant darkness and whirling wells of night and silence that gradually give way to a haze of green and gold that turns to leaflight and sunlight and the trickle of hidden water.

He lies with her in a shady clearing, looking into eyes deep as forest pools. Her hair is woven with leaves. In their union, the boundaries that define Tyne Durwood rush swiftly outward, expanding until he encompasses forested mountains and hollows, fields and running streams, birds and animals and plants and rocks, a boundless and timeless infinity all contained in a single drop of rain clinging to a leaf. At the moment of climax he feels himself collapse inward at a terrifying velocity, imploding to a packed point of energy no bigger than a seed.

He wakes to find himself holding only a delicate framework of white bones bound with flowering vines. Among the bones the wind plays a plaintive, familiar melody.

The third doe went where nobody wist, among the leaves so green-O.

171

Listening, he can feel the tickle of leaves growing in his hair and sprouting from his jaw in a burgeoning beard.

Where'd you go? he tries to say. What's happening to me?

But the only sound that emerges from his lips is the rustle of leaves.

Jared fights to keep from blacking out. It wasn't a hard fall; he's had harder, like the time Conlee pushed him out of the bed of Ward's pickup onto the gravel roadbed back when they were twelve. As the blackness recedes, he registers the fact that he's cold and wet, lying on his side. There's something digging into his cheek and his head hurts like hell. Maybe he did black out after all.

Rolling onto his back, he sees a crisscross of leafy branches outlined against pale sky. Where's that light coming from at this hour of the night? There's pain radiating from the side of his head, and gingerly he reaches up to find a gouge in his right temple, crusted with what feels like dried blood.

Wait – *dried* blood?

When he tries to sit up dizziness swamps him. It takes a while, moving a few slow inches at a time, to prop himself against a nearby trunk where he rests, astonished at how weak and thirsty he is. What's going on? A few minutes ago it was night; now, from the look of the brightening sky, it's nearing sunrise. But trying to think makes his head hurt, and he tells himself he'll rest a little more and then the answer will come to him. Leaning his throbbing head against the tree, he closes his eyes and immediately opens them again.

Something's coming, something big, crashing through the trees. A bear, or maybe . . . It's coming closer. He hears the swish of branches, leaves kicked aside. Not far away now. Maybe it's his buddies looking for him, or maybe –

Jared opens his mouth, but nothing comes out. Using the tree for support, he manages to get to his feet. The sound is close now. As the exploding lights inside his head subside, all at once he can see movement among the shadowy trunks, a lanky shape thrashing through the trees.

"CW! What the – ?"

The old man doesn't hear him. Wherever he's headed, he's in a hurry; another dozen steps and he'll be gone.

"CW! Wait!"

This time his shout registers; CW stops abruptly. When he turns, Jared sees he's holding something against his chest.

"Who – who's there?" The voice is a quaver.

"It's me. Jared. Where – " Jared stops for breath; that last shout used up all his reserves. "Where you goin?"

CW hesitates. Then: "I gotta . . . gotta bring him to the oak."

"Bring who?"

The bundle in CW's arms stirs. Jared's breath catches.

"What you got there?"

"It's him. The baby."

172

"What baby?"

The old man's answer emerges as a sob. "Kathy's baby. Kathy's . . . and mine."

Jared hears the words, but they don't make sense. Kathy's baby? CW's sister-in-law, his brother Gordon's wife, who never missed a chance to remind everybody in Durwood they were all going to hell? *Kathy's and mine?* It's like a dream, shards of reality bizarrely rearranged.

"I gotta do it," CW says. "This is how it's supposed to be."

Jared feels like a man overboard, grabbing for the rope and missing. Is CW really carrying a baby through the Noon Woods at dawn? Either he's dreaming, or something has gone terribly wrong. If it's not a dream – and every passing moment makes that possibility seem less likely – then whose baby is it, and how did CW get hold of it? And what for?

"I don't follow you," he says. "How what's supposed to be?"

"The child of the greenwood belongs to the oak." The way CW says the words makes them sound like a lesson dutifully learned. *Child of the greenwood* – that what the old folks in Durwood say when somebody shows a special talent, like Skip Vernon with his fiddling. *Oh, that one's a child of the greenwood all right.* Followed by a sideways look, a little laugh. The tale is that once upon a time, on a fine spring or summer night, couples risked making love in the Noon Woods in the hope they'd make a child with a touch of the Bright Land in its soul.

"Wait. You sayin that kid was conceived in the Noon Woods?" He's playing for time, trying to figure out how to get the baby away from CW, who's tough as an old tree; Jared's not sure he could take him, even at his best. And right now he's far from his best.

"It was always only Alma," CW says. "She was the only one for me. We didn't need the greenwood to make our children, Alma and me, we made our own magic wherever we were. But after she died, I used to walk in the woods at night . . . and one night there she was. Comin toward me through the trees, naked, her body white as the moon.

"I didn't know what to think, and when she came and kissed me, I kissed her back. She said, Take me, Connor, you might look just like my husband but you're twice the man he is. Take me now. And I – I did."

The old man sinks down on his heels, bent over the baby in his arms. Jared stares at him. Everything he thought he knew about this man is blown to smithereens, questions drifting like wisps of smoke amid the wreckage. Is CW saying that he – not Gordon Senior – is Gordie's father?

Comin through the trees naked, her body white as the moon. What on earth had got into Kathy? Jared knows he'll probably never get answers to those questions, but there's one answer he really needs right now.

"The baby, CW." He keeps his voice soft. "Whose baby is that?"

"Child of the greenwood."

"Yeah, I heard you. But where you takin him?"

CW hunches tighter and the baby wails in protest. "It's the way it's supposed to be. The womenfolk know. The child of the greenwood belongs to the oak. Momma always said the oak must have its due, or the bargain would be broken."

Jared understands he's quoting Granny Dee, but – "What bargain?"

"Roan's bargain with the white doe. *And for each year that he gave a drop of his blood, for as long the woods stood tall no harm should come to him or his.*"

A crazy image flashes through Jared's mind – a tree growing up through his chest, roots working their way into his heart. What the hell? Just how hard did he fall?

"Well, if the woods gotta stand tall, I guess we better hope Gordie Fu – hope Gordie calls it quits," he says, and bites his lip. If Gordie is really CW's son, how much more bitter the betrayal. Gordie, a child of the wood? It's enough to make you cry.

"Keep the bargain," CW mumbles. "Child of the greenwood."

Gibberish. Jared shakes his head. The movement triggers a series of red-hot hammer blows inside his skull; between the searing beats he tries to think. He's missing something here. Bargain. *For each year that he gave a drop of his blood* . . .

All at once he understands, with cold clarity, that in his own mind CW owes the blood of his son by his brother's wife, conceived in the greenwood, in exchange for the safety of the community. Didn't Granny Dee always insist on carrying the birthcord of every Durwood newborn to the Noon Woods to hang on Roan's Oak? A primitive practice Jared had been glad to see Sally abandon – but such customs had an origin, a point at which they'd made sense to somebody.

For each year that he gave a drop of his blood . . . Did his blood mean not Roan's blood, but his blood*line*?

"CW, wait." Jared starts talking before he even knows what he's going to say. "Listen, you're not thinkin straight. Roan and the doe – that's just a fairytale. And that ain't Gordie you got there. Gordie's all grown up now, remember? That baby ain't him. You're mixed up, CW; you been through a lot lately, we all have. But what we gotta do right now, we gotta get that baby back to its momma and daddy."

His thoughts have caught up with his words and he's beginning to figure out a few things. The only babies Sally's delivered recently are Shelby's and Molly Upshaw's, so it's got to be one of those two. Shelby's baby has an obvious birthmark, and the other one is a girl. If he can get this information across to CW, convince him to look at the kid, to connect ever so briefly with reality, maybe –

The old man's talking again, head bowed so low the words are all but inaudible.

"She cried when it was done. Said all she ever wanted was a child, a soul to bring to Jesus. Said things had got so bad between her and Gordon that he wouldn't touch her. I felt sorry for her. But I had to tell somebody what happened, so I told Momma. She didn't fuss, she just reminded me how it was supposed to be. About the child and the oak. I didn't do nothin bout it then –

how could I? But maybe it's not too late."

Pale light flickers on the lenses of his glasses as his head suddenly lifts. He falls silent, chin raised high. Jared finds himself doing the same thing, the two of them like a pair of hound dogs scenting the air.

Smelling smoke.

◆◆◆

Liz stands at the edge of the clearing in the dawn stillness, surveying the litter of broken branches and scattered wish tokens, the aftermath of last night's attempted banishing spells.

The black crevice in the oak is silent now, but every branch boasts thick green clusters of leaves, and a dozen shoots have sprung up between the horns of the mangled crown. She's out of breath, arms aching, legs wobbly. Cautiously approaching the tree, she sets her burden down among the roots and unzips her case. As the sound rasps through the stillness, a breath of wind stirs the leaves above her and she freezes, waiting for it to subside before removing the bundle of sketches and the painting of the Green Man.

You didn't create him; he's always existed.

But he's using my drawings the way he used Roan. As a host.

She supposes she's known all along that Roan's Oak harbors the relentless spirit of the Green Man – that the force pushing through her, using her to expand its reach, is concentrated here. As a breath of air ruffles one of the drawings, the horned guardian shape seems to lift its head from the paper and look at her.

It's time to do what she came for. There are nearly four gallons of gasoline in the can she lugged from the cabin, listening to its rhythmic sloshing every step of the way. With her functioning hand she crumples the drawings and stuffs them into the dark opening in the tree. The painting goes last; she avoids its hollow gaze as she shoves it in.

Now fot the gas. She uncaps the can, heaves it up and tilts the oily stream into the hole. The smell catches in her throat, making her eyes water as it soaks the paper. When the drawings are saturated, she takes the box of matches from her pocket and clumsily attempts to light one. The first sputters out, but the second catches and she tosses it into the hole.

For a moment – a moment that seems to expand infinitely while she waits, feeling the ache in her legs and a relentless pressure in her skull like a fist squeezing her brain – there's nothing, and then the paper ignites with a *whump*. Above her head the leaf-laden branches of the ancient oak suddenly stir. Too late: wind can only help her now. As it gathers force, she hears a desolate wailing rise above the crackle of flames and sees the trees around the clearing's edge beginning to sway in response.

Without warning, fire explodes from the hole in a rippling ball of heat. The force of it propels Liz backward so hard that she falls and her head snaps back. The world turns to spangles, a cascade of dazzling color through which she can still see Roan's Oak, engulfed now in a billowing orange shroud. From the opening in the burning trunk comes an unearthly keening and she hears her own voice join in, mourning the closing of the door between the realms.

The heat from the licking flames is intense. Her walking stick lies on the ground nearby, but her useless fingers will not grasp it. The numbness is seeping up her arm, turning out the lights one by one as she lies watching the oak burn. Around her the clearing glows like a furnace; flames shoot upward toward the brightening sky and burning leaves fill the air, drifting and falling around her. Watching a smoldering fragment land on the back of her hand, seeing the flesh blacken, she can feel nothing.

Through the rippling wall of fire, the dark opening in the trunk begins to swell. Within it, as if at a great distance, there's a figure intermittently visible through the veil of flame. As it comes closer, walking shakily, leaning on a spiral staff like the one on the ground beside her, Liz recognizes Tyne Durwood.

A fiery spasm shakes the conflagration. When it subsides, there's another figure at Tyne's side, plunging past him through the crackling flames. It's Jared Gorton, something cradled in the crook of his arm. Behind him Tyne has stopped and stands leaning on his staff. Is it really Tyne? Through the flames she sees a leafy beard that flutters in the scorching wind.

He's waiting for her. There isn't much time; around him the doorway is already crumbling, dwindling. Darkness forms at the edges of her vision, a black knot slowly tightening. Beneath her the ground is swaying, tilting, and now she rises lightly, easily, sight and sensation rushing back as she feels herself become lithe and long-limbed, narrow hooves scarcely touching the ground as she leaps across the space that divides her from the tree.

Borne on the smoke is the impossible fragrance of apple blossom. With a final bound, she's through.

☀ 21 ☀

Sinking her shovel into the ground, Morgan smells charred earth on the fresh spring air.

The people of Durwood are all around her, scattered across the burned acreage where Roan's Oak once stood – natives and newcomers busy planting the dozens of young oak trees in the bed of Jared's truck. There's Skip Vernon helping Molly dig out a rock, Harley Cole offering Tamara a swig from his pocket flask, Susanna Sayles carrying a seedling to her mother. The Upshaw, Reese, and Lewis babies nap side by side in their carriers in the spring sunshine, watched over by May Vernon and Tiny Reese, who sit stitching quilts in their canvas chairs nearby.

Morgan notices CW leaning on his shovel, resting his stiff back. He seems to be recovering from the death of his son eight months ago; Tyner died the day of the fire, stricken by a heart attack while sitting at his computer – something called "non-ischemic heart disease," apparently not uncommon in cases of spinal cord injury. He'd never known about the fire that burned more than seventy acres of the Noon Woods before being brought under control. From the split and scorched stump of Roan's Oak, the blackened wasteland stretches away on every side. But a portion of the old forest was saved, and these new trees will grow in time.

As will Durwood. Jared and Sally stand whispering and laughing as they take a break from the planting, heads close together over her bulging belly; in another month or so CW will have his first grandchild. Jared seems more content with life in Durwood these days. According to the doctors down in Lenoir, he's lucky to have made a full recovery from the head injury that left him lying unconscious in the Noon Woods for more than seventy-two hours. And if Jared himself is unable to explain what he was doing there, or how he managed to find the Upshaws' missing baby – well, those are just a few of the unanswered questions about the time period surrounding the fire.

Fawn Creek Timber came and hauled their skidder away, and that's the last anybody has heard of any logging plans. Nor has there been further news of the lawyer Hal Everdale since his wife found him pinned beneath one of her

---

sculptures with a cracked pelvis. Since Hal's departure Mariela has put the property up for sale and moved in with Chad.

Gordie Durwood hasn't been back either. A state trooper told Ezra Vernon that somebody answering Gordie's description was picked up wandering along Highway 321 with leaves stuck to his clothes and hair, unable to speak, using his fingers to talk to the empty air.

And then there's Liz, who vanished the day of the fire – vanished so completely that at first people thought the blackened skull found by the Fire & Rescue Squad in the charred remains of Roan's Oak must be hers, until forensic scientists in Charlotte discovered that it belonged to a man killed probably two hundred years ago by a brutal blow to the head.

All efforts to discover Liz's whereabouts have met with failure, and Morgan wonders if they'll ever find out where she's gone. Her own grasp of the fraught interval just before the fire is tenuous at best; trying to recall the specifics is like trying to grasp water, and there are days when she almost forgets that it ever happened. For instance, did something not quite kosher take place between her and Nick? Why does she keep having a fleeting image of him asleep in her front yard, curled up stark naked at the foot of her dogwood tree? In any case, she has a sense it's for the best that he left Durwood and went back to give law school another try.

Patting down the earth around her seedling, she sets her shovel aside and heads for the undamaged part of the forest, hearing the voices and clink of tools diminish as she enters the trees. Overhead, spring leaves tremble in a haze of translucent green. Stopping to watch a bright red cardinal preening itself on a branch, she hears a swish of leaves behind her and turns to see a pure white doe moving through the trees not a dozen feet away, turning its narrow head in passing to regard her with eyes like dark forest pools.

As the rustle of its passage dies away, she becomes aware of another sound, a kind of musical murmur coming from somewhere deeper in the woods. Sunlight yields to luminous green shadow as she moves through the trees in search of the source. Distant one moment, startlingly near the next, it draws her onward – some invisible creek trickling serenely in its pebbled bed, a contented little song of water and stone.

All other sounds have faded. She wanders dreamily through the trees, abandoning her search at last to settle among the spreading roots of a tree. Watching the dance of sunlight among woven branches, she can scarcely keep her eyes open; and as she slips into a doze the babble of the hidden creek grows louder, singing of seeds taking root, greenery emerging from the earth to spread a living cloak over everything in its path until only hollows and hillocks of rustling green remain.

Is she asleep or awake? The air carries a mulchy fragrance of soil and moss and leaf mold underlaid by a drifting animal tang. Dappled light caresses her. Wanting to feel the soft breeze on her skin, she drowsily loosens her clothing. The touch of the air is so intimate, so strangely provocative that it nearly wakes her – but not quite. Instead she surrenders to her doze, nestling into the embrace of the welcoming roots.

The mossy smell grows stronger as a shadow traverses the sunlight. The second doe he kissed, sings the water.

Among the leaves so green-O.

The Noon Woods are already old in the tales of the first white settlers and even before, in the legends of the Cherokee. The local people attribute the name to the notion that only at midday can the sun's rays penetrate the forest's dense canopy; but in truth the name has nothing to do with the English word noon, or with matters of daylight at all.

Made in the USA
Middletown, DE
27 July 2022